ZERO BALANCE

Eviscerating the Snake Series
Book 2

BY

ASHLEY FONTAINNE

Much love! to you both! Kat a/k/a Ashley

World Castle Publishing
http://www.worldcastlepublishing.com

This is a work of fiction. Names, characters, places, and incidents are products of the author's imagination or are used factiously and are not to be construed as real. Any resemblance to actual events, locations, organizations, or person, living or dead, is entirely coincidental.

World Castle Publishing
Pensacola, Florida

Copyright © by Ashley Fontainne 2012
ISBN: 9781937593933

First Edition World Castle Publishing February 1, 2012
http://www.worldcastlepublishing.com

Cover: Lindsay Anne Kendal
Editor: Maxine Bringenberg

A SPECIAL THANKS TO:

The incredibly knowledgeable Mr. Russ Johnson of the Phoenix Herpetological Society.
Kathy L. Hall, Esquire Extraordinaire for her brilliant legal mind and friendship.
My Love: for ALWAYS believing in me
My son: I love you more than life itself!
The biggest thank you goes out to all of my fans! Your support means everything.

PROLOGUE:

"Revenge, at first though sweet, bitter ere long back on itself recoils."
– John Milton, *Paradise Lost.*

"Jury selection for the trial of Olin Kemper, former managing partner of the Phoenix based accounting firm, Winscott & Associates, is scheduled to begin Monday at the Yarkema County Courthouse. Mr. Kemper is accused of the murder of Gina Milligan 33 years ago in Summerset. His arrest last year for this local, legendary case has catapulted Summerset into the national spotlight, filling the hotels and restaurants located in and around this tiny berg to well beyond their capacity, as news crews from all over the United States have descended upon this normally quiet town like a horde of hungry locusts. Roger Clanton and Nicolas Rancliff, lead attorneys of Mr. Kemper's dream team of lawyers hailing from Scottsdale, refused to answer reporter's questions moments ago as they entered the courthouse, but inside sources told us that Mr. Clanton and Mr. Rancliff filed a change of venue request due to the notoriety of this case and their concerns about obtaining a fair and impartial jury from the pool of local citizens. National legal analysts are divided on their opinions as to whether or not Judge Marshall Hall will grant a change of venue, as well as the odds on Mr. Kemper taking the stand in his own defense. Key prosecution witness, Mr. Robert Folton, who was originally charged as an accomplice with Mr. Kemper, already

pled guilty and, in exchange for his testimony against Mr. Kemper, was given five year's probation for his part in the case.

The debates on these issues, along with Mr. Kemper's guilt or innocence, are just as heated between lifelong residents of this close knit community, which has caused an invisible line of stark contrasts separating longtime friends and close family members on each side.

Stay tuned for our continuing, live coverage of this trial, beginning Monday at 8:00 A.M. This is Jan Patakee reporting for Channel Six News."

* * * *

"That's a wrap guys. Make sure you include the video clips from Kemper's bond hearing as well as the security footage of the courthouse from this afternoon. Oh, and don't forget that picture of Gina!" Jan said, barking the orders to her camera crew as she tossed her microphone over to her lead assistant, Tony. She stomped quickly in her four-inch stilettos back to the relative comfort of the news van and plopped down in the front seat, slamming the door quickly in her attempt to keep the fire brick oven air from sneaking inside with her. She flipped open her compact and assessed the damage the searing heat had done on her makeup, and cursed herself once again for taking this job in Arizona over the one offered to her in Mississippi. Then again, if she were in Mississippi right now, she would be a slimy pile of sweat, makeup and hairspray from all the humidity, so maybe Arizona wasn't too bad after all, since all the heat was doing was making her skin feel like dried out sandpaper.

In the two years that Jan had been an on the scene reporter for Channel Six, she had begged, borrowed and occasionally broken a small law or two in her attempts to be the first to break a big story. Up until 9 months ago, when the news broke about Olin Kemper's arrest and the huge shakeup at Winscott, she had thought herself doomed to cover the boring, blasé life of Phoenix and its abundantly rich and snooty citizens. Out of all the mundane reports she'd covered back then, the ones that were the worst involved the overly plasticized, hoity toity society wives that perched themselves high upon their gilded thrones as they perused the lowly commoners beneath them with their Botox-frozen eyes, barely able to see over their inflated tire-lips. On more than one occasion she had forced herself to walk away rather than spend the night in jail for popping one of them in the face after particularly brutal comments about her ethnic heritage from a few of the nastier hags reached her burning ears. Of course, their faces were so full of injectable chemicals she doubted they would have felt a thing anyway.

All of that changed the day she was the first one to hit the airwaves with the news of Olin's arrest since one of her drinking buddies, Tiffany Hemscott, happened to work as a minority partner at Winscott.

Jan was savvy enough to understand during those first few minutes of conversation with Tiffany that this was going to be an explosive story, and quite possibly shove her into the national spotlight (and maybe the global one as well.) if she played her cards right and continued to stay one step ahead of the other reporters by becoming the new best friend, rather than just an occasional wine taster, with Tiffany. She knew her well enough to know that a few glasses of Pinot were enough to loosen Tiffany's tongue, and made sure that they went out at least twice a week to the bar down the street from Channel Six for the latest insider scoop on Winscott.

Jan finished her touchup and snapped her compact shut. Glancing around, she realized that neither Tony nor her idiotic camera crew dorks had made it back in the van, so she reached over and blared the horn several times. They needed to get moving to get this footage edited and ready for the evening news. After her last honk, Tony slid open the side door and everyone piled in, with Tony jumping up front into the driver's seat. He smiled over at her, his dark brown eyes dancing with feigned excitement, and did his best impression from *Driving Miss Daisy*; "Yes ma'am! We is ready!"

Jan cocked her head and released one of her trademark evil smirks at him, her overly bleached pearly whites shining in the sun, and said, "Let's go boys. I have a national viewing audience that is just *dying* to see my smiling face as I report on this case!"

Tony fired up the van and the glorious cool air blew Jan's thick, raven hair from her face. She picked up her cell to call their producer and let him know they were on their way back, but before she touched the screen, it lit up with an incoming call from him. "Okay, so Jason has E.S.P.," Jan quipped to Tony as she answered. "Hey Jason, I was just about to call you. We are on our way back."

"Change of plans, J.P. Just have Tony upload what you have already and send to me. You won't have time to make it back to the station before cutoff. You need to head up to Robert Folton's ranch off of Highway 93. Now."

The tone of Jason's voice made the adrenaline immediately jolt through Jan's system. She recognized it from numerous other occasions when a breaking story was about to unfold. She motioned for Tony to pull over and put her phone on speaker as she set it down on the console so she could grab her notebook. Barely containing the excitement in her voice, she replied, "What's the lead, Jason?"

"We just heard through our contact in Summerset that a search is currently underway for Robert. Apparently, he left Monday on horseback to survey his herd and hasn't returned, or contacted his family, although he promised his wife he would return yesterday. She is frantic that he is a day late and contacted the Summerset Police Department, which is now spearheading the mounted search and rescue."

Jan could hardly write as Tony had immediately sped back up and headed down the rough road towards the outskirts of Summerset. Still trying to jostle words down while Tony drove, Jan asked "Jason, who else knows this?" hoping and praying that the answer was what she wanted to hear.

"Only us, so let's keep it that way. Get there as fast as you can and set up for a live feed. This could be the story of the year," Jason barked, quickly disconnecting from the call. Jan let her huge, toothy grin spread across her darkly tanned face as she looked over at Tony and said "Punch it!"

CHAPTER 1:

TWO WEEKS PRIOR

Audra-Dreams Unleashed

I woke up from my restless slumber completely encased in a cold, damp sweat that caused my thin silk nightgown to adhere to my soaked skin like wet tissue paper. I tried to recall whether or not I cranked the air conditioner down to a cool 70 degrees before I crawled into bed earlier, since my bedroom suddenly felt like a sweltering steam room. Slowly, as not to jostle the clinging wetsuit any more than necessary, I glanced to my left to the nightstand to make sure my fan was still blowing on me, and to my surprise it was. *Good grief, the middle of April and my body is acting like I just finished running a marathon in July in some humidity laced tropical jungle.*

My eyes closed briefly while I listened for the slight noise of the air conditioner hoping that it was just on the fritz, rather than my sudden combustion and subsequent meltdown stemming from internal sources. Unfortunately, I knew the latter was the answer as the air conditioner hummed quietly in the darkness around me.

A deep, heavy sigh escaped my lips into the lonely silence of my room. Purr Baby, who was curled into a tight little ball on the pillow next to me, twitched slightly and began to emit a low rumble from her furry white chest. A brief grin danced across my lips at that familiar sound, relishing the calming effect Purr Baby's presence always seemed to have on me, even during my darkest moments over the years. My grin became a full-fledged smile as I realized that I would have gone stark raving mad had it not been for that soft pile of fur next to me during the last tumultuous eight years of my life. It was uncanny how at times she intuitively sensed my moods and would gently appear at my side, quietly purring as she rubbed her soft head on my legs. It was almost as if she was letting me know that she was there for me when I felt so lost and alone.

Cat lover for life, no doubt about it.

Sweat dripping down me like I just sprayed myself with a water hose, I closed my eyes once again and tried to steer my thoughts to all things cold: glaciers, ice cubes, the North Pole, ice skating, but to no avail. At the beginning of my sufferings from these stifling explosions of body heat three weeks ago, I assumed I was in the early stages of menopause. I was pushing 40 and the women in my family tended to go through the change early, so I reluctantly went to my gynecologist seeking relief of the annoying symptoms. When Dr. Kidson called me back three days after my initial appointment and happily informed me in her best perky voice that my hormone levels were completely normal and that I had many child bearing years left, I immediately knew the cause. My vividly ominous dreams, broken slumber and sweat surges were brought on from external sources of stress and not from a lack of hormonal balance.

Great.

Since my body wasn't responding to thoughts of cold and continued to exude copious amounts of sticky liquid and my heart pounded heavily in my chest, I tried desperately to focus my attention on the rhythmic breathing of Purr Baby. My mind refused to cooperate, becoming a racetrack, and my thoughts careened around the corners like an Indy Car driver zooming around high on cocaine. I gave up trying to corral them and just let them run wild, staring silently at the ceiling.

I had never been a heavy sleeper, even in my youth. The subject of my sleep habits was a topic of discussion that my mother loved to share with others. She would dramatically recall what a difficult child I had been to raise, and that my ridiculous slumber schedule was the reason her youth fled so quickly. "That girl never allowed me a full night's rest until she was six." she would say, her hands flitting about her head. That storyline usually segued into why she never bore any more children, since her lack of rest would surely have pushed her into an early grave.

My parents: I finally reconnected with them after Gina's funeral following years of keeping them at arm's length. Even before the loss of the baby and my "promotion" to equity partner, our relationship had dwindled dramatically, starting when I entered college. Even though I was their only child, my parents tended to focus more upon their own agendas. My father's medical practice grew by leaps and bounds, and my mother spent her time split between shopping with her friends for their overpriced couture at Biltmore Fashion Park, or flying off to some luxurious vacation destination with her friends. I became nonexistent to my father when he realized that my talents were miles away from anything to do with bodily functions or medicine, especially when I began to display a real knack for math and finances at an early age. And of course, my mother could not comprehend why I shunned the upper elite society that I was raised in, preferring to keep my head shoved in books. To me, crunching numbers while my head was buried in a book rather than underneath the bright fluorescent lights of the local boutiques that she loved to frequent was much more exciting. It was beyond her limited vision to understand why I wanted to work in a field that had mostly been dominated by men, and not focus on finding a rich, suitable husband to settle down with. By the time I was awarded a full scholarship to Arizona State to the highly coveted W.P. Carey School of Business, my parents were barely able to muster any excitement for me. Only sheer determination to put on a show for their friends allowed any sort of feigned enthusiasm upon my graduation with honors and acceptance to Harvard College of Business. When my mother spoke about her "career-oriented daughter" at the society events she inevitably dragged me to, I could tell it pained her.

For the first few weeks after our reunion, things were a bit strained between us all, especially as the news stories went from being local to national. Reporters from around the country hounded them for interviews about me, the "Warrior of Winscott" as one headline labeled me. My parents' aversion to talking about me actually ended up being a good thing during that time, as they never once granted an interview. I knew, however, that the reasons for their denial to all the vultures did not stem from a familial protective vibe over me; it stemmed from a sense of shame over the fact that I had been raped and kept it hidden from them for so long. Throw in the fact that they feared being asked, "Gee, Dr. & Mrs. Tanner, in five years you hadn't physically seen your daughter, even though you only lived 20 miles away?" It didn't really matter what the reasoning behind their perpetual silence with the media was, really; I was just glad that they kept quiet, and that at least we were working on being a family once again. We did so in our own quiet, snail paced way. I was just now coming to terms with the realization that I had spent most of my adult life trying to excel and obtain accolades from not only my employer, but also my less than interested parents, and that and determination to succeed killed my child and almost cost me my life.

Staring at the empty space above my bed, I blinked twice as I tried to adjust my eyes to the darkness around me, knowing that sleep would not descend upon me anytime soon. I was accustomed to waking up to uncontrolled images swirling through my head after I lost the baby years ago. Back then, my tendency to pop awake during the wee hours of the night began as I experienced unsettling dreams that centered on disjointed visions of me hovering over an empty crib, arms aching as I frantically searched through piles of blue blankets for my son; or suddenly shooting straight up out of bed to the haunting sounds of the muffled, distant cries of my unborn child, yet unable to find the location of his feeble voice. My hands would involuntarily caress my flat stomach while I sobbed.

The first few months after my miscarriage, I attempted to console my wounded mind and spirit by telling myself during the brightness of day that these nightmares would soon cease as time passed. All fresh wounds eventually heal after the gaping holes that caused them close, leaving only a jagged scar as a reminder of the incredible pain. I remembered just enough from psychology class years ago in college to comprehend that the dreams were just my brain's way of dealing with the physical trauma of losing the baby. The fluctuation of hormones wreaking havoc with my thoughts would end eventually if I just shoved the pain down further. I learned that lesson while still a small child: out of sight, out of mind. Looking back on that thought process now with a clearer head, I realized that burying my emotions in a cesspool already full of putrid waters from older, fetid thoughts was not the ideal way of dealing with the tragedies that life tended to spew out.

When my husband James left me not long after I lost our son, my mind spun quickly into a deep, post-partum sinkhole. My nights became a jumbled dance of waking to find myself sobbing uncontrollably, hugging my pillow to my face, it's soft, feathery fibers soaked with the tears of my devastation. The overwhelming sorrow that my heart just couldn't contain anymore then shifted to continual hours of zombie-like stares into the empty ceiling as my eyes refused to stay shut. I assumed this was a mental safety valve to keep me from wading through the nightmarish dreams again. God, I had shed so many tears during that six-month time frame that I could envision them being enough to fill up a small swimming pool.

All the crying stopped abruptly when rage overtook my soul, searing my tear ducts dry for almost five years. My dreams shifted into vile, bloody images of retribution after being raped. The dreams of a despondent mother searching, longing for the child she would never really know and then the feelings of alienation and wandering alone through a cold, harsh world all shifted violently into nightmares; nightmares that bounced from overwhelming fear as I relived my trauma through disturbing memories, over to viscous, animalistic scenes of me hacking all of those people responsible for my unending mental anguish into pieces.

Those years of burning, dry hell totally engulfed my damaged body and already weakened mind. The fury that welled up inside me from after that horrendous night completely immersed my psyche. I would lie awake planning for hours the downfall of them all. My demented thoughts floated around in my mind, stretched out in the same spot where I was now, staring at the same, boring ceiling. Those vengeance fueled visuals then changed over into marathon nights of tirelessly reading and studying every single thing I could while I delved into each partner's own personal buried treasure trove of sins, once I had unlocked them. My mind was solely focused on making all of those slimy snakes accountable for their actions; and in some cases, inactions. My obsession became like a disease, slowly feeding upon my soul until not much but a hollow shell remained. Now, almost nine months after that explosive day in the conference room, here I was lying awake again, realizing how sick and darkly possessed I had actually become. It was during those murky, revenge filled years that I became a predator that stalked its prey. The irrepressible urges to obtain my own personal justice consumed my entire being while I slowly buried myself in the deep, gloomy well of self-imposed exile. I had imprisoned myself as I sank further and further to the bottom of the well, covering myself with the dirt of others as I went.

The dreams that jolted me from my sleep this evening, as well as ones that I had experienced during the last three weeks, were not ones borne of fear, anger or intense sorrow. Instead, they were oddly haunting scenarios, one of which centered around me traipsing through an eerie forest at night, full of a tangled mesh of barbed vines that clung to my heavy legs, ripping and pulling as they tried to yank me down deeper into the darkened depths of the blackened forest floor. Another saw me running through endless hallways, trying to find my way out, yet I seemed doomed to trudge through them alone, tripping and falling as I felt the walls around me close in and cut off my air supply. Good Lord, would I ever be able to find the shut off valve to this rampant mind of mine?

I couldn't help but crack a wicked grin at the incredible irony my life had evolved in to. I spent so many years working my mind and body into a complete frazzle, first through college and then at Winscott. Clearly, I was obsessed with showcasing my abilities and perfecting my work above all others, thus gaining the recognition and respect I so desperately craved from my parents. That ambition became an obsession. Succeeding was my guiding purpose and nothing else mattered. My goal, ever since I could recall being old enough to truly have one, was to be the head of a successful company, a businesswoman that was strong and capable yet tough as nails when necessary. A powerful woman that had it all: career, spouse, children and always seemed to be able to balance the three in perfect harmony, unlike my mother. Her only sense of self-worth came from what designer she wore on her boney back, or the make of the car she drove. Now here I was, a partial tidbit of my goal finally obtained, yet I was still wide awake in the stillness of the night, completely drenched in my stress-induced sweat, unable to sleep uninterrupted for an entire evening. Maybe it was the knowledge of Olin's upcoming trial that spurred my insomnia on. I had less than two weeks to mentally prep myself to open old wounds, yet again as I would be forced to sit in the same room with that lecherous reptile and watch him attempt to slither out of his punishment. Not only was I expected to testify, along with Robert and countless others, but I promised Mrs. Milligan that I would be there by her side the entire time.

Oh, Mrs. Milligan: just thinking about that sweet, strong lady made me immediately feel guilty for worrying about my own trivial thoughts and emotions. God only knows the emotional twister that she had ridden for over 30 years now. Her words *"Let it go"* always reverberated through my mind when I thought about her. I couldn't bear the thought of letting her down, so I knew, for her sake, I must try harder to stay strong.

In the past few months, Mrs. Milligan and I had gone from being strangers that were united under the shadow of sadness to being extremely close. I had never been the type of individual that would randomly pick up the phone and call my mother to share my day or just to hear her soothing voice (since actually, she possessed a very irritating nasally pitch that I could only stand for a few minutes before my ears bled). However, I found myself doing just that with Mrs. Milligan. At first, I told myself that my conversations with her were just to check on her well-being; politeness to an elderly woman that seemed to need checking up on; but if I were to be completely honest with myself, I was drawn to her maternal kindness. Her strength and compassion were foreign emotions to me, and things I had never experienced with my own mother. She was such an enigma. When I looked beyond the frail appearance and witnessed the stoicism and bravery she possessed, I also sensed the grace and sadness that she balanced inside her. To still be able to truly smile and enjoy life after the tragedy that no mother should ever suffer was far beyond my ability to comprehend. I still yearned for my son and I never saw his face or held him in my arms, whereas Mrs. Milligan had spent years with her daughter. The staggering sadness of that loss would have driven me over the brink into utter madness. The one thing that puzzled me the most about her was her unyielding faith in God and her absolutely unshakeable belief in not only the existence of a Heaven, but that Gina was there waiting for her, along with her deceased husband. Although she didn't speak of these things often, when she did, her face would become calm and serene, aglow with a youthful vigor that would, for a brief moment, wash away the ravages of time that had tromped unmercifully across her face. Listening to her speak about these things would leave me with a strange sense that I was missing something from my own life. Some intangible ideal that my black and white brain found utterly ridiculous, yet my heart whispered I desperately needed.

Fully awake now, I let out my breath slowly. I gave up trying to lie still and gently crept out of bed so I wouldn't wake Purr Baby and went to the bathroom to rinse my sticky forehead and guzzle some cold water. The water cooled my skin and calmed my nerves. I briefly wondered if the stress was brought on from becoming "the boss" and all the responsibilities that came with being the new managing partner, and how I had obtained that coveted title. I realized now that all my years of strategizing the downfall of everyone was as far as my late night obsessive planning sessions had gone. I never really gave much thought to or made preparations for how my life would change after those plans finally came to fruition.

The first few weeks after my takeover and the rippling after effects of Olin's arrest were almost a blur now. The publicity nightmare of the fraudulent audit and bankruptcy that Sprigg Oil & Gas eventually entered in to kept all of us hopping from one disaster to the next. The loss of numerous clients over the whole sordid affair kept my mind constantly shifting from one fire to another. Then, two months after I took over, Eric abruptly announced his early retirement and left the firm, which really crippled the already hobbled horse. Most of his clients that hadn't already sought accounting services elsewhere left soon after he did, and the loss of his clientele had a huge impact on our bottom line each month. To my surprise, Nicole stepped up to the plate and truly attempted to convince some of Eric's larger clients to stay. But even with her staunch efforts, she could only procure a successful retention rate of about ten percent, which of course, wasn't much help.

Tensions on the tax floor did not help matters out any either. After the flames died down from the volcanic eruption in the conference room, the rumors continued to spread like molten lava. The gossip grapevine trailed all the way to Kevin's house and crept right into the ears of his wife. Divorce proceedings immediately began, and Kevin didn't stand a chance in hell since not only was his soon to be ex a lawyer, but a scorned woman as well. *Hell hath no fury*. There seemed to be a very distinct line drawn in the sand in terms of supporters of Kevin versus supporters of Miranda on the floor, and working conditions were strained, to say the least. Then the lawsuits began; fifteen of them so far, which was not too surprising considering the monster that Olin was, but the shocker was that Kevin was involved. Apparently, these women, after experiencing Olin's behavior, had sought solace and help from the quiet partner, Kevin. According to their affidavits, Kevin would comfort them and promise his help, bed them, and then afterwards, act like nothing ever happened. Good God, if only the cash flow was available, I would consider asking him to resign. It would be worth the cost of his buyout just to remove his smarmy presence from Winscott.

Our biggest bleeder, naturally, was the tremendous loss of all of our oil and gas clients. They literally scattered like ashes in the wind after the news broke about the Sprigg situation and Olin's arrest. The media coverage spread like a summer wildfire and soon, Winscott's name was right in the trenches of accounting hell. I realized, a bit too late, that I failed to work out the intricate details of the domino effect that taking Olin down would have on the firm in terms of the financial backlash. Out of Olin's 600 plus client base, less than 100 opted to stay with the firm. That revenue stream loss was pumping out of our doors faster than a spewing severed jugular vein releasing its crimson fluid.

Surprisingly, most of Robert's clients had decided to stay and were now in the capable hands of Carl. I could only assume that they took Robert's plight into consideration and maybe even had some twisted sense of respect for him. He finally stood up and admitted his personal wrongdoing in not only his part of Gina's death, but the whole Sprigg mess. All of these issues weighed heavily on me each day. When you added in the fact that the air at work was thick with the underlying current of distrust from most of the partners and employees, each day was hell. This distrust in the firm and each other caused our turnover ratio to spike dramatically. My stress level had been at its peak for the first three months after taking over. My inability to sleep was kept on the back burner, for it just seemed a natural response to all the pressing issues that were swirling around me on a daily basis.

However, about five months after my ascension, the roller coaster slowed down to a more reasonable teacup ride. The blood thirsty media sniffed out fresher wounds from other bleeding corpses to swoop down and feed upon. As they dissipated, it allowed us to begin patching up our wounds. The frenzied departure of over half of our clients, countless employees and media attention began to slow down to a steady drip rather than the gushing geyser they had been.

Surprisingly, Nicole's business valuation niche was booming, which helped not only with our profit and loss each month, but also with her attitude at work. After Eric left, it seemed that her plan to bury herself even deeper than normal under mounds and mounds of paperwork was keeping her occupied. It was also keeping her bank account, and her sanity, afloat, since she possessed nothing else now to occupy her time. The loss of Eric from her life, pathetic as it seemed, was devastating to her. Nicole never had children and what few family members were still living all resided in eastern Georgia; and I could not recall her ever mentioning any female friends, so she was pretty much alone now. Eric had been her life. They had been together for years, and for him to just suddenly announce his retirement plans to travel around the world with his wife and grandkids almost destroyed Nicole. In some aspects, I did feel sorry for her, and viewed her now in a different light than I had previously. It finally dawned on me, that day in the conference room, that behind the makeup, high fashion couture and foul-mouthed exterior, Nicole was just like any other woman. Under her carefully placed veneer was a woman that actually possessed emotions other than the greed and anger I uncovered. I watched her struggle to control her face from crumbling into a pile of sorrowful tears upon her realization that she was not the apple of Eric's eye like she had assumed she was. When confronted with the fact that he was just like the majority of other men—he followed his penis in whatever direction it pointed—she changed, almost overnight. She had shocked me even more when she had come to my office a few months ago, in what I can only surmise was her version of an apology, and offered to help in any way possible. She had some ideas to help stem the flow of money that was leaking out of every conceivable crack and laid out her marketing plans. When I agreed, she then went out and executed them as only she could. She hadn't retained many of Eric and Olin's clients, but the ones that she did paid well, and she actually began to soften up at work. I was getting reports back that she was seen every now and then smiling at other employees, which was a first. I found it fascinating to observe her stages of transformation into a real human being and marveled at how when her reality check hit her hard, she stood up, brushed herself off, and proceeded to pay the bill as only a strong, southern-bred woman could.

My nemesis was still in jail, which finally allowed my mind to begin to relax a bit and afforded me, at least for a glorious few months, to sleep uninterrupted for about four hours at a time.

Until three weeks ago.

I couldn't quite grasp why I was suffering from such overwhelmingly crushing dreams. Every time I awoke from one, like tonight, the sensation of my chest being squeezed by some unseen vise was beginning to take its toll on me. I knew Steve was right: I needed to visit with, at the very least, a rape crisis counselor. Better yet, a therapist who could help me to work through all of the traumatic events that I had endured alone in repressed silence. But, I was such a private person that I just couldn't bring myself to plop down on some cold leather couch and spill out the most horrid details of my life to a complete stranger as I stared at their ceiling. Hell, I hadn't even been able to express my emotions to James during our marriage after the loss of our son, and we had been married for eight years. Of course, James never had been the type that could sit still for more than a few minutes and listen to someone talk about their feelings, much less comprehend the emotions of another person, so I never even tried.

James: he was a powder keg of adrenaline that raced through life at only one speed: supersonic. We met during a party at Harvard as he was finishing up his last semester of law school, and I was immediately drawn to his reckless pursuit of life, money and excitement. His exuberance left me breathless at times while I tried to keep up with his breakneck speed. For the first few years, I rode that high. But once my own career took off and my schedule put me far away from home almost three-quarters of the year, James's enthusiasm for money began to wane. Suddenly, he decided he wanted to start a family with a wife that stayed home while the husband went out and earned all the bacon. Of course, that attitude and thought pattern won my parents over immediately, and sometimes I felt like the only reason they continued to have any type of a relationship with me was just so they could see James.

After the first six years, our relationship suddenly became flipped flopped, as now I was the one running full bore and he wanted to slow things down and spend more time together. This sudden shift in priorities made me wonder what happened to the man I married. It was almost like he wanted to recreate the Cleavers.

And I was no June.

Making sure that protection was a top priority for the short stretches I was actually home, I held off as long as I could without getting pregnant. I soon found out that nothing is 100 percent effective except abstinence when I found myself with child. My under-enthusiastic emotional response to this was soon boosted to happiness as James's thrilled demeanor began to rub off on me. Unfortunately, our relationship was held together strictly by the thin cord of expectant parents. His resentment of my devotion to work and refusal to cut back on hours went from being a small curb we could step over to a large brick wall that separated us. That wall eventually became a prison that neither of us could escape, especially after I locked myself in "mental solitary" after my miscarriage.

Thinking about James now only left me with a small sense of melancholy for our eight years of marriage, for if I broke our relationship down to the barest essentials, our connection with each other never passed the superficial stage. We were too young and both of us lacked the insight and ability to share ourselves with each other on a truly emotional level. Of course, when you each are traveling at the speed of light in different directions, opportunities for the linking of two souls tend to pass by in a blurred frenzy. Soul searching conversations never materialized, leaving our connection tenuous and easily broken.

Steve, on the other hand, possessed the uncanny ability to listen and really hear the undertones of what was being said, as well as the almost freaky sense of perceiving what was behind the words. Those attributes, most likely, were what made him such a great detective. At dinner earlier tonight, the subject of my inability to sleep came up again and he lightly suggested, once again, that I needed to see someone about it. When I reiterated how I wasn't comfortable doing so with someone I didn't know, he seemed a bit puzzled. His gorgeous face was overshadowed by concern as he questioned why I had been able to tell him, when he had been a complete stranger at the time, but couldn't talk to a professional better trained to handle the delicate nature of my issues.

Right now, I wished more than anything as I stared at my pathetically tired reflection in the mirror, that I could answer that question as well. Of course, then the rest of our conversation burst into my head as Steve reminded me that I was going to have to split open my life, splayed out for the world to see, during Olin's upcoming trial. The judge in the case had already determined that cameras would be allowed in the courtroom, and if I couldn't handle a one on one couch session with a shrink, how would I handle the national exposure?

I honestly had no idea.

I peeled off my damp gown and padded quietly over to my dresser to retrieve a dry one, and then headed to the kitchen. As I rounded the corner, I glanced at the microwave: 3:45 in the morning. I chuckled softly as I thought about the crazed father in *The Amityville Horror* that always woke up at 3:15, so at least I needn't need to worry about my house being haunted or me slipping into murderous insanity since it was past that time. It seemed that my brain just seemed pre-programmed to wake up about this time as it overflowed with too many thoughts. I decided I would at least put it to good use and get some work done.

Coffee started and computer booting up, I sat down at the kitchen table and briefly yearned for Steve's strong arms around me. I kicked myself mentally for not letting him spend the night after dinner earlier. I felt the warm sensation of desire weave through my body just at the mere mention of his name, yet I was still unable to succumb to my longing for him. In the past two months since we officially began dating, Steve had been so kind, patient and tender with me, letting me be the one that reached out for his hand first and the one who initiated our first tender kiss, but I was unable to allow things to move any further. Each time Steve got too close, I would feel my stomach knot up so tight that the sensation of being punched would overwhelm me, and had closed the valve tightly on any amorous intentions.

God, I really did need therapy if I was ever going to be able to work through my angst and fear and allow myself have any semblance of a normal relationship with a man again. The look in Steve's eyes as he left me standing in my doorway this evening was a mixture of sadness and disappointment. I knew I wasn't being fair to this wonderful man and that knowledge caused me to feel even more anxiety, which then just compounded my issues further. It was a vicious cycle that I knew only I could end. A heavy sigh left me as I filled my coffee cup up with the steamy, robust liquid, and I decided right then that I wasn't going to let Steve's glorious presence slip through my grasp. My marriage to James crumbled due to our inability to cope with feelings and I was determined not to let that happen again.

I walked over to my purse and dug through it until I found the card Steve had given me months ago of a rape crisis counselor/therapist, and then I sat back down in front of the computer. I quickly typed out and sent the counselor an email and requested a call back to discuss my situation and available appointment times. I smiled a bit as I acknowledged to myself that I had just taken another first step down my long road to rebuilding a new life that would be full of possibilities and excitement rather than fear, anger and remorse. That idyllic vision was going to be a difficult one for me to attain. I had spent so many years focusing on nothing but my revenge that my tunnel vision became black and clouded, almost as if I had been locked in a dark cave for years and then was released into the blinding sun for the first time in ages. I knew that it was going to take time for the eyes of my soul to be become accustomed to the light of day once again.

As I sat and contemplated all these rambling thoughts about redemption, recovery, reconciliation and my potential romantic interludes with Steve in the pre-dawn hours of the morning, the sound of an incoming Skype message pulled my attention back to the computer screen. The message was from Steve and simply said "Go back to sleep." which made me laugh out loud. As I began typing a message back to him, relishing his online presence and obvious watchful eye over me, I smiled and thought *I can do this*.

CHAPTER 2
Piper-Executing the Plan

ONE WEEK PRIOR

MONDAY

Males: They are rather easy targets to manipulate if you lower yourself to their sensory levels and prey upon one of their three basic needs: food, ego stroking or sex. I have used all three tricks in a variety of combinations over the years and discovered that sex—or the tantalizing lure of potential intercourse—is the best tool to wield for the quickest results.

I finished applying the final touches of mascara to my contact lens converted light green eyes and walked into my closet. Pushing the hidden button, I stood back as it recessed into the room that housed my various props. As the lights came on and showcased my numerous costume options, I tried to decide which look would best suit the reclusive herpetologist that I was meeting with this afternoon. Considering that he spent most of his days either milking poisonous snakes or staring through a microscope, I figured that a demure redhead would suit my purposes for the day as I reached for the long mane of wavy copper.

Returning to my makeup table I adjusted the wig, letting its flowing waves cascade down my shoulders and back. Sliding on a pair of dainty eyeglasses, giving me the "sexy reporter" air that I hoped would render Dr. Moore into pliable putty in my hands, completed my look. I stood up and surveyed the entire ensemble and decided that the subdued black skirt and white shirt would need a bit of *va-va-voom*, so I crammed my feet into the highest black pumps I could find in my closet and looked again. One more little morsel: I unbuttoned my shirt to just above my décolleté. With just a small dab of perfume strategically placed behind my ears and between my breasts, I was ready; time to play my part of "interviewer" to my "interviewee", Dr. Moore. I grabbed my black leather satchel and double checked for the empty syringes and the full syringe of liquefied Ambien. They were tucked safely away in the side pocket, right next to the small insulated lunch sack, so out the door I went. The thrill of the hunt made my heart pound a bit faster than normal.

Irritated at the Monday morning rush hour traffic, I finagled my way through the hordes of sheep on their way to their pathetic jobs in their pathetic little cars, their pathetic little lives just plodding along. Normally, it was a two-hour drive to the tiny field office in McNeal that Dr. Moore worked at, so I had plenty of time to rehearse every possible scenario that might occur during our meeting. Considering the ridiculous congestion, I knew I would be a bit late if I didn't step on it.

My initial contact with him was a week ago, under the guise of "Bridgette Summers, reporter for a start-up magazine entitled *Reptiles Today*." When I explained that Arizona was next on the list of states that our magazine was interested in showcasing for a two-part series on the venomous snakes of the United States, I could almost feel his excitement projecting through the phone lines. My research had led me to choose Dr. Moore as my "interviewee" for several reasons. His remote location in the desert of Southeastern Arizona and the fact that his specialty was producing anti-venom were strong points for sure. But, his bland biography I found online was the clincher. It was patently obvious that Dr. Moore was a loner that enjoyed the company of scaly creatures rather than humans.

In other words, he would be an easy target.

I wound my way through the endless twists and turns of dusty back roads until I came over a small rise and found the research lab. Quickly glancing around, I only noticed one vehicle other than my own, so luck was with me. I let the grimy dust settle around my car while I checked my reflection in the mirror one last time. Everything had to be in place. I dabbed a bit more shine to my lips then stepped out of the car. Before I could even take three steps towards the front entrance, the heavy steel door opened and the silver colored head of Dr. Moore popped out.

"Welcome, welcome Ms. Summers. Right on time, yes, right on time. My directions were on the button, were they not?" he stammered, unable to take his beady little eyes off my chest. I knew then that this would be a piece of cake.

"Dr. Moore, I presume?" I asked coyly as I batted my falsely elongated lashes at him at the same time I extended my hand. He nodded his head in agreement, his wire rimmed glasses lightly bouncing on his protruding nose. "It's a pleasure to meet you," I said, flashing my best smile.

Dr. Moore released my hand and stepped back, holding the door open for me. I walked inside, immediately accosted by a smell that overwhelmed my nostrils. Years of smelling horrid stenches at Haven Hills allowed me to keep my composure and not react to the reeking odor that now pounded my olfactory senses, as my eyes tried to adjust to the sudden change from the brightness of the Arizona sun to the darkness of the lab.

Dr. Moore's biography failed to mention that he looked exactly like a hobbit, save for the pointy ears and clothes. I quickly surmised this was the reason he decided to spend his life as a recluse in the desert. Why he chose to work around fanged creatures that could kill him in a matter of seconds was beyond me. He could have been a desert dwelling hermit without keeping company with vipers. It was obvious that he did not often entertain females here by the way his ravenous eyes glided across my body. I couldn't help but wonder how long it had been since he had actually fucked a woman. Quite some time, I suspected, which made the avenue I was going to take today an easy choice.

"Thank you so much, Dr. Moore, for allowing me the opportunity to see firsthand all the wonderful and exciting work you do here. To think, you risk your life each day just so others can be saved by the life giving anti-venom you create." I gushed as I strolled over to the long table in the middle of the room. I made sure I kept my distance from the glass cages that were to my left. As I walked, the sound of my heels must have agitated the snakes because the room suddenly filled with the sound of their rattles. I stopped at the table and placed one hand on it as I turned around slowly, making sure that I looked a bit unsteady on my feet. Dr. Moore was right behind me and noticed my falter, immediately reaching out to steady me.

"Ms. Summers, are you alright? I hope it's not the smell; I know to outsiders, the reptilian odor can be…well, rather repugnant."

"No, no, it isn't that. I am just a bit tired from the drive. I have only lived in Arizona for a few months and my body just hasn't acclimated to this heat. I will be fine, I promise, I just need to sit down," I said as I sat down on the nearest stool, making sure to cross my legs so my skirt hiked up well into the middle part of my thigh.

Dr. Moore continued as he took a healthy slurp of his coffee, "Please, let me get you some water."

"I am fine, really. Let's get started, if you don't mind. I do have a deadline to make," I said as I set my satchel on the table and dug out my notebook. "Let's start off with the most obvious question that our readers will want to know; what is the most poisonous snake found in Arizona?"

Dr. Moore quickly stopped thinking about my wellbeing and my exposed thigh. He was now in his own little world, rambling about all the snakes that were indigenous to Arizona, as well as the differences in their venom. I played my part well and nodded my head at the appropriate times, expertly playing the pretense of taking notes although I really wasn't listening, until he said, "…and of course, the most dangerous one to humans is the

Crotalus scutulatus, more commonly known as the Mojave Rattlesnake."

"Oh! And just what makes this particular snake so deadly?" I purred as I glanced over at him.

"Well, it's venom is a neurotoxin and hemotoxin, rather than just containing hemotoxins alone, as most pit vipers do; which means rather than causing tissue death by destroying red blood cells, the venom acts on the central nervous system and can cause respiratory failure by disrupting the synaptic responses in our neurons. Death can be quite quick and excruciatingly painful," Dr. Moore said with an almost reverent awe creeping into his annoying voice.

"So that's why what you do is so important. The anti-venom must need to be administered quickly, which I assume means that hospitals must have some on hand at all times. How long does it take for you to create a—oh, what would you call it?—a batch?"

Dr. Moore went over to the stainless steel refrigerator in the corner and opened it wide as he motioned for me to come over, and said, "See this top shelf here? Those are all vials of the venom from the nine *Crotalus* that I have here at my facility. It took me a full day to obtain these samples and after you leave, I will begin the process of injecting the hosts to produce the serum."

Time to bring out the damsel in distress.

I slowly walked over to stand by him at the fridge and made a point of looking confused, with the slightest bit of apprehension in my voice, as I replied, "Hosts? You aren't referring to those precious little horses I saw out back when I drove up, are you?"

Dr. Moore looked at me as though I was a simple child and replied, "Oh yes, the venom must be injected into a living creature that has a similar cellular structure to humans. Their bodies create the antibodies to the venom after injection, then I harvest the anti-venom from their blood. The entire process takes up to an entire week, just to produce enough serum for three hospitals."

He'd just walked right into my trap. *Snap.*

"Oh, my, well that is fascinating Dr...." I said as I reached out for his feeble little arm, feigning a dizzy spell. "Oh, I'm sorry; I'm feeling a bit woozy."

Dr. Moore grabbed my arm and led me back to the stool and said, "I apologize for upsetting you, Ms. Summers. The process of obtaining the anti-venom must be a bit much for a layperson. Please, sit right here and I will get you a nice glass of cold water."

"Thank you, Doctor. You are too kind," I said in my best please-take-care-of-me voice.

When he rounded the corner, I reached into my satchel and grabbed the syringe full of Ambien; 100 melted milligrams to be exact. I squirted the cloudy liquid into his thankfully black coffee, recapped it, and slid it back into my bag. I put my arms on the table and rested my head on them, the act of "close to fainting" complete.

Dr. Moore came bounding around the corner on his little hobbit feet and almost spilled the glass on me. He was in a frenzy to help the poor, distraught looking pitiful female resting on his workbench. I couldn't help but wonder if he was hoping I would pass out so he could really take a look at me, because that was probably the only way this moron ever saw any action: from comatose women. God, this was the ultimate "taking candy from a baby" scenario. I couldn't have picked a better mark.

I looked up at him with my best doe-eyes and gushed, "Thank you so much, Doctor. I am sure this will help." I demurely slid my lips over the rim of the glass and drank. "Please, join me for a few moments while I regain my composure," I said, looking over at the empty stool on the other side of the table where he had set his coffee mug. "I guess I should have taken you up on your original offer of water when I first came in."

Dr. Moore scurried over to his chair and sat down, his mind obviously empty of the snake discussion and now fully consumed with the hunger for my breasts and thighs. I took the glass and held it to my neck, allowing some of the water to trickle down my chest. Hungrily, he snatched up his coffee mug and swallowed several long gulps, his eyes betraying his lustful thoughts.

He was mine now.

I let him ogle me all he wished, for I knew that in a few moments, he would be out cold. I set down my water and picked up my pen again, asking a few more questions about his work. He droned on half-heartedly about the subject as he was having difficulty focusing on anything other than my damp cleavage. After about ten minutes, he pulled his glasses off and rubbed his eyes, his words starting to jumble together and become nonsensical. His head began to loll around like a bobble head while his eyes rolled back in his head. He mumbled, "…not….well" and then BAM! His head hit the table with a loud thud, knocking his coffee mug onto the floor, breaking it into tiny shards. I didn't move and just stared at him for about 60 seconds, watching for the slightest movement. When I didn't see any, I reached across the table and poked him with my pen.

He was out cold, the drool beginning to form a small pool around the edge of his mouth on the hard table.

Quickly, I picked up the glass he had given me and ran over to the sink and dumped the water out, then put it in my bag. I grabbed a pair of rubber gloves from my purse and put them on, then went over to the open fridge and gently removed three full vials of the Mojave rattlesnake venom. I carefully set them on the counter, my hands shaking a bit from the excitement. One by one, I extracted the creamy liquid death into the syringes.

Once I had repacked my fully locked and loaded weaponry into their new little home that was nice and cold, I left the refrigerator door open and walked over to the snoozing doctor. I placed the empty vials next to his curled up right hand and then walked around to the other side of the table and stretched across it. With my gloved hand, I pushed two of the three vials onto the floor, each shattering into thin slivers around his feet. The noise was startling and made the snakes begin their incessant rattling again, and I froze for just a brief moment. I held my breath, staring at him to make sure he was still asleep; which of course, he was. Hell, I had given him enough Ambien to knock out a few of the horses he had outback for a few hours. He wasn't going to wake up soon.

Standing across the table staring at him, I was suddenly struck with the thought that he looked eerily similar to Dr. Hopkins from Haven Hills. Strange, I hadn't noticed that before when he was awake and yammering on about snakes. He had been like a prepubescent boy telling his locker room buddies about the first boob he touched. Now that his eyes were closed and his head turned slightly with his glasses gone, his silvery hair mussed and covering part of his leathery cheek, the resemblance was strong enough to make the bile rise up in the back of my throat. I looked away and caught the reflection in the mirror behind him and jumped a bit, not realizing at first that the redhead in the mirror was me—crazed eyes and all. I felt a bit unsteady on my feet and glanced back over to the table. Oddly, it was Dr. Hopkins sitting there, staring silently at me, his hands folded in front of him. His black eyes pierced into my soul, waiting impatiently to begin another torture session of "Olin doesn't love you, he is like a poison to you, Piper." I let out a small squeal and clamped my eyes shut so hard that bright, colorful lights burst behind them as I stood there trembling, awaiting the mental pain I knew was coming.

I don't know how long I stood there shaking before I finally smelled the snakes.

The stench of them brought me back to reality as I opened my eyes and realized I was standing in the research lab of Dr. Moore, not the rubber covered room that Dr. Hopkins had conducted his "therapy" in. My shoulders were aching and sweat was pouring down my neck and back, my ember-colored synthetic locks stuck to my neck. I realized that was because I was standing behind Dr. Moore with a large metal canister of some sort, that I had no recollection of picking up, raised high above my head. Lowering my aching arms slowly, my eyes bounced back and forth from one section of the room to the next as I tried to construct exactly how long I had been standing over him. I shook my head from side to side, hard, wincing in pain as the muscles in my neck protested, trying to gather my composure. This was Dr. Moore; I was no longer at Haven Hills. Dr. Moore was of no use to me anymore and I detested the idea of leaving any loose ends behind, but did that mean that I should bash his skull in just because he reminded me of my own personal demon? I looked back down at his small frame and thought that one good whack on the temple would finish him off, and he was probably light enough that I could manage dragging him to my car. But then I wasn't sure what I would do with him next after that. The thought of digging a grave in the arid dirt around his compound in the searing heat outside did not appeal to me. Besides, I wasn't ready for the body count to start stacking up.

Yet.

Then I felt a surge of overwhelming anger at not only Dr. Hopkins, but Nick's betrayal, Ralph's suicide and Olin's previous rejection of me, and my vision becoming clouded with red fury. *What the fuck? Live by the snake, die by the snake you dirty bastards*! resounded deep inside my head. My body reacted before my brain thought my actions through, and, as though watching from a distance, I saw myself snatch up my satchel and look at the canister that was still in my other hand. With Herculean effort, I launched it at the glass cages that housed the Mojave's. The sound of shattering glass, violent hissing and the rattling of the venom filled monsters reverberated through my ears.

I yanked the door open and leapt out; no time to survey the sun baked vistas to ensure that I was still alone. If someone were to walk up now I would just scream "Snakes loose!" and be gone, as most likely, so would they. Even in heels, I made my way quickly through the dirt back to my car, mindful of the contents in my bag as I placed it gingerly in the passenger seat, and then cranked up the car, leaving a trial of dust and debris in the dry air behind me.

It took me ten minutes longer than when I arrived earlier to make it to the main highway since I was a bit paranoid about hitting the heavy ruts. I didn't want to lose the prizes inside the glass vials. If I broke one, I sure couldn't go back now and obtain more. Once on the pavement, I finally released my breath and let a sly grin spread across my face as I thought, *Although a slight detour in my original plans for Dr. Moore occurred, Phase One is complete.* Now, I just had to hurry home and change into my other hunting attire. I needed to deliver one of my newly acquired gifts to Robert.

Olin would be so proud.

CHAPTER 3
Robert-Riding for Redemption

"It's only for a few days, honey. This trip will be my last opportunity during the next couple of weeks to enjoy some wide open spaces and fresh air. Besides, I need to check on the herd and make sure all the calves are healthy before the trial starts. I promise, I will be back by Wednesday, so that's only two days from now," I said to Stacy while I cinched the saddle up tight on my favorite mare, Sahara. I did my best to produce a true smile for my lovely wife. I knew those brown eyes were glaring at me behind the dark sunglasses she was wearing, and I really couldn't blame her for being irritated that I was leaving.

But I had to go clear my head before Monday.

"I just don't understand why you won't take Juan or Manuel with you. You are breaking your own strict rule that no one is to go out alone on overnight trips, especially during the spring when the snakes are everywhere. It's too dangerous," Stacy said, trying her best not to let her sultry voice morph over into a whine. "I told you I have a feeling about this; I don't want you to go." She removed her sunglasses and leaned in closer to me and whispered, "I'm scared, Robert, and not just because you will be alone, or because I don't want you to cross paths with an aggressive snake. I can't put my finger on exactly what it is, but I just can't shake this uneasiness in the pit of my stomach. Please, babe, stay? For me?"

It took every ounce of strength and determination I had not to give into her pleading, and I knew that if I didn't leave now, she stood a good shot of swaying my thoughts over to the cool sheets upstairs that we just messed up earlier. I grabbed the reins and mounted my horse (rather than my wife) and smiled. "I can break my own rules because I won't fire myself," I said, reaching down with my free hand and stroking her long black hair. "Stop worrying, lover. I'll be back before you know it. Besides, Sahara here hates snakes even more than you do, and I guarantee she will steer clear of them." Stacy grimaced and quickly jerked her head away from my hand, putting her sunglasses back on with one quick snap of her wrist. She curtly dismissed me and turned on her heels, trudging off towards the house, her back rigid with anger. Sahara, sensing it was time to go, snorted loudly and stomped her front leg impatiently, awaiting my nudge to go. I took one final glance at the lovely backside of my bride and gave Sahara the cue. She responded with another snort and then took off out of the barn, her strong gait kicking up a cloud of pale dust behind us.

I let Sahara have her head for the first few miles, relishing the hot breeze on my face and the strength of her muscles under my legs. The sound of her pounding hooves pushed out all other random thoughts in my head. The desert scenery passed by in a blur of colors as we made our way down to the interior basin of the first 200 acres. Slowly, I eased back on the reins and coaxed Sahara into a mild trot as we were now entering more rocky terrain. I patted her dripping neck and cooed, "Good girl. Thanks for clearing my mind."

In the past few months, we had made this journey numerous times and I knew that Sahara could find her way, so I relaxed the reins and let her lead. In a few miles, she would stop for a drink in Boulder Creek all on her own. It would take half the day to get out to the campsite anyway, and honestly, I was in no hurry.

I reached back into my saddle pack and retrieved a bottle of water, slowly sipping as we made our way through the outcropping of cottonwood and juniper trees that would lead us to the peak of the vista as we made our way up the trail. I smiled as I surveyed the beauty of the blooming trees and brush flowers. They were just as vibrant and breathtaking as they had been in my youth. This was the first time since my college days that I was actually out in the wilderness during April, since that was always crunch time for accountants. Unless you were dead, in a coma or minus a vital appendage, missing work during hell month was not allowed.

God, I sure didn't miss those days.

The last nine months of my life had been a strange conglomeration of varying emotions. The first few days after my arrest, I was suicidal. The weight of everything came crashing down on top of me all at once. My worst fear was that I would lose my precious Stacy once she found out she was married to a monster, one that kept a huge, dark secret from her for our entire 25 years of marriage. I shuddered a bit at the memory of those desperate hours when I had no idea whether or not she would stand by my side. Then I smiled inwardly, recalling the moment she walked in, attorney in tow, and bailed me out of jail. She never said a word to me in the process. She didn't have to, for I could see in her big brown eyes that she wasn't going anywhere. She held her head high with her shoulders thrown back just a bit, almost daring anyone to say something to her for standing by me.

What an ironic twist of unforeseen events. Now, I rode atop my favorite horse, dressed in my old, dirty jeans and tattered cowboy boots, surveying the land that my father raised me to love, rather than rotting in jail. I was overcome with almost palatable serenity. No deadlines; no stressed out clients with their ridiculous demands on my time and energy; no being away from home and missing out on momentous events in the lives of my children; no ill-fitting monkey suits. No longer was I forced to view the outdoors through my window, and no more squabbling partners jockeying for the reins of the firm.

No Olin.

God; that was the best part; to finally be free of the heavy shackle he placed around my neck so long ago. For me, it was akin to being granted rebirth. The heaviness that I carried with me for so long, the nights of terror filled dreams that were only dimmed by drunken stupor, were almost completely gone. I hadn't had a drink in months now. To finally be rid of that dark, sordid secret, painful as it was to extract it, was wildly liberating.

A few days after Stacy bailed me out, I sat down and told the whole sordid mess to her and the girls, the words pouring out of me, just as they had that day in the conference room. The difference was that this time, the emotional level was much higher. It was one thing to admit my part in Gina's death to colleagues and cops, but to my wife and children—well, that was the worst. The shame, humiliation and outright anger at myself, my inner weaknesses and stupid mistakes, opened up in front of the three people that meant the most to me, was the most difficult thing I ever had experienced. Even the death of my parents paled in comparison. When I finished my story, I couldn't even look up into their eyes, fearing I would see their love and respect for me gone, replaced with disgust and shock at what a horrible person I really was. To my never ending surprise and utmost gratitude, my youngest, Shannon, with the wisdom of only the young and pure at heart, saved the day when she leaned over and held my hand and said, "Daddy, it's okay. We know you didn't hurt her, you couldn't. You were just in the wrong place at the wrong time, with the wrong friend. Shoot, you can't even put down one of the sick cows, you have to have Juan or Manuel do it." And then she smiled the most beautiful smile I had ever seen, her raven hair shimmering under the lights while we sat on the porch. Everyone started laughing at her candid comment. Stacy and Shawn immediately came over to where I was sitting and put their arms around me, embracing me for the person I was now, not the monster I had been.

Remembering that day caused a lump to form in my throat and made my chest heavy with love. I knew from that incredible moment that I was truly a blessed man; that no matter what happened to me after that, I could handle it. My precious family was by my side and forgave the sins of the younger me.

I focused my attention back to Sahara before I wound up blubbering like a baby. She slowed down as we came up the edge of Boulder Creek, and I swallowed hard and dismounted, letting her meander over to the water's edge and drink her fill. I followed her, gently running my rough hands through her heavy mane. Staring out into the endless terrain in front of us, a tear of happiness made its way down my cheek. Even though I was alone, my hand instinctively jerked and wiped it away, smiling to myself as I realized I was just a big softie at heart. Being out here on my land that was just as surely a part of my family as my inherited genetics, I felt the sudden rush of peace and tranquility come over me. I felt lighthearted and carefree, which was exactly the reason I had come out here before the trial. I needed to commune with not only nature, but the ground that held the blood of generations of my family, drawing strength from the dusty sediment as my ancestors once had. I tried once to explain the strange tie I felt with this ground to Stacy, but bless her heart, she just didn't understand. She was a city girl, although years of living with me had somewhat "countrified" her, so I really didn't expect her to have the same attachment to the endless, arid acres of land as I did.

Sahara's cold, wet muzzle brought me out of my lost thoughts as she playfully nibbled at my arm, her way of suggesting it was time to go. I patted her neck softly and then gently checked each of her hooves for embedded rocks while she patiently waited. Once finished, we resumed our trek towards my favorite place out of the 24 thousand plus acres I owned. We still needed to travel another few miles before we arrived at camp. Sahara's excitement from before was tempered now by the heat, and her pace slowed to a steady walk, the sun bearing down on us both.

Holding the reins lightly in my gloved hands, I thought about the day that I accepted the prosecution's offer and decided to testify against Olin. After countless grueling hours of questions, along with one detestable trip later to where we buried Gina, the conclusion was made that I was indeed telling the truth. My part in Gina's death was relegated to failure to report it and hindering prosecution. While Stacy and the girls were thrilled that I wouldn't be spending any time in jail and that my testimony would be the clincher on sending Olin away for life, I still struggled with my emotions. The fact that I possessed no recollection of what happened between the time Olin and Gina poured my drunk ass into my truck, to waking up naked in the backseat, haunted me. That was the stickler for me: why was I naked if I indeed, did not rape her? Who took my clothes off, and why? That question alone caused me great internal strife, for only two people truly knew the answer to that question, one of which was dead and the other— well, his word, either way, could not be relied upon. I needed to learn to come to terms with the fact that I never really would know if I had indeed defiled that sweet young thing until the day I stood in front of my Maker.

We plodded along in the miserable heat, Sahara's hooves the only sound other than a stray bird. In the quietness, I remembered the look on Audra's face that day in the conference room, staring at me with such disgust and hatred while I poured out the words for the first time in my life. I remembered how I almost choked on them as they spilled out. If someone had asked me prior to that day if I thought that Audra was capable of pulling off what she did, I would have laughed and told them no. Although Audra was one of the finest accountants in the state, her demeanor and personality never gave the slightest clue as to what was bubbling below the surface. Of course, I tried to stay as far away from her as possible. I knew the moment I walked into her office two days later and saw her swollen lips and blackened eyes what really happened to her after her meeting with Olin. I remember leaving her office and running to the bathroom to throw up, kicking myself for being such a pussy when it came to dealing with Olin. I let my fear of the sins he held over my head outweigh the anger I felt towards him, and for that, I would never forgive myself. If I could have instantaneously grown balls big enough to stand up to Olin that horrid night so long ago, none of this would have ever happened. He would have been in jail, never gone to work at Winscott and drug me right through the muck with him, and Audra would never have suffered the way she did. She would never have tossed the giant boulder into our lake that caused a ripple effect that destroyed numerous lives that day she shredded us all.

Part of me understood completely why she chose the route she did, for all of us played a part in her rape just like she said; each of us knew what kind of sorry bastard Olin was yet never did anything to stop him…albeit, for different reasons. I must admit though, I did feel a bit of sympathy towards some of the other partners that were trying to pick up the pieces of their shattered lives after that day. The only one I kept in contact with was Carl, who actually turned out to be quite the staunch supporter through this whole mess. When he told me that Eric retired and left Nicole, I felt a twinge of pity for her. Even though I knew that their relationship was a sin and never really condoned it, I witnessed enough stolen looks between the two of them to see the depths of Nicole's feelings shining through. I imagined she was devastated at not only his betrayal of her, but also his hasty departure.

Sahara rounded the bend that led down to our favorite little spot, nestled in at the edge of a large, open expanse, overlooking vista that was full of beautiful trees that gently swayed in the hot breeze. Her snorting brought me out of my reminiscence of the past briefly. She made her way over to the small circle of rocks that I set up weeks ago as a fire pit and stopped. I jumped off her wringing wet back and quickly removed the hot saddle and pack I had with me, then grabbed the large jug of water out of it and poured its refreshing coolness down the length of her back, rubbing her down as I went. She stomped and snorted a few more times, like she was saying thank you, then wandered over to the nearest expanse of open ground. Immediately, she dropped down and rolled in the dust, making her dark bay coat turn a light chestnut. I laughed at her for a moment, then turned around and began assembling the small tent I brought with me. I was thoroughly enjoying the mindless task of preparing my little camp, bustling about quickly since it would be dark in a few hours and I really needed to gather some wood for a fire.

Twenty minutes later, the sweat was dripping down my face and back, so I removed my shirt, throwing it inside the now upright tent. I made my way across the dusty ground towards the trees, climbing quickly up the small trail, forged by countless feet traipsing it prior to mine. Once I reached the top of the hill, I stopped to catch my breath and take in the view. The colors of the desert were like a salve to my heart.

I found plenty of broken limbs and dead, smaller trees that I chunked over the edge towards my camp, smiling as Sahara decided it was some sort of game and ran around in circles each time I threw a piece of wood. Her dog-like antics had always cracked me up ever since she was a small foal, romping and playing with the numerous farm dogs rather than the other babies in the pasture.

I peered over the edge and decided that enough wood was procured for at least a full night's worth of a roaring fire and descended the hill, dust and debris shooting up from underneath my boots. It took me almost another 20 minutes to haul all of the wood back over to the pit, but soon, it was all there and the fire was crackling loudly in the quiet, desert air. Dusk was just beginning to settle over the western horizon and the magnificent colors in the sky were almost so perfect that they looked like a painting.

God, what a beautiful place this was.

I sat down and drank in the sunset, letting the emotions that no man wants to admit he possesses run free through my mind. This brief moment in time, this silence that I so desperately craved, this freedom in the open expanse of the land that was now in its fourth generation of Folton ownership, was what I needed. This was a place where no one except the occupants in the Heaven's above would see, so I wept and prayed to God. Although the words were screaming forth from my heart, they never crossed my lips. They were silently flung into the air towards the sky, begging the Almighty for strength to stand up to Olin on Monday. Pleading to make things right that had gone so horribly wrong years ago. Beseeching Him for forgiveness for whatever part I played in Gina's death, and for not stopping Olin from raping Audra. Tears of thanks for blessing me with the most wonderful wife and beautiful children ran down my sunburned cheeks at my unworthiness to be gifted with such love after all the terrible things I had been a part of.

Physically and emotionally spent, I opened my wet eyes to the darkness that now surrounded me, the vibrant sunset long gone. Shocked that I spent so long in silent prayer, I realized that I needed to find Sahara and feed her, along with myself. I stood up and clucked for her, and her dainty whinny sounded softly from about 50 yards to my right, her hooves clacking on the rocks as she made her way over to me. I went into the tent and grabbed the bag full of oats out of the saddlebag and walked over to the small tree that I normally tied her to. I rattled the sack hoping it would speed up her slow gait. Her ears perked up and she crossed the remaining 20 yards in a quick trot, and almost knocked me over in her excitement to shove her nose in the oats. I grabbed the lead rope and secured it to the tree, and after she finished her dinner, went back to the tent to stow the empty bag.

And that's when I found the booze.

I stood there and stared at the full bottle of bourbon that had obviously been in my saddlebag for quite some time, since I hadn't touched a drop of the liquid in months. With the help of my loving wife, I decided that it was best for me to face all of the demons in my past with a clear head from now on, rather than a bourbon soaked one. Surprisingly, putting the poison down didn't cause me the pain I assumed it would. But now, in the stillness of the night, the bottle stared at me, its contents quietly whispering my name. They called out to me, like the voice of an old lover, begging me to wrap my lips around her cool, smooth rim and drink deeply from her depths.

To my shame, I caved, running back to the arms of the Jezebel that had been my companion for longer than my own wife. I snatched the bottle up and made my way out to the blanket, plopping down in front of the raging fire, admiring the amber color that seductively moved inside the bottle. I closed my eyes and inhaled the familiar scent, held my breath, and took a huge gulp. The fire raced down my throat and hit my empty stomach like a hot ember, and it lurched in protest. Before I could change my mind, I took a few more pulls at her glass breast, relishing every moment of the burn.

Setting the bottle down beside me, I stared into the fire, my head clouded and my vision swimming. The flames suddenly took on the shape of dancing demons, their fiery fingertips reaching out towards me in the dark. Oh God, I knew I needed to lie down and let this pass, so I half stood up, half crawled to the tent. I made it to the sleeping bag, sprawling out on top of it, too drunk to figure out the intricacies of the zipper.

That was the last thing I remember before waking up to the most incredible pain I had felt in my life and hearing a voice from the past announcing my impending death.

CHAPTER 4
Piper-The Hunt

I pulled the piece of crap, no GPS and cash-only rental over behind the outcropping of rocks I had spotted during a previous reconnaissance of the area. The jagged boulders jutted out almost to the edge of the road and curved sharply back, holding just enough room behind them to completely obscure a vehicle from the roadway, which is exactly what I needed: coverage.

I lost track of the hours of my life that had I spent slowly driving along this 100 mile stretch of road as I desperately searched out the terrain, noting everything of significance, from the closest people (over 75 miles away) to the layout of the arid land and the amount of traffic flow (practically nil). The five practice runs I'd made in the last week allowed me to memorize the route I needed to take to the spot on foot, even at night, so I wasn't too concerned that I arrived with only about an hour until dusk. Had I not packed my clothes and gear earlier, before my meeting with Dr. Moore, I would be sneaking through the woods at midnight. That would have caused some problems with my intricate plan.

My plan to kill Robert.

Stepping out of the little Honda POS, I quickly retrieved my gear from the trunk, slinging the backpack over my shoulder. I locked the car and stashed the keys under the small rock by the back tire. The fewer items I had to worry about the better, and in this heat, covered in black from head to toe–including my warrior painted face–I was already sweating and I had yet to start walking the four mile hike to the camp.

Fuck, the things we do for love.

After adjusting the straps of my pack, I then checked the laces on my black leather combat boots, making sure all bases were covered for this journey. I was on a euphoric high from my first kill, and my earlier encounter with the hissing monsters that Dr. Moore had been so fond of (*had, hee hee,*). I felt like I had dropped acid and ecstasy at the same time. Dr. Moore's tragic demise (*again, hee hee*) hadn't been nearly as up close and personal as Robert's would be tonight, so the anticipation was almost too much to bear.

I didn't really have any reason to end Dr. Moore's feeble little life other than the mere fact that he possessed balls between his legs. Yes, he bore a striking resemblance to Dr. Hopkins, whom I hated with a passion that was only matched in emotional intensity by my love for Olin, but...oh well, I needn't worry about that now. I couldn't help but wonder, had he actually been awake enough to have any, if Dr. Moore's final thoughts would have centered on his poor choice of career.

But Robert: now, I had many reasons for killing him, the most important one being to free Olin from that hellhole he was sitting in so we could be together. Our little jailhouse visits just weren't enough; I needed to feel the rush of his hands on me after waiting so many years. I couldn't wait to feel the exhilarated high that would overcome me when I watched Robert gasp and sputter for his last, extremely painful breath. Just thinking about that made my steps come quicker, the muscles in my body taut with the anticipation of the kill. My senses were heightened to the sights and sounds of the surrounding environment, my coordination and balance working in harmony. Picking my way easily through the dense scrub brush, I wound my body between the trees towards my destination.

After about two miles, I stopped briefly by a craggy, meandering creek and leaned against a boulder that doubled as a seat as well, and a cloak. It was recessed enough to allow me to sit back and be out of sight, in case some rough cattle-puncher decided to walk up on me. I took my backpack off and set it carefully beside me, double-checking its contents to make sure everything was still intact and in its proper place. Satisfied, I grabbed a bottle of water and leaned back, glancing at my watch to discover that it was only 8:30. Fantastic. I was making great time. Grateful for the moisture sliding down my parched throat, I greedily slugged back a few gulps of water. Looking up at the beautiful Arizona sunset, I recalled how so many nights, locked up in my cell-like room at Haven Hills, I had dreamt about being outside; to be free from the wretched Dr. Hopkins and his incessant prattling about my numerous "psychoses" and my "obsessions" with the wrong men. He may have the letters "M.D." after his name but really, what did he know about the inner workings of not only my mind, but my heart?

Not a damn thing.

Love: I had been in love three times in my life: the first, my ex-husband, Nick. That dark, sultry face, those huge, limpid brown eyes that stared right through me, the gentle touch of his hands on my body; oh, now he was something! He was fresh out of law school and I had just graduated with my accounting degree when we met as interns at Winscott. I ended up staying after my internship, but he left after being offered a position at Ketner Law Firm in Scottsdale, where he was now a full partner; and on the team of lawyers for Olin, which was rather shocking, since I divorced him over Olin. Our courtship was brief and he proposed amidst candles and champagne with a huge rock that almost blinded me. For the next several years our life together consisted of brief interludes that rarely included a romp in the sack. We both travelled so much that we were never home long enough to have a relationship, so we grew apart.

After the first five years, I realized that our biggest issue was the fact that I didn't have the right equipment between my legs to entice him to bed. That little bit of information was forever ingrained in my vision from the time I caught him in a compromising position with his newest in a long string of many assistants, Greg. An impromptu visit to surprise my husband ended abruptly when I walked into his office and saw Greg bent over Nick's desk as the receiver. Walking in on that little escapade shocked me, but not as much as it should have. My feelings for Nick had already changed over into the brother/friend realm as I realized I no longer yearned for his touch and actually, was quite repulsed by it on the rare occasions he tried to initiate sex. In the back of my mind, I always knew he was a rump ranger. After hastily yanking his pants back up, Nick had chased me to the parking lot and cried, begging me to stay. Sadly, this panicked display was not because of his "love" for me, but because he couldn't bear the thought of the scandal and how it would affect his ability to become a partner. So, we came to an agreement right there in the parking lot: we would remain legally married but were free to pursue our own agendas. This freedom was contingent upon discretion, and in exchange for my part in the charade, I was to be given free reign with the finances, no questions asked.

For the first few years, that arrangement worked out just dandy for me. I went on an excessive buying spree. I bought, without Nick ever even looking at it, a five million dollar estate that was nestled in the hillside and had panoramic views of Camelback Mountain and the Phoenix skyline. I spent another two million dollars furnishing it, and then once that little project was completed, went out and bought myself a brand new Mercedes.

But, I was still bored and lonely. By then, I had made minority partner and my travelling days had diminished quite a bit; and, I started working closer with *him*.

I felt a tear slide down my painted cheek at the mere thought of Ralph, and knew I needed to get going; no time for sitting here cruising down memory lane. None of all that pain mattered now anyway, since I had my Olin. Quickly, I packed my water away and secured my pack and hopped off the rock to begin my journey again. I tried to concentrate on the trail that was now dark and that my footing needed to be sure and steady, but oh, I should never have thought about Ralph. In mid stride, I stopped and slapped myself twice, hard, trying to rid my mind of images of his face.

Good God, I had loved that man with a passion just as strong as the one I now felt for Olin. Funny, thinking about the two of them at the same time used to make me feel a sick, twisted sense of guilt, almost like I was cheating on Ralph with Olin; but that was just silly, since I never actually had the chance to consummate my physical longing for Ralph before he killed himself. God knows I tried on countless out of town audits that he took me on, but he always spurned my advances. He was such an honorable man. He had looked so sad when telling me that he felt like a mentor to me, and that would be wrong of him to take advantage of me in that way. Hearing his chivalry made me want him all the more.

The distracting images would not leave and I began to worry that they might harm my plans. Slapping myself silly wasn't working, so I resorted to a measure I knew would. Reaching into my pants pocket, I retrieved the small knife hidden there, then quickly rolled up my sleeve and started slicing vigorously. The painful ecstasy raced through my blood and rushed to my head, wiping away all traces of coherent thought, save for the beautiful, burning pain. I shuddered slightly, almost orgasmically, and sliced once more, the blood now dripping onto the dry, desert floor. Replacing my knife, I rode the waves of glorious, mind numbing pleasure.

Clear headed now, my focus back on my prey, I moved at a quicker pace through the twists and turns of the trail under the bright desert moon, covering the final two miles in record time. Before I even climbed the rocks to my perch overlooking the camp, the acrid smell of smoke from the bastard's fire greeted me and I heard the faint whinny from his horse. Immediately, I slowed my steps down to a crawl, mindful of the noise that my footfalls would make if I misstepped. I quietly made my way up the rocks and across the short vista to the large grouping of Palo Verde trees at the edge, which was my designated lookout point. Pausing every few steps to listen for the telltale sounds below that would signal that I had been discovered made my trek even slower. Hearing nothing but the crackle of the fire, I made it to the trees and gently removed my backpack, setting it down beside me as I flattened myself to the dry ground, belly first, and peered over the edge, eagerly watching my former colleague: now my prey.

He had his back to me as he tended the roaring fire. His horse was about 20 yards away, tied loosely to the tree closest to his small tent. I quickly scanned the rest of his little camp, looking for the one item I counted on him bringing as part of my plan: a bottle of bourbon. I smiled a bit, thinking that he hadn't changed a bit since my days at Winscott; he was an alcoholic and always would be.

Just what I'd hoped for.

My eyes caught every movement the rat-bastard made while he fiddled with the fire and eventually plopped back down on his pallet of blankets. I watched him reach over and take a full, long pull of his bottle, and squinted a bit after he set it back down, trying to determine exactly how much was left. My hope was that he had already consumed plenty. My patience was rewarded when he stood up and began to make his way to his tent, stumbling twice and almost falling into the fire once.

It just couldn't get any better.

Crouched like a hidden tiger as my prey nested in his tent, the snoring of a dead drunk ringing throughout the valley, I waited for over an hour before I rolled slowly over and reached into my bag, extracting the syringe from its resting spot inside the cooler. Stealthily, I crept back over to the boulders and climbed down, knowing it would take me a good ten minutes to circumvent this small vista to the campground. When I was a little over 50 yards away, I picked up a small rock and threw it in the direction of his horse. Startled, it snorted and whinnied for a few moments. Like a statue, I didn't move as I waited to see if the noise from his trusty steed awoke the fucking prince. Thankfully, all I was greeted with was louder snoring.

Perfect.

I walked a bit faster this time, heading straight for his horse and untying its rope from the tree despite its vigorous protests. Big ugly thing, it didn't even wait for a slap on the ass; as soon as the rope hit its neck, it twirled around on its hind legs and raced off into the darkness. Again, I stopped and moved my blackened frame behind the cover of the tree, waiting and listening for sounds from the tent, hoping that the heavy thud of the horse's hooves hadn't disturbed my old friend. My ears were delighted to hear the obnoxious rattles blaring from his nostrils.

With my heart racing and my blood flowing through my veins as the adrenaline rush overtook me, I crept up to the tent and peered inside. Robert was passed out on top of his sleeping bag rather than inside it and a small lantern flickered in the corner, which was going to make this easier than I thought. I gently reached over and uncapped the syringe and began to unzip the tent, keeping my ears pealed for the slightest change in his nostril symphony. I took two steps inside, crouching down to my knees as I stopped next to his head, deciding that the best spot to inject him was in his exposed neck. Suddenly he rolled over, his arm hitting my thigh, and in my attempt to move too quickly, I lost my balance and fell over. I tried to protect my hand that held the syringe and in the course of doing so, landed hard on my left side, almost on top of Robert.

All the commotion brought him out of his drunken stupor, his swollen, red eyes trying desperately to focus as he blinked rapidly several times. Although I knew he couldn't actually see my face, he felt my physical presence and reacted to it, kicking out both legs and smashing his left knee into my temple. I grunted loudly and he screamed, his voice raspy and heavy from the booze and sleep.

"What the hell? Get off me!" he yelled as he tried valiantly to sit up and take a swing at his attacker; his lack of body control was almost laughable. With energy and excitement running through me now, I ducked, rolled over and set myself upright once again. My reflexes were almost catlike and my face was only inches from his as I answered him, "Olin says hello, motherfucker!" and jabbed the needle up to the hilt into the soft crook of his neck, releasing the entire contents of the poison into his bloodstream. Immediately, his face contorted in pain and his hands flew to his neck, clawing and twisting at the burning wound.

I leapt to my feet and took a step back, my senses taking in the violent scene before me. He was writhing around the tent floor now, his guttural screams piercing the night and ringing through my ears, and his body began to convulse as though he was being electrocuted. In his frenzy, he had actually torn pieces of his skin from his neck, and the blood was now flowing freely from the wounds. As the convulsions worsened, his hands fell from his neck to his sides, the screaming stopped and his breath came in great gasps as his eyes began to bulge out of their sockets. His skin was turning an almost ashy white when suddenly, ever so slightly, he turned his face in my direction, his pain-engorged eyes locking with mine. I smiled lovingly at him, hoping beyond hope that he might recognize me under this entire stealth garb as I knelt down beside him, reaching out with my gloved hand to gently stroke his face. For a brief moment, behind all the pain, I almost sensed a hint of recognition behind his eyes and my smile grew even bigger as I leaned over to his ear and whispered, "And the snake recompensed the rat twofold."

The backstabbing bastard struggled for his last breath, his eyes rolling back in his head. His body gave one final jerk and then went limp, his bowels immediately evacuating all over his sleeping bag, filling the tent with a horrendous odor that almost made me vomit. Turning away quickly, I made my way out and ran back to the spot where my satchel was then jogged for the first mile or so back towards my car. The vibrant moon was almost in the center of the starry sky, giving me plenty of light to maneuver across the rocky terrain as I slowed my gait down just a bit. The energy that flowed through me now was overwhelming and it spurred my muscles with renewed vigor; after a few minutes, I was running full speed again. The hot night air whipped across my face and filled my lungs with its warm vapor. In less than 45 minutes, I rounded the bend back to my hidden spot by the road.

Retrieving my keys from their shallow grave, I opened the trunk and flung my backpack into the dark space. I forced my pounding limbs to stay still for a moment so I could listen for the sounds of any traffic; hearing none, I unlocked the car door and started the feeble engine up. Backing up in the dark was a bit difficult, but once out of the hole, I slowly made my way to the edge of the road with my lights off and checked for any signs of oncoming vehicles.

It was clear as a bell. With that, I gunned the engine and the car shot out into the road, its little lawn mower engine humming a protest to my heavy foot. I turned the lights on and made my way along the twisty roads, and smiled at the image of Robert's distorted face, another memory forever ingrained in my head. It was a shame that Olin didn't get to see that lying sonofabitch suck in his last breath; I would need to recall every detail when, at last, I could hold him in my arms and share all of this with him.

The road whizzed by and I headed back to Phoenix under the cloak of darkness. I began laughing uncontrollably and tears rolled down my sticky, dirty cheeks as I thought, *One down, two to go.*

CHAPTER 5
Audra-Releasing the Demons

WEDNESDAY

The soft, black leather recliner—no couch, thank God—was at least comfortable in this uncomfortable situation. The silent yet patient face of Charlene Bray, the counselor I had contacted a week ago on Steve's recommendation, stared back at me. I had been surprised when she contacted me later that morning and had an appointment open for the following Wednesday: today. I couldn't help but wonder if Steve had something to do with that, since most of the time, therapists were booked far in advance.

I had just finished spewing out the last eight years of my life to her, including the day I eviscerated the snake in the conference room, and ended by regaling her with the tale of my recent nightmares. Although she was a professional therapist, I could almost sense her struggling to retain neutrality when I described how Olin was led out in handcuffs by my now detective-boyfriend, her eyes widening slightly as she took furious notes. I expected to see smoke rising from her pad any moment if she wrote any faster. My mouth was parched and felt like I had swallowed several cotton balls, and as I took a few gulps of water from the bottle I brought with me, Charlene finally finished her copious scribbling and looked up at me. Her huge brown eyes had questions running around behind them and I could almost see her internal search to pluck out just the right one to ask me.

55

"Audra, after all you have experienced over the years, especially the last five, why do you think you decided seeing a therapist now was necessary?" She tossed the question out in front of me almost like a hunter setting a trap full of bait for its prize to sink its teeth into. And of course, I bit.

"It's the dreams. I don't understand them or have the slightest inkling what they might mean. As I told you earlier, I am accustomed to dreams and nightmares, but the ones in my past have always stemmed from events that *already* occurred: my inability to please my parents, my miscarriage; my divorce; my rape. The dreams that followed each of those events, as awful as they were, made sense to me. Lose a child? You dream about searching for them. You experience the demise of a marriage? Your dreams tend to center around your broken heart and abandonment issues. Violently raped? You tend to relive the trauma through dreams and plot your revenge. But these dreams are so different. I can't seem to shake this overwhelming sense of foreboding when I wake up from them, like there is some foreshadowing, something I should be learning from them; yet I don't know what that lesson could be. I don't just feel alone, I feel forsaken, all the light sucked from me as I trudge through darkness and malevolent, unseen forces attempt to pull me deeper in, plunging me into oblivion. The physical sense I have upon awakening is that of someone sitting on my chest, slowly pushing the air out of me as I struggle to breathe. I have experienced fear in my dreams before, but this feeling...well, it's petrifying," I whispered, embarrassed to admit out loud how utterly helpless the nighttime scenes in my subconscious seemed to render me as I spoke them aloud: to an almost childlike state.

"Interesting perceptions you have on dreams, Audra. The one that I find the most remarkable, where I believe we should focus our attention for our first few sessions, is your association of being raped with revenge. I noticed that you didn't say, 'Violently raped? Relive the trauma through dreams and learn to heal' but rather, 'plot your revenge.'"

For a moment, I didn't quite understand what she was trying to tell me with her statement. The silence between us lasted for a few moments as I let that question sink in and stared out her office window into the vibrant, endless blue sky outside, searching for the hidden meaning behind her question. Why did she pick up on that tidbit after *everything* else I said earlier? I felt a bit of anger rise up inside me; being asked such a ridiculous question irritated me. This woman obviously had never experienced the humiliation and degradation that the act of rape has on someone and therefore, had no right to question my choices of response to one.

I was surprised at my immediate flare of anger and forced myself to let it subside. After all, it was only a question. Before I could say anything to her, Charlene leaned forward and asked quietly, "Audra, what are you thinking of right at this moment?"

Clearing my throat, I pulled my gaze away from the vast blue horizon and looked across the room into her probing eyes and replied, "Surprisingly, anger."

"And why does your emotional response to my question surprise you?" Charlene prodded, her pen absentmindedly tapping her strong chin as her own answers were filling her head as she awaited mine.

"Well, my first assumption would be because it was a simple question which invoked an immediate angry thought process from me, as my first consideration was that you have no right to question my reactions after being raped. I guess I sort of feel like your question was encased inside some hidden reprimand for me choosing revenge over healing, like I wanted that to be my path," I said, lifting my chin up faintly and leveling my eyes with hers in a small show of defiance, almost as if I was daring her to tell me I was wrong.

Charlene leaned back in her chair and set her notepad down as she folded her hands in her lap. Her eyes were full of unasked questions as she looked at me, sensing my anger as though it were a visible entity to her trained eye, her eyes focused on my hands. I followed her gaze and realized that I was sitting like a rigid doll at the edge of the seat, and that my fingers were gripping the armrest so tightly that they were turning white. I immediately let go, forcing myself to ease back into the cool folds of the chair and control my pounding heart. I softened up my gaze and said, "I apologize, Charlene, for reacting like such a child. I normally don't get that angry, or have such a lack of control over my emotions, especially over something as trivial as a simple question."

Charlene cocked her head ever so slightly and her eyes bored into mine again. I could almost feel her presence inside my head as she trudged her way through the myriad of thoughts, and probably felt a bit dizzy from all the twists and turns as she went.

"Audra, do you realize you just apologized to me, the therapist you hired to listen to, and hopefully help guide you through, your thoughts and emotions? I am here to help you to understand yourself better, to give you the tools to assist you in coping with the tremendously difficult emotional and physical stressors from your past, as well as the ability to overcome these tragedies and be a stronger person for them. I am not here to judge you for anything you say to me or for any actions or ideas that you may have thought of or acted upon. I am also not here to solve your problems; rather, I'm here to walk along side you as a steadying force as you learn to work through them and peacefully coexist with them: to accept them for what they are, incorporate them into your being, and move along with your life in a healthy direction. However, my questions are specifically designed and chosen to make you ponder what you truly are feeling, why you are feeling that way, and how best to work through those emotions. Therefore, what I am saying to you is that apologies are not needed, or necessary, although I would like for you to contemplate why you felt the need to do so after our session today; and also, consider the reasons for the anger you exuded towards me when the word "revenge" was brought up, to discuss at our appointment next week."

As I sat there and listened to Charlene speak in her best professional drone, I couldn't help but wonder, even though I hated to admit it to myself, if she had a point. Why did I become immediately defensive when the subject of revenge came up?

What was it about that word that triggered such a quick and angry response? Maybe it was because, for the first time since the attack, I allowed my inner thoughts and emotions to be spoken aloud to another person (other than Steve, who was only aware of the surface issues, not the deeper seated ones, since I wouldn't allow him to be). Maybe it was because the old Audra was trying to break through, to reach out of my subconscious as some sort of an inner voice from the past; the voice of reason and sensibility; the one that whispered to me that night that I should have called the police and had the bastard arrested; something other than shutting myself off and releasing the dormant animal that resided in me. Maybe it was the fact that I knew, somewhere deep down, that I sensed the feelings of regret and remorse for the entire last five years of my life, yet buried them. I abhorred the snakes and their slithering ways and could only concentrate on making them pay for what they had done to me; but really, I ended up sinking down to their pond scum level and rolling in the stagnant muck right along with them as I did things that I never knew I was capable of. Was it possible that the realization that I was no better than those I hated with such a passion had just hit me? Was that what had made me so angry?

It was too much for my already overtaxed brain to focus on, so I stood up quickly and grabbed my purse. I whipped out my checkbook and said to Charlene, "How much do I owe you for today's visit?"

She smiled awkwardly at me and quietly said, "One hundred and fifty." The look on her face, those questions that loomed silently behind her eyes, were just too much for me, so I scribbled out the check and twirled to leave as Charlene asked, "Audra, would you like to schedule another appointment for next week?"

My hand was on the doorknob and I stared at the silvery circle without blinking for a few seconds before I answered her. As I twisted the knob and opened the door, my voice barely above a breathy whisper, I said, "I will be at Olin's trial, and I don't know how long that will last." Hanging my head in quiet shame, I continued, "But even if I were free, I am not sure I could come back." I fled her office like someone, or something, was chasing me.

CHAPTER 6
Audra-Realizations

Once inside the relative safety and familiarity of my car, the sweat on my forehead beginning to dry under the forced air from its vents, and I closed my eyes and tried to control my breathing. I had known before I walked in to Charlene's office that morning that the session was going to be difficult, since she was going to ask me to delve deep into my life and open up wounds that I had covered with hidden gauze long ago. The reaction I had expected to experience from airing out my "dirty laundry" was a few shed tears and maybe some pent up anger, but the overwhelming sensation of fury that had engulfed me was shocking.

Try as I might, I just couldn't understand the reason behind my response. I thought back to the day of Gina's memorial service and the sense of relief and finality I'd experienced when I watched her ashes float into the wind-swept meadow. That feeling stayed with me for months as I convinced myself that I had accomplished what I initially set out to do. Honestly, I didn't have much time to contemplate my actions as I was immediately immersed in the day to day struggle of running Winscott, along with all the chaotic occurrences that fell into my lap from day one. Maybe it really was the upcoming trial that was bothering me; I knew I would be required to dredge up those dark moments again, and my life would become an open tablet for not only the judge and jury to witness, but also the entire nation. Every word that came out of my mouth would most likely become the newest morsel to be picked apart by the scavenging media.

I leaned back in my seat and thought about Steve's worries in terms of my inability to discuss my innermost thoughts with strangers. My actions had just proven him right; I couldn't even make it through a measly one hour session with a counselor without becoming angry and running for the hills, so to speak. How in the hell was I going to make it through my testimony, which was less than a week away?

Starting my car, I made my way out of the parking lot and to the freeway, planning to get back to work and prepare for my Friday meeting with a potentially huge new client. God knows I wouldn't be able to concentrate on much for the next few weeks once the trial started, but I decided I just couldn't bring myself to put on my game face for the office. I grabbed my cell and called Gabrielle.

"Audra Tanner's office, Gabrielle speaking," said her chipper voice through the phone.

"Gab, it's me. I have a few other things I must do today that I have put off for way too long, so I will not be coming back today. Will you please tell anyone that calls for me that I am out of the office and won't be back until tomorrow? If it's urgent, tell them to email me, but don't let them talk you into forwarding their call to my cell because I won't have time to answer it." My voice started trailing off as I was distracted by the road that I had been aimlessly driving on for the last few minutes, and then my brain registered the fact that, judging by the familiar scenery on Highway 93, my body had decided we were heading to Summerset.

I could hear the worry in Gabby's voice as she replied, "Sure thing, Audra. If there is anything you need me to take care of on this end, let me know. Did you want me to relay your messages to you, or would you prefer to wait until tomorrow?" she asked, slyly trying to see how I would answer her question, so she could assess the likelihood of my completing any work today.

"Unless there is a major fire that needs tending to, no calls," was my clipped response as I slowed down and pulled into a gas station, dreading the thought of stepping out into the heat to fill up.

"Well, no, nothing pressing. But Janette Lancaster called to confirm your appointment for tomorrow night at 6:30. She was rather adamant about getting an answer from you today. I told her that the meeting was still on your calendar and that you had not informed me of any changes, but she wanted a firm commitment today. I can call her back if you like," Gabby said.

Good grief, this woman was sure pushy. But, then again, she was going through a really messy divorce and a lot of money was at stake for her, so I could understand why. I knew I really needed to be the one to call her back and confirm, but I just didn't want to listen to her drone on again about all of her soon to be ex's business ventures and all of their homes that needed to be valued. Although grateful to have the chance to score a huge new client, I pushed the call off to Gabby.

"Would you mind? Please tell her that yes, we are all set for Friday and that I will see her at Zargenta's," I said, immediately feeling a twinge of guilt for peddling off something that was really my responsibility on Gabby. She had been such a godsend to me the last few months, working tirelessly right alongside me, all the while planning her elaborate wedding. "Oh, and once you finish talking to her, take the rest of the day off, Gab. Go pamper yourself; you deserve it. The next few weeks are going to be rough."

Gabby's voice was a mixture of glee with a little bit of wariness mixed in as she said, "Gee, thanks boss! You're sure?"

"Go, girl. Just please remember to call Mrs. Lancaster first. I will see you tomorrow." And I quickly hung up before I could change my mind or she could start asking me questions that I didn't want to answer.

What I wanted was to see Mrs. Milligan, for if there was one person that I could truly open up to and entrust with my darkest fears, it was that blessed soul. There was something so open and inviting, so warm and tender about her, so tangible that it was almost physically pulling me towards her. I was about an hour into my drive through the mountains when I decided it would be rude not to contact her before I just showed up on her front stoop unannounced. As I hoped, she was delighted that I was coming to visit, and told me to drive safely and she would be patiently waiting on the porch with her special blend of iced tea.

As I ascended higher up the mountain and away from the heavy traffic of Phoenix, my jumbled thoughts centered round my sanity, or lack thereof. My immersion into the rancid depths of retribution's sinkhole had perhaps been too long, and I wondered if I would ever truly be free of its lingering stench. I was quite adept at fooling myself, for short periods of time at least, that I no longer harbored any ill feelings towards Olin and the other pit vipers; that I was past all the rage and had finally come to grips with what happened to me; and that I let it all float away with Gina's ashes.

But that wasn't the truth.

Although I didn't seem to be inundated as much by the all-consuming thoughts from before, the rage still reared its ugly head at seemingly insignificant times, like today. A simple, introspective question immediately ignited internal combustion. Before, all my emotional responses tended to hone in and set up residence with the anger, not allowing me much room for any other emotion. Now that other emotions were trying to surface, my brain seemed to resort back to its previous state, which I despised. I didn't want to feel angry or any emotion associated with it, but it was almost a comfort zone for me, and more familiar than the newest gut wrenches that I felt upon waking up from the lonely dreams.

My hands shook a bit as a thought finally emerged from the shadowy corner of my brain and stepped out into the bright sunlight, causing me to drive faster and faster through the mountains. I was so confused at this sudden turn of events, for this was the first time I realized that was the core of what I was feeling: anger's distant relative, guilt. And I didn't like it at all.

I turned the radio up full blast to drown out this disturbing revelation as I careened down the road, forcing myself to only concentrate on the lyrics and the road to rid myself of this moment of self-discovery. I was screeching at the top of my lungs to *Runnin' Down A Dream* by Tom Petty when I realized I had almost missed my turn into Mrs. Milligan's driveway. I hit the brakes harder than I intended, causing dirt and gravel to kick up all around my car as I swerved into her drive, barely missing her quaint little country mailbox. I came to a complete stop amidst the gritty cloud I had stirred up and shut the engine off. As I stepped out into the blaring heat of the sun, I heard a small snicker coming from the direction of the front porch, which I knew was there somewhere behind the dust, and heard Mrs. Milligan's gentle voice call out, "Well now, that is sure some way to make an appearance."

I couldn't help the wide grin that made its way across my face at not only her soothing voice, but also the fact that, despite its numerous critics, music did seem to have the ability, even if just for a moment, to soothe the proverbial *savage beast*...or at least to cause my beast to hibernate for a bit during my drive.

I made my way to the porch and sat down on the front swing next to Mrs. Milligan. All it took was one smile and her gnarled hand gently wrapping around mine and for the next few hours, she listened while I opened my mouth and let the words that had been trapped inside me for so long tumble out.

CHAPTER 7
Audra-Reborn

It was well after dark when I finally hugged Mrs. Milligan goodbye around her frail, soft neck. As our embrace ended, she clasped her strong, gnarled fingers gently around my face, her cloudy green eyes beseeching my own, and said, "Don't forget, child, what you learned today. Forgiveness is what truly cleanses the soul and wipes away all tears as the tumor of hatred is removed. Anger and fear will never stop festering inside you if you never remove them. What has happened is in the past and cannot be changed. You can only look forward now; but please dear, don't drag these heavy bags behind you, for in the end, they will become too much for you to carry and will pull your forward progress to a dead stop. You felt your pain, lived out your anger, sought your revenge and *it's over now*. I told you once to 'Let it go', but neglected the most important part: 'Let it go and let God' handle this."

I nodded in silence, grateful for her no nonsense words of wisdom. Of all the years I had been on this earth, I had never once experienced someone crawling inside my heart and soul like she could, immediately locating the source of my struggles and pointing them out, making me come to full terms with them while she gently stood at my side for moral support.

Earlier, after I had finished whining and complaining about all my jumbled thoughts and feelings after I arrived in a cloud of dust, she opened up her own heart and shared with me what the last 34 years of her life had been like. I listened not just with my ears, but my pain-filled heart. Her words somehow sunk deep inside me, peeling back the countless layers of hatred, anger, distrust and sorrow that had stacked up for years. They had been encased in a blackened knot that she finally broke through. I realized about halfway through her tale that although poignant, her words held a deeper meaning for me; strangely inviting, almost as though they were being spoken by someone, or something, else. She shared her love of God with me, and how she relied on Him for strength and power to get her through her painful journey of losing her daughter, and then the death of her husband. Her voice was a quiet whisper that floated over me, showing me that the missing piece of my life was that relationship; I just was clueless as to how to get there.

Her wise eyes saw my confusion and she had excused herself from the porch, quickly returning with a well-worn, leather covered book in her hand, and placing it in my hands as she said, "This will answer all the questions you have, my dear." She sat back down, smiling at the fact that my eyes had widened at the thickness of the Bible. "Don't worry, honey. Gina was an avid reader and marked it well. Just follow her notes; they will lead the way to the answers you seek and hopefully, quiet your dreaded nightmares."

Now, Bible in hand and her words ringing in my ears, I smiled back at her lovely face. "Thank you, for everything. I agree with you: there is a reason why we are in each other's lives," I said, staring down at the cracked leather cover of Gina's Bible.

"Yes, you are our Avenging Angel," came her quiet reply as she smiled, the thin skin crinkling around her eyes, and clasped her hands to her chest as her eyes closed, almost if she were reliving the dream she had of Gina so long ago. Under her breath, I would have sworn I heard her say, "You look so much like her," as a tear slid down her face.

I smiled back at her as the color rose in my cheeks at her pet name for me and replied, "Yes, you know what role I played in your life: now for me to find out yours in mine." Holding the tattered Bible up in front of me, I said, "I assume my answer lies somewhere inside these pages?"

"Avenging Angel, it's nice to meet you: I am your Guiding Light." she quipped, immediately grinning from ear to ear as she took her hands and shushed me from the porch. "Now, skedaddle girl! Go see your man before he is sawing logs in his bed, dreaming about you."

The laughter between the two of us filled the quiet night as I heeded her advice and headed to my car and climbed in, gently setting the Bible down in the seat in the same place that less than a year ago, I had placed the urn of its previous owner. Once again, Mrs. Milligan entrusted me with something so precious and valuable I couldn't bear the thought of letting her down, and promised myself that as soon as I could, I would investigate the words on the pages that she seemed so intent upon me reading. As I pulled out onto the darkened highway and headed towards Steve's house, I laughed out loud when I pictured how my parents would react when I told them I was reading the Bible. They both were staunch, card-carrying atheists that would flip out, thinking I had been brainwashed by some crazed religious cult, and would probably insist on me going to some sort of de-programming unit for immediate treatment. Their reaction alone was worth me reading the pages of this book.

My thoughts of shocking my parents and causing them a few more sprouting gray hairs were interrupted by the chirping of my cell phone from Steve's incoming call. It was almost ten o'clock and I was sure he was wondering where I was, since I told him earlier that I was on my way, but then became caught up in Mrs. Milligan's life story.

"I was just about to call you," I said. "I am about 15 minutes away."

"Well now, I was beginning to worry about you, then I remembered, 'Why, that's the Warrior of Winscott and no one messes with her.'" he said, laughing at his own joke. He knew how much that newspaper article's new nickname for me caused me to see red, for the embarrassment was overwhelming, and unwelcomed.

"Oh, funny man. Did you want me to come over or not? One more crack like that and I will turn this car around and head straight back to my place." I quipped, hoping he sensed the playfulness in my voice.

He did, and responded in his best impression of Clark Gable as *Rhett Butler*. "Why ma'am, I would be distraught beyond consoling if you changed your mind and did not offer me the chance to bask in your glorious presence this evening. I do apologize for my rude behavior and promise it won't happen again."

We laughed and chatted for the next few minutes as I made my way up the twisty mountain road towards his house. I had only been to his place twice before, and never in the dark, so I was gladly trading quips with him on the phone. I was a city girl and the darkness of the mountains still caused me a bit of apprehension. Fortunately, my GPS worked just fine out here in Redneckville (my pet name for his farm) and led me right to his drive. He was sitting on the porch waiting for me, beer in hand and that gorgeous grin across his face. We hung up as I stepped out of the car, and I threw my phone in the seat, determined to not let the constant notifications and calls distract me from what I came here to do.

He stood up, reached over to the small cooler beside him, and pulled out an ice cold beer (which up until I met him had never once crossed my lips, but now I loved it.), handing it to me as his fingers gently touched mine, sending shivers running up my spine. I returned his smile, looking deeply into his eyes for the first time, and watching the mixture of happiness, lust, confusion and questions that floated around behind them. This was the first time I ever came to Summerset without planning ahead of time with him, and I had recognized the intrigue in his voice earlier when I called and told him I was there visiting Mrs. Milligan and would stop by to see him later in the evening.

I stood there staring at him, drinking every bit of his presence into my soul, the rush of desire filling my mind and making me almost dizzy. I waited for the gut punch to slam into me and render me unable to finish what I came here to do, and was surprised that it never materialized. I didn't say a word as I moved closer, my hand now resting on his chest, the thumping of his heart strong with excitement, my eyes never leaving his as I whispered, "I'm ready."

He never said a word as he stared deeply into my eyes, searching, almost as if he was waiting for me to bolt as I had done in the past. His nervousness was almost palatable and his questioning thoughts evident behind his brown eyes that were heavily hooded with desire. His calloused, rough hand reached out to my face, gently cupping my chin as he leaned his lumbering frame down and gently kissed me, and as our lips locked together, the only thing I felt was desire flow through me. Sensing the hunger for him in my response, he pulled away briefly, face flushed and eyes gleaming, and said, his voice husky and low, "You sure?"

My answer was silent as one hand reached around his lithe torso, pulling myself tightly into his fully ready frame and the other pulled his head towards mine and kissed him like I had never kissed another, and finally, we united as one under the bright, Arizona moon.

* * * *

THURSDAY
Audra-A New Day

I awoke the next morning to the sounds of bellowing cows and sat up quickly in the bed, momentarily confused as to where I was; then the scent of my lover gently wafted to my nose as I jostled around in the sheets, and I realized I was in Steve's bed, alone. I noticed a small note from Steve on the pillow next to me that read:

"Babe, duty called this morning and I had to leave early. God knows I didn't want to climb out of that warm spot next to you, after dreaming about this moment for months now. It looked like

71

you were sleeping so peacefully, I couldn't bear to wake you up. Breakfast is in the kitchen and the coffee is steaming. Call me when you are up and on your way...last night was amazing and, well...worth the wait."

I smiled at his sweet words, just for a split second, then sat up straight in bed in a panic, noticing that it was light outside and realizing I was not just going to be late to work, but would miss most of the morning. Good grief, what time was it?

I leapt out of bed like my feet were on fire and sprinted around the bedroom, retrieving my clothes that were strewn all about the room from last night's passion-induced frenzy. As I snatched them up and raced to the bathroom, I cringed at the thought of wearing the same clothes once again, then remembered that I never made it in to work yesterday, so at least no one there would be aware that I was wearing the same outfit for the second day in a row. Once showered and dressed, I spent what seemed like an eternity looking for my bag, which I finally found shoved underneath Steve's bed. *Good grief, how did it get there?* I wondered as I snatched it up and ran into the bathroom again to do the five-minute makeup drill. I gave up on drying my mound of hair and just pulled it back into a slick ponytail. I glanced quickly at the final results, wincing at my appearance, and then bolted for the kitchen, rummaging through the unfamiliar cabinets until I found a coffee mug that I didn't think Steve would miss. Filling it up to the brim with coffee, I raced to my car, eager to get on the road.

Engine roaring and air on full blast, I headed out onto the small, two-lane highway towards Phoenix. I finally glanced at the clock—I put off doing that while getting ready, afraid to really know what time it was—and was shocked to discover that it was only 8:20, which allowed my breathing and heart rate to slow just a bit, since it wasn't as late as I thought. I reached into my purse to find my cell so I could call Steve and check the undoubtedly numerous calls and emails I had missed during my "interlude" last night with Steve, but I couldn't find it. Briefly, I panicked and thought I might have left it at Steve's and almost turned around, but then I recalled throwing it on the front seat last night before I jumped him, and sure enough, there it was under my purse.

I listened to my messages and forwarded a few of them to my office phone, making mental notes to remember to listen to them when I made it to work. Of course, keeping my head focused on work issues would be rather difficult today, just like yesterday, but for entirely different reasons.

As I drove down the winding mountain roads out of Summerset, reliving my incredible evening with Steve, for the first time in years, I actually felt relaxed. I remembered the first moment I felt that spark of electricity between the two of us the day of Gina's funeral and how his impressive stature shouted to my soul "safe haven", yet I held him at bay for so long, my intimacy issues overriding my libido.

Not anymore.

A sweet, tingly shiver ran through my body as I recalled our lovemaking from last night. His note was right: it was well worth the wait. I smiled a bit, thinking that I was now feeling what the romance novels my mother loved to read would describe as, *"The world truly did just melt away as we embraced and I was surprised at my uninhibited sexual response to his strong touch."* Cliché I know, but somehow, fitting and true: my crazy, messed up world really did melt away, at least during those glorious hours he held me in his muscular arms, enveloping me in a luxuriously warm, sensual embrace. His presence next to me allowed my eyes to remain shut all night, and somehow, managed to fend off the dreams from their nighttime ritual of torture.

I felt like a new woman.

Mrs. Milligan had hit the nail on the head yesterday evening when she chastised me for bottling everything up inside and only sharing my innermost thoughts with "...an old, wrinkly woman..." that could only listen, when I needed to open my eyes and look at the man that was standing right in front of me, waiting patiently for me to peel back the layers of security wrapped around my heart and embrace his love. "Honey, men like Steve are a once-in-a-lifetime find, like a diamond buried in the dirt: sometimes you must dig through the nasty, sticky mud to find them. You see yours, shimmering in the sun, yet you have failed to pick it up. You just remain there, staring at your dirty hands and looking at the long climb behind you, rather than at the gem in front of you. Don't just stand there staring girl. Snatch him up, honey, before some other treasure hunter does!"

I smiled as I recalled the look in her eyes as she beseeched me not to risk ruining a potentially incredible relationship with Steve. There was a mixture of sadness lurking behind her eyes as she spoke as well, and I assumed it stemmed from the love of her life no longer walking the earth with her. It was at that moment that I realized I didn't just *need* to, but *wanted* to, cleanse my soul from past muck and make room in my heart for Steve.

I was just about to make the turn onto the main road that would take me to the freeway, lost in these thoughts and telling myself that I would conquer all these trials one step at a time and become a better human being for them, when I realized I was humming, which was something I hadn't done since high school; and for the first time in years, it dawned on me that I was actually happy. God, it was such an incredible feeling: so foreign, so alien, and so fantastic. Could it be that this link, this deeply rooted connection I found with Steve was the culprit? I thought about that for a moment and although our night last night was, well, quite spectacular, what I was feeling was much more intricate than that.

It was hope.

Hope that I could change; hope that my tainted views on humanity were wrong and that there were wonderful, kind, affectionate and caring people still left in it; hope that I could let my internal shield crumble and feel an emotion other than hate or rage; hope that my life would no longer revolve around everything Winscott, good and bad. Most importantly, there was hope for my own redemption from the guilt-ridden nightmares through making amends to those I hurt in the past, including myself. Mrs. Milligan was right: carrying around this hate was becoming more burdensome to my psyche than the actual physical events that caused it, and I needed to let go and forgive, especially those individuals that were only riding the fringe of agony's coattails for their silence and not the actual act. Granted, the hidden deceptions and numerous sins I uncovered about the other partners were morally reprehensible, but wasn't my exposing them, using their own sordid lives as a lever to wrench hold over them for my own personal mental salve, just as wrong? Did my justified rage at Olin overflow my mental reservoirs and spill out through the open door into their world, causing me to stand right in beside them, which really didn't make me any better than they were? I used my anger as some sort of blinding shield to hide behind as I wielded means and measures that were not normally part of my internal repertoire. True, Olin was a horrid, nasty man that deserved to be locked away from society and finally pay for his deplorable crimes; but what about the others? How were they any different from countless people throughout the ages that turned a blind eye when a crime was committed? Was the punishment I bequeathed them with truly befitting their crimes of looking the other way? My initial reaction to this probing question, which I answered that night in my office, was hell yes, they deserved every single bit; but thinking about it now, I did have doubts.

Yesterday's discussion with Charlene about this guilt for my own actions made me mentally run for cover, but Mrs. Milligan wouldn't let me hide behind the anger anymore. In her gentle, determined way, she made me take a hard look at the things I did, and pointed out that obviously, at least subconsciously, I held deep regret for them as well. Although she used a lot of Biblical perspectives on redemption, recovery and recompensing for things, which I still wasn't quite sure I bought, she did make some extremely valid moral points on my behavior, and I was determined to start turning things around in my life, since, as she deftly pointed out, only I had the power to do so. As we talked last night, I promised myself, and her as well, that I would start, right then, to make the most of each day and maybe work on rebuilding bridges that I had burned, even though I wasn't entirely sure how to accomplish that; but I vowed I would try last night as I drifted off into heavy sleep in Steve's arms.

I smiled as I felt peace and tranquility wash over me, mixed with a huge dollop of desire, as I my thoughts wandered over to Steve again. Something about him, something I was unable to pinpoint and name, yet surely felt, made me not only feel safe, but accepted. He accepted me for all my faults, all the broken pieces of my tangled life and all my scarred, heavy baggage. He knew what junk I brought into this relationship with me and willingly seemed to pick up some of the bags and walk alongside me, not even batting an eye at their weight in his hands. When he looked at me last night, I swore I felt his eyes pierce all the way inside me, their intense heat turning my shield into a pile of melted metal. God, what a man he was. I had to stop thinking about him and focus on my driving before I ended my ride at the base of a tree.

All that giddy, school girl glee had caused a stupid grin that was plastered across my face, but when my phone rang and I saw that it was Steve calling, my euphoria came to an abrupt end when I answered and heard the edginess in Steve's voice after the perfunctory greetings.

"Where are you?" he asked, a bit too warily.

"Gee, miss me already?" I said, a bit unsure by the tone in his voice as to whether I should be scared or not, so I tried to lighten the conversation, more for myself than for him.

"I'm serious, Audra. Where are you?"

Irritated now with his tone and secrecy I replied, "About a half mile from the interstate; why, what is wrong, Steve? Please, tell me. You are officially freaking me out here."

Steve cleared his throat and said, his voice softer than before, "You need to turn around and come back to my place."

Incredulous, I blurted, "I am doing nothing except remaining on my course to Phoenix until you tell me what is going on!"

There was a brief pause, and finally he said, "That early call to work this morning was about Robert. We just found his body, Audra, and we're almost positive he didn't die from natural causes."

Oh shit.

CHAPTER 8
Gabrielle-Wedding Jitters

My morning started out exceptionally bad for a Thursday: the air conditioner croaked sometime during the night in our building, and although Jeff—and other hot, irritated tenants as well, I'm sure—called building maintenance several times, he was greeted by the sound of the droning answering machine, informing callers to leave a message. After his fourth phone call, Jeff left them one long, rambling message that I am sure the recipient would never forget, especially if they spoke Italian.

Jeff and I finally decided our best option was to take a cool shower, since help was not coming anytime soon, throw on workout clothes and get ready at our perspective places of employment, although that was obviously a much simpler task for him than for me. The few little items he packed in his gym bag paled in comparison to the crap shoved in mine: makeup, hair dryer, deodorant and undergarments, just to name a few. It was moments like this, as the sweat began to trickle down my once clean back, that made me wish I could travel back in time to find the person that decided it was socially necessary for women to adorn themselves with all this ridiculous attire to be considered attractive; once I found them, I would alter history and release the shackles of generations of women from all this frivolous nonsense by making sure that moronic individual (male, I am sure) never started this trend.

Once on the road and headed towards work, I made the HUGE mistake of thinking I had a bit of extra time on my hands and stopped for a cup of coffee. Said coffee then proceeded to immediately spill all over my gym bag that contained my work clothes after the idiotic driver in front of me decided they should just suddenly slam on their brakes in the middle of the road for no apparent reason. The day almost began with the hood of my Mustang up their ass! Fortunately, this was narrowly avoided at the last second as I swerved sharply to the right and grazed the curb. I slammed on my brakes and the smell of the burned, blackened rubber hit me immediately. Breathing hard, I flipped the dumbass driver the bird.

The proverbial "final straw" occurred when I pulled into the deck at work and, after retrieving my bag, noticed my car was sitting at an odd angle, and discovered that was because the right front tire was almost completely flat. I stood there for a moment, sweating heavily now due to the heat as well as my anger, my coffee stained clothes and other contents making my gym bag smell inviting but heavy as hell, as I stared at the flat. I was late, didn't have anything to wear but sweats that really were "sweaty" now, no makeup on, hair in disarray and now forced to deal with a flat. Could the day get any worse?

I hurried through the deck to the elevator. As I passed by Audra's designated spot, I noticed that she hadn't made it in yet, which was rather worrisome. She had not been herself the last few weeks, and then when she basically blew off the entire day yesterday, I really became worried, especially with it being tax season crunch time. When she didn't come back yesterday, the back-office whispering began, and I was thankful that she told me to go home early, because some of the comments that made their way back to my ears were enough for me to seriously consider a good, old fashioned slap in the head to those that were running their mouths.

Riding the elevator to our floor, I thought about how frightened she must be, knowing she was not only going to testify in front of a packed courtroom, but be broadcast live on television.

I couldn't imagine, for I was terrified for my little part in this whole thing, which would be minimal compared to hers. Of course, there was a tiny bit of me that was glad she wasn't here yet so I could sneak off into the bathroom and attempt to do something with this wild mane of mine and at least slap some lipstick and mascara on my face.

The elevator doors opened and I was thankful that no one was in the lobby as I darted into the bathroom, flinging my pack on the counter and quickly digging out my tools. As I reached up and attempted to unwind my hair from my ponytail, my fingers became entangled as my engagement ring became firmly stuck in a mass of hair and cloth.

Just freakin' wonderful.

Leaving as much hair intact as possible while freeing my hand, I realized that was one more item that I needed to add to my "wedding to do" list: hire a professional hairdresser, not only for myself, but for my entire bridal party. I should have thought about that earlier, since the wedding was just a few months away. Damn, things were so crazy between work and house searching (since we KNEW we didn't want to stay in that apartment anymore. Any doubts as to justifying the expenses of becoming homeowners were completely wiped away after this morning's fiasco.) that it just slipped my mind. Hand extracted, I began brushing through the knots, wondering if that little bit of planning wasn't something that should have been suggested by my wedding planner, the ridiculously expensive Heidi Morgan-Thomas. Oh well—I made myself a mental note to call her today and see if she would at least be willing to assist me in finding someone.

What I really wanted from her, which she had been unable up to this point to secure, was to help me finagle my wedding reception to take place in Chandler at the highly sought after venue, The Castle at Chandler. They were booked years in advance, but my research on Heidi contained one major theme that drew me to her: she would get you what you wanted as long as you were willing to pay for it. For the last two weeks I had sort of hounded her on whether or not she felt she stood any shot of procuring this site for me; however, she had skillfully dodged my calls, emails and texts, responding only briefly to some, promising to let me know as soon as she heard something. My mother was trying to steer me in the direction of another venue, worried that we would end up with a fully planned wedding and no location to hold it in. I was beginning to think she was right, although admitting that (even only in my head) was rather revolting; and besides, I wanted to be a true princess, just for one day, since I was marrying my prince.

Hair now presentable and makeup slathered on, I was just about to walk out of the bathroom when my cell phone vibrated in my bag. My heart jumped for a moment, hoping it wasn't Audra calling, wondering where in the hell I was. I dug around until I finally latched on to the thing, breathing a sigh of relief to see it wasn't work, but almost didn't answer it since the number was one I didn't recognize. But at the last second, as I slung my coffee-scented bag onto my shoulder, I decided to flip it open.

"Hello?"

"Gabrielle? Gabrielle Lincoln?" came the unfamiliar, breathy feminine voice over the line.

Hesitantly, I responded, "Yes. Who is speaking?"

"Oh, I am so glad I have the correct number. Heidi's assistant, Karrie, has such a heavy accent, I wasn't sure that I wrote it down correctly." said the voice, almost sounding out of breath. I smiled, realizing she must be from *The Time of Your Life*, Heidi's wedding planning service, for she was right: Karrie possessed such a thick accent that I refused to speak with her anymore over the phone, preferring to keep my lines of communication open with Heidi through either email or texting.

"And your name is?" I asked, kicking myself immediately for sounding so rude. This was the first time in over a month that someone from Heidi's office actually returned my phone call, so I needed to at least be courteous.

"Oh, I'm so sorry for neglecting to introduce myself. How utterly rude of me. I am Diane Martin, a consultant with *The Time of Your Life*. Due to Ms. Morgan-Thomas' extremely tight schedule today, she brought me in as a favor to you since we have good news: The Castle at Chandler actually had a cancellation the day of your wedding."

I stopped so quickly that the bathroom door slammed into my back, almost knocking me over, but I didn't care. My venue was available. The place I'd dreamt of having my wedding ever since I was a little flower girl at my Aunt Celine's wedding was within my reach. I was going to float down that winding rock staircase, my cathedral train gently floating behind me as all eyes watched every delicate movement amidst the deliciously scented flowers and candles adorning every available space. I could hardly form a coherent string of intelligible words as I sputtered, "Ms. Martin, please, are you serious? This isn't some kind of joke, is it?"

Ms. Martin chuckled loudly into the phone. "Honey, I know, we are just as shocked as you. That place NEVER has a cancellation, but apparently, the scheduled wedding was called off due to, um, shall we say, indiscretions from college that the soon to be bride neglected to tell her mate about? Anyway, the place is yours if we can be there by ten for you to sign the contract and provide them with the deposit."

I literally dropped everything I was holding except the phone, which was now thoroughly glued to my ear in my excitement. Oh, I couldn't believe what she just said! I would take 100 mornings like the one that I just suffered if this was my reward. I realized a bit too late that I was actually doing some sort of strange happy dance in the hallway by my office and stopped, trying to regain some professional composure. I felt like a little kid that just was informed by her parents that they were going to Disneyland. But then the words, "...be there by ten..." surfaced and I winced inwardly, knowing that would be a problem.

"Oh my God, Ms. Martin. I can't believe it! This is the best news I have heard in weeks. Pardon me for asking you to repeat yourself, but did you say that I needed to be at their offices by ten to sign the contract?" I asked, hoping that maybe, just maybe, in all the excitement, I misunderstood what she said.

"No, you heard correctly. Ms. Morgan-Thomas is a personal friend of the manager and pulled out deep, long reserved favors for her to keep her lips sealed on the cancellation so you can get there and 'seal the deal.' But of course, the window of opportunity is extremely slim, and you must leave…well, right now, to make it in time. I am sorry about the short notice but this *just happened*!" Ms. Martin said, her voice cracking under her own excitement.

I was at a loss as to what to do since my car was sitting in the parking lot, limping like a horse that had thrown a shoe: no good to me now. Even if I hung up right this second and called someone to come and change the flat, I wouldn't make it to Chandler in time since it was already past nine o'clock. I raced through my mental contact list, striking off everyone that popped up: Jeff worked on the other side of town and stood no shot of making it here in less than 15 minutes, even taking into consideration the breakneck speeds he normally drove. Mom and Dad just left yesterday for a long weekend in Las Vegas, and most of my friends worked on the other side of town as well, their lives just as busy as mine, and I didn't want to be the kind of "emergency" call friend in desperate need of help. Damn!

As the silence from my end stretched out longer than I should have let it, I guess Ms. Martin sensed my quandary and said, "Ms. Morgan-Thomas insisted that I be at your beck and call today and you seem a bit lost here, and time is ticking. Ms. Lincoln, is there something wrong? Something I may be of assistance with in some way?"

And then it hit me as I said, "I really hate to ask, but this has been the morning from hell, truly, and my car is now sporting a flat tire and…"

"Say no more, Ms. Lincoln. Diane to the rescue. My car is nice and cold and has four tires completely full of air. I understand from your file that you work downtown, and I just left Arnelle's Catering, so tell me, how far is that from you? I will be delighted to pick you up and drive you there."

I lit up like a kid again and actually did what some would consider a 'fist pump' in the air, excited that one major hurdle was just cleared as I responded, "Arnelle's is only four blocks from my office. I am at 3789 Van Buren…"

"I will be down at the corner in less than five minutes. I'm in a black Mercedes. Hurry girl, we are wasting time chatting when we could be driving!" and before I could answer, the line went dead. I was so excited that I stood at my desk and kind of turned in a circle, not sure which direction I should take first. Audra was still not here and I needed to let her know about my whereabouts. I panicked for a moment when I thought about the deposit, since I knew that I didn't have anywhere close to the 15,000 dollars required, but then I remembered my dad giving me the "wedding emergency" credit card for just such occasions as this. I realized that up and running out of the office without telling anyone where I was going was not very professional at all, but I decided that I would just call Audra on the way and then send out an email to the receptionist as soon as Ms. Martin and I were on our way to Chandler.

I waited impatiently at the elevator bank for the doors to open, eager to get downstairs. I tried calling Jeff from inside, but I don't know why I even bothered, for this elevator was notorious for killing phone connections. As the doors opened in the lobby and I emerged (Okay, I leapt out, my excitement making my legs spontaneously throw out a ballerina move) I saw Ms. Martin's black Mercedes shining in the sun through the glass doors. I quickly tried calling Jeff again and this time, it went straight to his voicemail.

"Baby, the most wonderful news! The Castle at Chandler is available ON OUR DATE! I am heading up there right now with Ms. Martin, one of Heidi's assistants. I have to be there by ten to sign the contract and pay the deposit, and my car has a flat left front tire, so Ms. Martin is driving. I love you, can't wait to marry my prince in our castle. Woo hoo!" I gushed as I opened the glass doors and practically burst into a spring on my way to Ms. Martin's car.

God, this day just did a complete one eighty. I thought as I opened the door and slid into the cool leather seat. Ms. Martin stuck out her hand, smiling brightly as she said, "Perfect timing, Gabrielle. Now, let's get on the road. We have a date to fulfill your destiny." she said, a large grin sliding across her full lips.

"Thank you so much for helping me today. I can't believe this is happening. My fiancé is going to flip! Oh, and my mother. She will be beside herself that she missed this when she comes back on Monday. Do you know that when I was little, we would sit outside out by the pool and watch the sunset together and plan my wedding? Those are some of my favorite childhood memories! Oh, I'm sorry Ms. Martin, I am rambling here, but it is such a rarity when one of your lifelong dreams comes true." I said, the flush of heat exuding from my cheeks as I realized the woman probably thought I was some type of drug addict by the way I was yammering on and on.

"You go ahead and 'ramble' away honey. I am just as excited to be a part of this experience with you. And believe me, brides are usually a jittery bunch anyway; you know, so much going on in their lives that it becomes quite overwhelming, causing even the shyest of women to became raging monsters." Ms. Martin answered, her eyes never leaving the road as she deftly weaved in and out of the traffic. Damn, for a wedding planner, she sure did know how to drive the hell out of this car. I kept my eyes focused on my lap instead of out the window, for the speed at which we were travelling was making the scenery whiz by so fast that it made me feel a bit nauseous. I dialed Audra's cell first, but oddly, it went straight to voicemail, so I opted for an email, concentrating on hitting the correct keys on my phone, and typed an email out to Audra and a few others at the office, letting them know what was going on and that I should be back this afternoon. As soon as I hit send, I prayed that Audra wouldn't be too upset with me for this, but it was just one of those emergency situations (albeit, a good emergency) that couldn't be foreseen or helped; then I immediately kicked myself mentally for worrying. Audra was the best boss I ever worked for and we were on the road to becoming close friends, and I knew she would understand.

I decided to change the subject a bit so I didn't come off as some self-centered *Bridezilla* whose sole focus was on her wedding, so I commented, "Ms. Martin, you are a fantastic driver. Where in the world did you acquire your skills? A closet NASCAR fan are you?" I quipped.

Her grip became a bit tighter on the wheel and her jaw clenched ever so slightly as she replied, "No dear, I've just spent a lot of time on the road, clearing my head when it becomes too full of things. That's why I bought this car: nothing better than German engineering when you want to become one with the road. Besides," she said, her bright red lips curving into a slight grin, "we need to get you to the church on time, so to speak."

"Well, I must say, you are handling this car like a pro. My fiancé would just die to get behind the wheel of this gorgeous piece of machinery. A Mercedes has been his dream car ever since I've known him," I rambled, hoping that if I could engage her in some type of conversation, she would slow down just a bit, since this high speed was really making me queasy. I reached down and grabbed my bag, hoping that somewhere in its depths there was a leftover Tums or Rolaids, or something to settle my turning stomach. Hell, I already looked like a gym rat that just rolled out of bed, so the last thing I needed was to was roll up to one of the most prestigious addresses in all of Arizona looking like I was there to clean the pool or mop the floor.

"I must apologize for my attire Ms. Martin…" I said, quickly popping the lone Rolaid I had found into my mouth, hoping it would take effect quickly, but before I could finish my thoughts, she held up her hand in protest.

"Not another word. Rosemary won't give your clothing more than a quick glance. She is much more interested in what's inside your wallet, trust me. Besides, you are such a beautiful young woman, you could don a burlap sack and still turn heads."

I laughed lightly and felt the blood rush to my cheeks once again, as I always did when someone commented about my looks. Although it was nice to hear compliments, I still couldn't grasp why so many people felt that way, for when I looked in the mirror,

I just saw the reflection of a normal girl staring back at me; but I did appreciate the fact that she was trying to ease my worries about my appearance.

The silence between the two of us obviously lasted longer than either of us felt comfortable with, and I was wracking my brain trying to think of something to say that didn't center around my upcoming nuptials. Thankfully, Ms. Martin cleared her throat and broke the awkward silence as she said, "I noticed in your file with us this morning that you work at Winscott. I imagine, if you don't mind me saying so, that things have been rather tense around your office lately, what with the upcoming trial and all."

Damn, I wish I had thought of some topic first, because I immediately felt my stomach knot up at the mere mention of work, and I was out of Rolaids. It never failed: every single time someone realized where I worked, they always wanted me to throw them some juicy piece of insider gossip to munch on, hoping that I would oblige them. Most of the time, I steered clear of truly answering their probing questions by curtly cutting them off by replying how much I adored working for Audra, or just completely changing the subject over into territory I was willing to talk about; and in the instances where it was an option, simply walking away. Of course, that option was not available to me in the small confines of Ms. Martin's speeding Mercedes, and I really couldn't change the subject without coming off as downright rude to this stranger who was kindly whisking me away to make one of my life long dreams come true. So I opted for the short answer, hoping she would recognize by the tone of my voice that I didn't wish to elaborate on the subject.

"Yes, they have been."

My plan failed as she replied, "I bet. It seems that the media has enjoyed tearing your firm to shreds, especially that former boss of yours...oh, what's his name?" she said, unwilling to change the subject.

"Olin."

"Yes, Olin. That's it!" She chirped, snapping her fingers at the mention of his name. "Such an odd name, you would think I could remember it; Heaven knows they have splashed it across the screen enough times over the last few months. I mean, the reporters are acting like this is the next O.J. Simpson trial!"

I couldn't stop the grin that spread across my face at that analogy because she was right: it did, at times, feel like we were smack in the middle of the newest "trial of the century", although the number of Olin supporters was basically nil; at least, in my experience. Once, a few weeks after Olin's arrest, I overheard Carl in Audra's office talking about the media frenzy and his newfound sympathy for those involved in OJ's trial, for the constant media scrutiny was, at times, unbearable.

Ms. Martin finally slowed down as we exited the interstate and now were on a two-lane road that led into Chandler. I finally lifted my eyes and glanced out the window, since we were no longer traveling at the speed of light, wondering why in the world someone decided to build a huge castle in this location. The stretch of road we were on now was rather desolate looking, like something out of a movie where a crazed hitchhiker goes on a killing spree and buries the bodies in the dry desert ground, and then steals their car. That thought made me shudder just a bit, so I focused my attention back to Ms. Martin and her nosy questions.

"Yes, sometimes it has felt that way. For a few months, the media left us alone, but in the last few weeks, as the trial grows closer, they have been driving us absolutely batty. Hopefully, once this sordid mess is over, things will return to normal; that way, I can refocus on my wedding preparations," I said, deciding that her perception of me as a self-centered bride was better than continuing this conversation about Olin and the firm. I must admit, even though I was rather nervous at the prospect of being called as a witness by the prosecution, I would be relieved once it was over and my life became that of a normal person again.

Ms. Martin rattled on for several more minutes, asking me all sorts of questions about the firm, the partners and Olin, and I did my best to answer with as little information that wasn't already public knowledge as possible. She seemed most interested in my take on the crime that Olin was charged with, and at one point, flat out asked me, "So, Ms. Lincoln. May I call you Gabrielle?"

"Of course you may."

"So, Gabrielle, do you think he did it? You worked with him, right?" she asked, eagerly awaiting my answer.

"Yes, briefly, for about three months," I cautiously replied.

"Well, did you ever sense that he was capable of such a thing? I mean, did he ever make you nervous when you two were alone…you know, did you ever get the impression that he was violent?" she asked.

"That is a hard question to answer, Ms. Martin, for I have so many other things on my mind right now, most important being planning my wedding. I will say this though; no one deserves to be located behind steel bars more than Olin Kemper does," I responded, my words trailing off as I turned my head towards my window, hoping that my harsh words would signal to her that I didn't wish to discuss this subject further.

There was another awkward pause in our conversation, but my plan to shift the conversation to another arena worked as Ms. Martin finally replied, thankfully changing the subject, "Oh honey, don't let the intricate details of your nuptials drive you crazy. I tell all my brides to sit back and enjoy this time, relish the thrill and the excitement, for all this planning lasts much longer than the actual ceremony and reception."

"For the most part, I have enjoyed the planning phase, except for thinking that I would have to use another venue, which I really didn't want to be forced into, because as I said earlier, I have had my heart set for years now on getting married at the Castle. My mother has been trying to persuade me to look at other locations, as well as Ms. Heidi, but even as close as we are to the wedding, I just wasn't ready to let that dream go. I am so glad now that I didn't." I said, the giddy little girl's voice in my head leaking out a bit through my voice. "I am still in shock. I wish my mother could be with me today, for she would be just as happy as I am, maybe more."

"Yes, that is a shame that she couldn't make it, but I am sure she is enjoying Las Vegas. Imagine how surprised she will be when she returns and you tell her your great news!" Ms. Martin said, doing her best to try and make the 'worried bride' happy. I smiled a bit, knowing that she was feigning excitement for me when in reality she probably couldn't care less about my happiness, for after all, we were complete strangers and I wasn't even her client; which meant she wouldn't be getting any compensation for this emergency trip to Chandler.

Before I responded to her comment, my cell phone vibrated in my lap and I glanced down to see who was calling, hoping that it was my mother responding to my earlier text I sent her about where I was currently heading, but it wasn't: it was Audra.

"Oh, excuse me Ms. Martin, I must take this call," I said as I answered, "Good morning boss! Did you get my message?"

"Morning! Yes, I just now read your email. I am so excited for you. What wonderful news! Have you "sealed the deal" so to speak?"

Internally, I breathed a sigh of relief, thankful that her voice didn't betray any irritation at my absence from work as I responded, "No, not yet. We are about 15 minutes away still. I am sorry to leave you in a lurch boss, but this came up at the last minute and it was an opportunity that I couldn't pass up!" I said, hoping that she would understand.

"Gab, please, don't worry about it. I am so thrilled for you and Jeff, and I do know how much this means to you. I am not anywhere close to being at the office anyway, so don't worry about it. I won't be in until around one o'clock this afternoon and all we really need to concentrate on is preparing for my meeting with Mrs. Lancaster tomorrow. Oh, by the way, did you call her back for me yesterday?"

"Yes, I sure did and everything is all set for tomorrow night at Zargento's. She will meet you there."

"Great. Thank you so much for handling that for me. I really wasn't up to par yesterday to handle pulling off a long, drawn out conversation with her. Good grief, but that woman can prattle on,"

Audra said, and I laughed a little bit too loud, and I noticed in my peripheral vision that my laughter startled poor Ms. Martin.

"No kidding. She seemed rather perturbed that it wasn't you returning her call, but I think I smoothed things over well, so I just know you are going to land her as a new client tomorrow night." I said, smiling over meekly at Ms. Martin. I hoped my conversation wasn't annoying her, for I knew I didn't care for someone blathering away on a cell phone when I was within earshot, so I tried to end the conversation discretely.

"Thank you, Audra, for being so understanding about today. Really, I do appreciate it and I promise, as soon as Ms. Martin and I are finished here, I will be back in the office."

"Gab, please, don't; no need for that. This is your wedding, for Heaven's sake. Princess Gabby and Prince Jeffrey. Oh, it will be spectacular, especially at The Castle. I will see you when you get back so we can give the proposal a final review and tweaking, if necessary. Have fun!" Audra said, disconnecting the call, her voice unnaturally chirpy and full of a lilt that I didn't recall ever hearing before. I smiled a bit, wondering if a certain sexy detective was the one responsible for her change of attitude. I sure hoped so, because the way that man looked at her made me almost swoon with desire, wishing that Jeff would look at me like that just once.

I leaned over and put my phone in my back pocket and turned to Ms. Martin, ready to apologize for my cell phone etiquette faux pas, but before I could utter a word, her cell phone rang and she quickly answered "Diane Martin, how may I help you today?" her voice sleek and professional. I smiled slightly, trying to cover it with my hand as I realized I was glad I didn't get a chance to apologize for my rudeness, since she obviously had no qualms about talking on the phone in my presence. As I glanced out the window, trying to determine how much longer we had left before our turn and to try and tune out her conversation, I glanced at my watch and panicked when I saw that it was ten after ten, which meant we were late. Good Heavens, after everything that happened today and the absolute frenzied driving of Ms. Martin to make it there on time, could we really have just missed our window of opportunity by a mere ten minutes?

I felt sick.

I looked over at Ms. Martin and noticed her cheeks were crimson red and her hands were shaking, her bright smile from earlier now gone, replaced by pursed lips that almost disappeared into her mouth. As she jerked the car over to the shoulder of the road and slammed on the brakes, her long, slender fingers were gripping the wheel so tightly her knuckles were turning an odd shade of white and a strange, almost physical electrical current was emitting from her. Instantaneously, I felt a heavy sense of dread overcome me as I heard her say, "This is outrageous! What an abhorrent display of unprofessional customer service! Do you have any idea the trouble we have gone through to get there? No, of course you don't, but not to worry: I will make sure that from now on, all our brides that even remotely suggest their wedding or reception take place at the Castle are told this story and steer clear of your venue!" Ms. Martin screeched into the phone, her voice beginning to hurt my ears and her words, my heart. After the craziness of this day and the high I rode all the way here, thinking Jeff and I were going to have our dream wedding, the sudden, crushing news that we weren't overcame me, and tears starting slowly flowing down my cheeks. Before I could stammer out the questions racing through my mind, like, "What happened? We are only a few minutes late! Why, why did they do this to me?" I reached over and opened the car door and quickly bolted out, vomiting the entire contents of my nerve-wracked stomach onto the dusty, desert ground.

Sobbing uncontrollably now amidst the vomiting, I vaguely heard the other car door open and feet walking in my direction, followed by Ms. Martin's concerned, yet oddly irritated voice, "Oh dear, oh dear, gosh, and I have no tissues for you..."

Normally I don't suffer from a weak stomach or have issues with projectile vomiting like I was currently experiencing, but the stress of my job, the wedding preparations and Olin's trial clearly were too much for my body and mind to process. I finally finished retching and leaned against the trunk of Ms. Martin's car for support, jerking my hand back almost instantly for the black shiny vehicle was burning hot after almost an hour in the baking sun. I almost fell over as I lost my balance, my head jumbled from the physical stress of just hacking up a lung, which in the stifling heat was what it felt like I just accomplished. Somehow, I managed to stay on my feet and finally made my way back to the opened passenger door and plopped down onto the now warm leather seat. Tears, along with sweat, were keeping my cheeks wet, and although I wanted to wipe my face off with my shirt, I dared not, fearing that there might be clingy remnants to it from moments before. I felt Ms. Martin's presence by me but didn't even look her way as I turned my eyes towards the road, recalling from my previous trips to the Castle that there should be a gas station in the next half of a mile or so; and sure enough, there was the Exxon sign in the distance.

Thank God.

Mortified beyond belief and my throat so raw I could barely speak, I looked up, my eyes squinting into the bright desert sun at Ms. Martin's face, and sort of just pointed in the direction of the gas station, mumbling, "Please, I need water."

Oddly, she just stood there and stared at me, her phone in her hand and her body rigid. For a second, I wondered if she was going to vomit herself, since so many people have a tendency to do that after watching someone else puke. Before I could give it much more thought, Jeff's ringtone sounded in the stillness of the car and I pulled the phone out of my back pocket to answer. Pulling myself fully inside the car now, I shut the door behind me. I started sobbing again when I answered, blabbing incoherently into the phone about the events of the past few hours, ending with my little side road episode out there in the middle of nowhere. It took me a full minute to realize that I was rambling into dead air when no response came from Jeff. *Smart move Gab. Now you have to tell him all of that all over again.* At some point during my blubbering fit, Ms. Martin finally made her way back to the driver's seat and we took off down the road, the refreshing cool air from the vents drying my flowing tears. We pulled up to the desolate, grimy gas station just as I tried calling Jeff back, but the call went straight to his voicemail. I managed a sniffle and a muffled "I love you" and hung up.

My voice was almost completely gone so I just sort of motioned to Ms. Martin that I was going inside and surely, she would comprehend that I needed to use the restroom. She nodded her head in my direction as she stepped out onto the parched dirt to fill her car with gas while I headed inside of the tiny building, the dirt kicking up heavily behind me. I quickly perused the place and had I been able, would have laughed at the decrepit building and ancient gas pumps. It was like something out of a horror movie, the kind that someone stops at and never returns from because some mutants or zombies have taken over. I was pleasantly surprised that when I entered the storefront, a cute little girl sat at the counter, looking bored beyond belief but otherwise, normal and definitely non-zombielike. I coughed as the dirt followed me inside and croaked, "Bathroom?"

She smiled a bit and reached behind her, grabbing a key the size of a cell phone off the wall, and handed it to me as she said, "It's around back." Oh great, an indoor outhouse.

I mouthed the words "Thank you" as I took the heavy key in my hand, coughing and sputtering all the way to the bathroom out back, my throat really on fire now. I finally unlocked the old steel door and stepped inside, overcome immediately by the rank smell of urine, dust and dirt, and my stomach lurched again in protest. My gag reflex tried to kick in after glancing over at the toilet seat that looked like it, as well as its interior, were leftover from the sixties. Setting the key down on the sink and turning the water on, I splashed my face with the tepid liquid. Damn, it wasn't even cold; which given where I was, didn't really surprise me, but I really wished that it was a bit cooler. I cupped my hands and sucked the water into my dry mouth, swirling it around as I did the best I could to remove that lovely bile taste that lingers after throwing up. I reached over to the paper towel dispenser, surprised to find that there were actually towels in it, and began to wipe my face dry, my thoughts swirling around the absolute craziness of this day. Really, it started off with me waking up to no hot shower, no coffee, wet hair in a mess, a rush to work, almost having an accident...

And that's when it me: the car.

I froze for just a split second as I focused my mind to recall the events of this morning when I was leaving Starbucks and spilled my coffee after the idiotic driver almost hit me. *The idiotic driver in a black Mercedes with no license plate.*

No, it wasn't possible. I was sure that Ms. Martin's car had a license plate, but I couldn't shake the feeling that was I wrong, so I stepped back over to the heavy door and opened it just enough to view the gas pumps and the back end of the Mercedes.

No license plate.

I quickly shut the door as if I just came face to face with a ghost. Again, I forced myself to think objectively, to recall every moment from the time I crawled out of bed this morning until right now, and as I came to the part in the conversation with Ms. Martin about work, I started to shake. I never filled out where I was employed on any paperwork from *The Time of Your Life*, or anywhere else that I could get away with leaving it out, because I hated the questions that would surely follow. My wedding was my focus, and I knew that if Ms. Heidi saw "Winscott & Associates" on the employment section, she would start nosing around, so I intentionally left it blank; so how in the hell did Ms. Martin know where I worked? Standing rock still for a moment, I tried to remember every word of our phone conversation this morning, and I was positive that I never mentioned what company I worked at, only the street address of the building, which housed numerous other businesses besides Winscott. I also had never said that my mother was in Las Vegas—only that she was out of town—yet, she knew that...how?

My heart began thumping wildly in my chest as my mind started to run with this new information and the adrenaline surge raced through me, the flight or fight response hitting me hard. Dear God, surely I was wrong. Surely I was just overly upset from the

94

events of today and was letting my imagination get the best of me. Hell, maybe I was suffering from a light case of heat stroke or something. No, it wasn't that: I was sure that something was amiss here, and I wasn't enjoying the territory my thoughts were racing to. I stood there inside the filthy bathroom and contemplated what my next move should be. Finally settling on a call to Ms. Heidi, I jerked my phone out of my back pocket to dial her number, my fingers trembling.

"*The Time of Your Life*, how may I help you?"

"This is Gabrielle Lincoln and I need to speak with Ms. Heidi *right now*," I said, hoping the apprehension in my gravelly voice would make an impact on the receptionist, since trying to get through to Heidi was next to impossible.

"One moment please, I'll see if she is in."

I stood in the center of the grungy sweatbox staring at years of graffiti on the nasty, dirt-covered walls, reading the filth that was written years ago, trying to occupy my mind while I waited impatiently, but unable to stand still as the anticipation was killing me. I was shocked when I heard Ms. Heidi say, "Ms. Lincoln. Perfect timing. I was just going to call you with some exciting news!"

I stopped moving around and stood perfectly still, unable to respond with much except a shocked, "Oh?"

"Yes, yes! Your venue is open. A cancellation was made this morning. You are going to get your dream wedding at The Castle!" she said, her excitement immediately calming my nerves and making me feel like an utter fool for my distraught visions of some conspiracy only seconds ago. I felt my body relax a bit at this news, knowing the lunacy of the day led me to fear for my life as I said, "Oh, thank God! Did they just call you?"

"Oh no, my dear, that is why I apologized earlier. The manager, Rosemary, called this morning and left me a voicemail, telling me that they just had a cancellation, but after the morning we've had dealing with the cops, police reports and cleanup crews, I failed to call you. I am sorry, but maybe this great news will make up for it?" Heidi said, her words peppy and bright, her tone forced a bit to sound apologetic.

I hung my head down in shame for thinking that poor Ms. Martin was some crazy lunatic that basically just kidnapped me, wanting God only knows what from me. My lips curved into a grin as I just shook my head, mentally giving myself a kick in the ass for being so overly dramatic. God, Jeff was right: I really needed to lay off the horror movies.

"No apology needed Ms. Heidi. Diane has been a Godsend, rescuing me this morning when my tire was flat and offering to bring me up here to sign the contract. She is a gem; you should give her a raise," I said, the burning in my throat still affecting the sound of my voice. God, I sounded like a 90 year old woman.

But then it finally dawned on me what she just said, "…called this morning…" and I recalled that I was inside this dirty bathroom because Ms. Martin, only moments before, received a call from The Castle, telling her the venue was not available. My heart sank once again.

"But, I don't understand; Ms. Martin just talked to them and they don't have any openings," I said as fresh tears began to slide down my cheeks.

"Who?"

I cleared my throat. "Diane. Diane Martin; the lady from your office that is driving me up to the Castle to sign the contract," I said, my voice trembling now.

There was a long pause before Ms. Heidi responded, "Gabrielle, what are you talking about? We don't have anyone here by that name."

"Well, then, who is she?" I whispered, my voice trailing off as fear instantaneously ran up my back in the form of cold shivers, my hands trembling once again and the heavy cloak of dread enveloping me. Before Heidi could respond, my senses picked up– unfortunately a split second too late–that I was no longer alone in the bathroom. I could hear faint chattering from my phone, but it didn't register as I quickly spun around and came face to face with Ms. Martin.

She was no longer wearing her sunglasses and for the first time on our trip today, her eyes bored through mine. They were ablaze with anger, so much so that I could almost feel the heat shooting from them, her fury etched deeply across her face as she said, her voice gravelly and low, "Name's Piper, bitch."

Before I could even blink my eyes, I heard a loud pop and felt the crushing pain explode in my head, followed by a flash of bright, intense light, then nothing at all as everything suddenly went black.

CHAPTER 9
Piper-Silencing Number 2

It took everything in me, every ounce of mental restraint, muscle control and strength, not to reach across the console and knock those bright white teeth out of that lying mouth of hers, driving their jagged edges down her scrawny throat, from the minute she sat her sorry ass in my passenger seat. Just having her this close to me, after all my months of planning, stalking and preparing for this moment, was a delicious fucking high. My body ached for me to kill her from the minute the door shut. Instead, I smiled widely after I noticed my white knuckled grip on the steering wheel, realizing that my thoughts of ripping her to shreds were getting the best of me, so I decided to concentrate on my role; but I couldn't help but ask the little disheveled tart about Olin, even though I knew that was dangerous territory for me.

She coyly tried to evade my questions, doing her best to turn the conversation in the direction she preferred to go, but I was relentless. Something inside me wanted to hear her say his name, since I knew it would be the last time that sensuous word would be spoken from her deceitful lips.

I tried to focus my attention on the road in front of me as I zoomed in and around the traffic, enjoying the fact that she looked a bit nauseous. I was doing my best not to stare too long at her, fearful that my eyes might betray my true emotions towards her, for even the large sunglasses on my face would not be able to contain my outrage at being in such close proximity to this evil whore. To think that this little hairball caused physical harm to my Olin made the bile rise up my throat, and my anger rose as I listened to her ramble on about how excited she was to have her "dream" come true by getting married at the Castle. Her persistent jabbering was making my stomach churn with every little giggle and smile she emitted. Good God, could she be any more obnoxious?

I steadied my resolve to continue with my plans for her, rather than succumbing to the intense, animalistic emotions now obscuring my vision; keeping both my hands firmly clasped around the leather-encased steering wheel rather than around her neck, focusing all my energy on playing the part of "Diane Martin, Wedding Planner." There was still ten miles to go until I reached the designated spot where I planned to stop along the isolated stretch of road to shut this bitch up, but every single moment was excruciating, and I wasn't sure I held enough intestinal fortitude to control my faculties that long.

I wanted this bitch dead, now.

I held myself in check pretty well, all things considered, until the little ringleader called. I could hear that bitch's voice through the phone, and it made the anger inside me ignite, like tossing fuel on an open flame, so much so that the road in front of me literally disappeared, replaced by a dark, red haze of fury. My foot pressed the gas pedal down harder, accelerating quickly, eating up the miles in a blur of speed.

Finally, both of the lying whores shut up, and I knew I couldn't wait any longer to execute my plan because at the rate I was going now, I would end up killing us both in a fiery car crash. While li'l Miss Priss fiddled with shoving her phone into her pocket, I reached down and hit "send" on the cheapo Wal-Mart phone, hidden nicely under my left thigh, and called my other cell, faking the call from "Rosemary" at the Castle. It didn't require much acting chops range to pull off sounding angry and perturbed, as I was well beyond those meager emotions. As I reamed out phantom "Rosemary" on the other line, my voice took on the pitch it takes when I am about to blow, so I immediately pulled the car off on the shoulder of the road before I smashed it into a tree. Of course, before I could even finish my "conversation" the bitch basically jumped out of my car and began puking all over the ground. As annoyed as this made me, since I was planning to knock her lights out with the heavy flashlight lying at my feet, I was glad she hurled her insides out onto the dry ground rather than my car, since riding back to her new temporary home would take a few hours, and I really didn't feel like smelling her vomit the entire way.

Besides, she would be weaker now and most likely would not be able to put up much of a fight; actually, giving her a nice rap on the head out here was a much better plan than my original one, for she wouldn't bleed all over my seats before I had the chance to bandage her wound. Rule number one of plotting someone's death; always be ready to respond to any last minute change of carefully laid plans.

For a few seconds, I sat in the cool confines of my car enjoying myself while watching her pale lips eject the contents of her stomach, relishing her tormenting heaves and pathetic sobbing. I finally pulled my attention back to the task at hand, since I knew she wasn't going to drop over dead from just throwing up or having a crying jag, and opened the car door, only to be met with a rush of hot, bone-dry air. I quietly snatched the flashlight off the floor as I stepped out onto the hot pavement, and carefully concealed it in the folds of my ample skirt, my heels sinking a bit into the heat-softened asphalt. As I came around the back of the car, I almost laughed at her feeble frame as she wobbled back over to my car, almost falling down as she tried in vain to lean against the hot steel for support. I tried my best to hide my amusement as I blurted out some random comment about not having any tissues as I made my way over to her body, now seated haphazardly in the front seat of my car. For a moment I stared at her, drinking in the helplessness that was exuding out of her, taking in the last moment she would see me as "Diane Martin" and enjoying her crackling voice as she begged for water, when her fucking cell phone rang, startling us both. I cringed on the inside as she started sniveling into the phone, breaking the "bad news" to the poor groom, furious with myself for wasting those precious seconds staring at her rather than bashing her skull in.

Fuck!

I really had no choice now but to get back into the car and drive the little whiny bitch to the gas station, since I couldn't really do much now. Damn! As I pulled out on the road, my mind was already working out the solution to this newest twist in my plans. I forced myself to remain calm and not just reach over and grab her by that knotted mess on her head and slam it several times into the dashboard. No, no, I needed to wait, but my body was reacting to my apprehension and started to shake. I needed a pressure release, now.

While the little bitch whimpered on and on into the phone, I pulled into the single pump gas station. Miss Happy Pants didn't say a word as she immediately jumped out of the car and headed to the building; I assumed so she could find some blessed water that she craved. I watched her disappear inside the door and as she did, I reached into my pocket and pulled out the small compact I kept with me at all times for such emergencies, lifted the long folds of my skirt up enough to reach my inner thigh, and started slicing quickly. Oh God, that rush of painful pleasure that greeted my brain caused me to shudder as the intense pressure in my head finally evaporated. I was still leaning against the doorframe of my car when the bitch walked back out, carrying what looked like a key. Covering my mouth with my free hand, I stifled the cackle I felt in the back of my throat at that site; li'l Miss Priss, forced to use an outdoor bathroom! Ha!

Inhaling deeply, letting the hot, parched air fill my lungs as I slid the blade back into my compact, I began the task of filling my car up, waiting for the little troll to finish pampering herself so I could introduce her to the next chapter of her short life. After a few minutes and a fully topped off tank of gas, the uneasy feeling that something was wrong crept up my back, immediately making my hair stand up on end as the sensation slithered its way up to the top of my head. What the hell was taking her so long? Then my stomach dropped like I was on some sort of crazy ride at an amusement park as the thought hit me; what if she figured out who I was?

I replaced the gas nozzle and walked towards the store to pay, ignoring the little counter rat as I threw the cash on the counter. I was almost to the door when I heard, "Is your friend alright?" come from the back of the counter.

Shit, now I had to converse with said rat.

I turned around and said, in my most chipper voice, "Oh sure, she just has had a rough night; you know, drinking away the memory of her cheating boyfriend," I said, eyeing this little dirt mite heavily, wondering if she would fit in the small cooler by the door, and exactly how hard it would be to stuff her in there.

"Ugh, men! Who needs them? I was just wondering, since she looked pale when she came in, and is still in the bathroom," the counter-rat replied.

Damn, I wish I brought the flashlight with me. My eyes quickly scanned the almost empty space, looking for something I could use to render her unconscious as I still stood by the door and replied, "I've tried telling her before that she is killing brain cells, but does she ever listen to her aunt? Nope, she just calls me to rescue her after she goes on a bender," I said, biding time while I scoped the place out.

"Gosh, I wish my aunt would do that for me!"

I finally found my weapon of choice by the counter; a tire iron leaning innocently against it, right next to a display of *Fix-a-Flat*, with a handwritten note that said, "Please Return Once Finished". Relieved to know that it was there in case I needed to use it on the dusty, miserable waste of energy if she got too nosy, before I felt the need to really worry she said, "Just tell her to leave the key in the bathroom; it doesn't lock anyway, and I bet she just wants to crash in a soft bed."

I smiled at the little waif, who unknowingly just saved her own life, and said, "Sure thing. Thanks!" as I pushed the glass door open and rounded the corner to the bathroom. Once out of site of the counter-rat, I slowed down and stopped under the tiny window, listening. I heard the water running and then stop, what sounded like crinkling paper, and then the door cracked open just a bit. Assuming she was coming out, I stood up quickly, pressing my back as hard as I could against the wall, and waited for her to walk back to the car, when suddenly, she shut the door and stayed inside. I heard her pace back and forth as she made the phone call I was hoping she would not make.

The sense of foreboding overtook me again. She must be mulling over the events of the day and finally put the pieces of the puzzle together, since I could now hear her garbled voice crackling into the phone, obviously talking to Rosemary, or at least someone at *The Time of Your Life*. I slid my shoes off and quickly turned the other direction as I sprinted back into the store, yanking the door open so hard that I almost tore the decrepit handle off.

Counter-rat was going to have to die today after all.

I didn't say a word as I barreled through the front door and headed straight to the tire iron that I had no intention of "returning." In one swift move, I slid past the edge of the counter and grabbed the ancient piece of metal. Spinning around, I split the skull of the young thing almost in two before she even had a chance to open her mouth and question my frantic moves, and as I watched her convulse for a few brief seconds, the *thud* of the metal making contact with her fragile skull played over in my head. Her twitching body and most of her brains leaking out onto the ancient Formica were enough evidence for me that she wasn't long for this world; but just in case, I reached over and yanked her tiny little plastic cell phone out of her bloodied hand and threw it on the ground, demolishing it with the iron, just like her head. I scanned the small store interior for any evidence of a phone line but didn't see one. I took one last look at the pathetic crumpled mass of blood, brains and matted hair and decided that I just did her, and the world, a favor. She was released from years of hardship and eating dust, working in this barren hellhole. Bouncing from one stained lover's sheets to another, her several litters of baby rats growing up and, in turn, living the same life she had, obliterated before they even took a breath.

I smiled and thought *Good work, Piper.*

That completed, I trotted back out the door and padded quietly over to the bathroom door again, just in time to hear her feeble voice, drenched in fear, reply, "Well, then, who is she?"

I was right: she did finally catch on that something was wrong. Not as stupid as I originally thought; I guess it just took longer for her brain to process information since it was too tied up in practicing what horrid lies about my love she would regale the jury with on Monday.

I could literally smell the fear from her as I quietly opened the bathroom door and slid inside, my bare feet moving me silently across the filthy, stained floor towards her. Her back was to me and she stood there, rigid as a board, shaking like a frightened animal as she finally sensed my presence. I smelled the sweat dripping from her, intermingled with the stench of her horror as I raised the heavy piece of iron in the air, high above my head, and planted my feet for a good, solid swing. She spun around and stared at me, her eyes bulging huge with terror, and I could see her struggling to process what was really going on. In that split second between seeing something with her eyes and her brain deciphering what it was, I introduced myself to her.

As well as the tire iron.

* * * *

"We are live outside the entrance to Folton Farms, the ranch owned and run by Robert Folton of Summerset, and a former partner at Winscott & Associates in Phoenix. Mr. Folton is the lead witness in the capital murder case against Olin Kemper which is scheduled to begin on Monday morning. But sources tell us that Mr. Folton's wife reported him missing after his horse wandered back to the ranch in the wee hours of the morning, without its saddle or rider. A search is currently underway for Mr. Folton through the coordinated efforts of the Summerset Police Department and various other county and state agencies. Mounted and air patrol units have the daunting task of covering over 20,000 plus acres in the soaring heat, beginning their search around four o'clock this morning.

105

As you can see from the scene behind me, family and friends of Robert's have gathered here in what seems to be a show of support for the family, with some of them even bringing horses of their own to assist in the search, as we have seen several take off in groups.

We were told minutes ago that a representative from the Summerset Police Department will be coming out to make a statement momentarily to presumably give an update on...oh, and someone is coming to the gate now."

Jan did her best to hide the excitement from her voice and face, the adrenaline rush hitting her hard, knowing she was getting a major scoop on all the other local and national newshounds that were oblivious to this latest juicy tidbit. They were probably getting still shots from town for their broadcasts tonight, and had absolutely no clue what was going on. She took in a quick shot of air through her nose and thrust her best professional demeanor forth as she turned around to face the speaker, microphone ready in hand to capture it all while making herself famous.

"The body of Robert Folton was just recovered about ten miles north of here. His body is being flown back to the State Crime Lab for a complete autopsy to determine the cause of death. No further comments or statements will be made until our investigation is completed. Thank you, Jan." Detective Ronson said, nodding curtly at Jan and immediately turning on his heels and closing the iron gate behind him before Jan could even utter one question. Jan let the camera catch those few seconds to regain her own composure, for she almost couldn't contain her joy any longer. The song 'Dirty Laundry' by Don Henley was certainly true, for she knew that her eyes most likely reflected the "gleam" from this juicy bit of news. She squared her shoulders back and faced the camera once again.

"That was Detective Steve Ronson from the Summerset Police Department officially breaking the news that Robert Folton is dead. While our thoughts go out to his wife, children and family

members at his sudden, tragic passing, we can't help but wonder how this will affect the trial of Mr. Kemper on Monday.

"We will bring you more updates on this breaking case tonight at six and ten. This is Jan Patakee, reporting live from Summerset for Channel Six News."

CHAPTER 10
Audra-Reality Hits Close To Home

LATE THURSDAY NIGHT

God, I was so tired. My muscles were screaming at me, especially the ones that ran up my back and neck, from staying taut and tense all day as I hopped from one fire to another. Finally, at almost eleven in the evening, my cell phone quieted down long enough for me to use the restroom and grab some water from the kitchen. Actually, I was surprised that the little electronic brain hadn't just exploded from the incessant usage it suffered today. Once the news broke about Robert, my phone literally blew up with calls, emails and text messages. Trying to screen all this while driving was quite dangerous and something that I wasn't very adept at accomplishing, so I finally just gave up and called the office, told the receptionist to put me through to Carl, and had him conference in all the partners at one time. That helped only an infinitesimal amount on call volume for a few brief moments; then, the media monster reared its ugly head once more, with the mouthpiece led by that obnoxious Jan Patakee from Channel Six. Good God, but that woman was insufferable!

My head was thumping from a raging headache, most likely brought on from lack of food and the many adrenaline highs and lows it suffered throughout the day. I fumbled around in my desk drawer in search of something to ease the pain and finally found some ancient aspirin crammed in the very back. Swallowing quickly, I leaned back in my chair and closed my eyes for just a bit, trying to calm my overly rigid nerves from the absolute insanity that overshadowed my earlier bit of happiness. I gently rubbed my temples, hoping that would alleviate some of the pressure.

Damn, it wasn't working, which was no shock to me, considering the last 15 hours.

I wanted to go back to the wondrous, joyful and highly energetic sensations from my night with Steve, but they were completely overrun now by the news of Robert's death. When Steve had told me on the phone earlier today, I felt those warm, luscious thoughts immediately vanish as my blood turned cold with shock. My first thought was that he killed himself over grief of his actions and, quite possibly, his fear of testifying against Olin. That mental road immediately led me to feel a huge internal twinge of guilt, so overwhelming that I had to pull off onto the shoulder to gain control of my shaking limbs, as Steve related his exciting morning as they discovered Robert's body. Obviously, he knew that I might feel that way and immediately tried to soothe those frayed nerves by reassuring me that although he couldn't say how, the coroner at the scene said Robert's death was most likely a homicide. Although that did relieve the guilt factor somewhat, it didn't completely chase it away.

Homicide: as I sat in my office chair and thought about that, my stomach began to roil for the umpteenth time today. I had spent 38 blissful years completely untainted by any such darkness and evil and now, in less than one year, I was confronted not just with another one, but one that was intricately entwined with the first. I forced my eyes open at that point, unwilling to let the mental images fill my vision, and stared out the window into the endless lights below. The view from my new office was quite spectacular and offered up a much better viewing alternative than what was lurking in my mind's shadows, so I kicked off my shoes and walked over to the couch I recently purchased for moments such as these: a comfortable place to stretch my legs and relax while I gazed at the serene view below. As I sank into the cool leather and kicked my feet up, I forced myself to think rationally about Robert's situation, and not emotionally.

So many people had reasons for wanting him dead. Maybe it was his wife, horrified by the knowledge that she spent her entire marriage sleeping next to a silent killer, or at least someone that was an accomplice to one. I thought about that for a moment as I sipped my water in silence, wondering how I would have reacted had I awoke one morning to discover that James had been somehow *involved* in a murder. It was a bit difficult to truly summon emotions from that since my emotional connection to James was at just about zero, so I tried to recapture the feelings of joy that once flowed inside me as we prepared for our soon to be parenthood and run with it, almost like watching an internal movie, as a life that never was meant to be played before me. If we would have made it through years of marriage and raising children and then suddenly, after 20 plus years, I found out what poor Stacy did, I could imagine the unbelievable rage that I would feel, and most likely, any horribly betrayed woman would, but could I kill him, or plot his death? Possibly, since I knew from personal experience that one tragic moment in life had the ability to alter the course your life was previously on, throwing you onto a road that you never thought you were able to travel.

Although I knew Stacy from various events over the years that she attended with Robert, and she seemed like a nice, sane person, I did not know her personally, so my ability to weigh in on whether she was capable of murder or not was severely limited. Of course, my judgments of other people's personality traits that I did know was obviously not one of my stronger qualities since I grossly underestimated several of them. I put her down as a mental "maybe."

It could have been one of Gina's relatives, since I seemed to recall several of them making public threats about ripping Olin to shreds right after his arrest. Maybe they were so enraged about not being able to wrap their hands around his neck that they sought out the next best thing in Robert. But of course, the top of the list was

Olin, since he stood to lose the most if Robert testified against him, but he couldn't have done it since he was in jail.

Unless he had help from the outside.

I sat up quickly at that thought, spilling my water all over the hardwood floors, but I barely noticed the wetness as a quick, cold tremble ran through my body. *That* was the reason that Steve was so adamant earlier on the phone, almost to the point of becoming angry with me, about me turning around and coming back to stay with him: he was thinking the same thing. Before I could delve deeper into this new train of thought and concentrate on just who that person might be, my office phone rang. I sighed heavily as I looked over to see what acidic news agency was calling me now, surprised to see that the call was coming from Gabby's house. Thank goodness, it was about time! I really needed her earlier today and she never came back from her meeting, or answered any of my numerous calls.

A bit perturbed and ready to unleash a bit of my stress out in the form of a good ass chewing, I snatched up the receiver and snapped, "Gabby! Where have you been?!"

There was a brief moment of silence before I heard the husky voice of a man say, "Is this Ms. Tanner?"

I recognized the heavy Italian accent immediately and realized it was Jeff. I was embarrassed by my blurting out at him, assuming it was Gabby, then it dawned on me; why was he calling me this late?

"Jeff? Yes, this is Audra. I'm sorry for…" was all I could say before he interrupted me.

"Yeah, Ms. Tanner, this is Jeff. Is Gabby there? I really need to speak with her," came the deep baritone voice, one that sounded a bit slurred from one too many drinks.

"No Jeff, she isn't. I assumed, after her excitement on booking The Castle today, that she just went home, maybe to celebrate with you?" I posed the timid question, and even as the words left my mouth, the stone that just dropped into my stomach sent the signal to my brain that something was terribly, terribly wrong.

"She left me a voicemail that she was heading to The Castle, but I never did talk to her. I tried calling her cell all day today, and at first it just rang and rang, but now it is going straight to voicemail. She said something in her message to me earlier that she had a flat tire, and I am worried that she..." his deep voice trailed off, too macho to reveal the true emotions that he was feeling.

"Jeff, when I talked to her today, she said she was riding with someone from *The Time of Your Life* up to The Castle to sign the papers, so she wasn't in her car..."

Before I could utter another word, Jeff interrupted me again and said, "I'm sorry I bothered you Ms. Tanner," and slammed the phone down loudly in my ear.

Gabby was probably out celebrating away her good fortune and her phone just died. She would probably roll in any moment to his worried arms, maybe a bit tipsy from all her celebratory drinks, and make it up to her future husband for scaring him. I wanted that to be the case, willed myself to believe that, but something was tickling the back of my mind, like the incessant prodding of invisible fingers drumming on a table, that she wasn't out boozing it up. I chalked that nervousness up to the raw emotions of the day and decided I was overreacting; and besides, Gabby's personal business was not mine. Who knows, maybe she got cold feet?

I decided after that odd phone call that I was sick of all the excitement contained in one very long day and that it was time to pack up and head home, since not only did I need to put the final touches on the presentation for tomorrow that I had yet to finish, thanks to Gabby's absence, but I needed to pack for an extended stay in Summerset for the trial, which was predicted to last for weeks. I quickly sent an email to myself with a copy to Gabby to remember to call and cancel my hotel reservations in Summerset since, after last night, I decided I would stay with Steve. Of course, even if last night never materialized, Robert's mysterious death would have been enough ammo for Steve to insist upon taking care of me anyway.

As I stashed my laptop in my bag, I heard heavy footsteps coming down the hall and for a moment, I froze, wondering who in the hell was still at work this late. My heart thumped wildly in my chest as I glanced around my office for some sort of weapon to use to defend myself, my stressed-out brain thinking the worst. I quickly snatched my scissors off the desk in one hand and my cell in the other as I braced my body for whoever was coming my way, adrenaline pumping through me now at lightning speed. As the footfalls drew closer, their heaviness gave way to the fact that it must be a male, so I held my breath, kicked off my heels and steadied myself for battle as I stared at my office door.

The footsteps stopped on the other side of my door, and just as I raised the scissors, ready to strike at the person on the other side once it opened, I heard a faint tap on the door, followed by a familiar voice saying, "Audra, are you still here?"

I let out my breath in one huge whoosh of air and dropped the scissors back onto the desk, along with my phone, at the sound of Carl's voice. Hysterical laughter was fighting to erupt as the surge of adrenaline levels that put me in fight or flight mode just split seconds ago quickly dropped, leaving me feeling a bit unsteady and a whole lot of paranoid. I found my voice and replied, "Hey Carl, come on in."

Carl pushed the door open with his foot, as his hands were both occupied carrying two glasses in one and a bottle of some sort of liquor in the other. He was smiling as he walked in and said, "Hey, I thought after today you might need a…," but that smile ceased and his sentence abruptly stopped as he looked at my face, which I was sure was lovely pale white from my earlier bout with fear. "Audra, are you okay?" he said, setting the glasses down on the edge of my desk.

Nerves shot to hell and legs full of Jell-o, I plopped back down in my soft leather seat and smiled awkwardly up at him as I responded, "Oh, I'm fine. I was just contemplating what orifice to shove those scissors into before I realized it was you," nodding my head towards the shiny weapon sitting on my desk.

Carl's pupils grew big for a split second as they followed my gaze to my desk, but his smile came back as he reached for one of the glasses he brought and quickly poured a drink.

"I thought you might need a drink after today, but I was wrong; I think you need the entire bottle," he said, smiling as he handed me a glass of the amber colored liquid.

The snide laughter that escaped my lips surprised not only Carl, but me as well. It came out like something that should have burst forth from some psychotic serial killer and not from a dainty businesswoman, but I reached over and accepted Carl's glass of liquid memory killer and said, "You couldn't have come at a better time, Carl."

Carl poured himself a drink and walked over to the couch in the corner and sat down, his gait a bit stiff and rigid, as opposed to his normally light stride. As stressful as the day had been on me, I knew it probably had been much worse on Carl, for he and his wife had been friends with Robert and Stacy for years, and Robert's daughters occasionally babysat his son. I took a small sip of the strong smelling contents of my glass, unsure as to exactly which kind of liquid fire it was since I never was much of a drinker, and wrinkled my face as it slid down my throat, deciding that it must be some sort of tequila.

Carl watched me struggle to get my first drink down and smiled; the melancholy smile of someone that is not really smiling at the current events in front of them, but rather, the images and memories swirling inside their head. He finally broke the quiet silence between the two of us and said, "It's not your fault, Audra."

I stopped in the midst of my second sip attempt and just stared at him, my mouth slightly ajar. For a brief moment, I wasn't quite sure how to respond to his statement, but before I could respond, he continued.

"The simple truth is that Robert couldn't handle the fallout anymore. He was like a deflated balloon: all the years of suffering and hiding his secret kept him afloat, like he was willing himself to continue just to feel the pain. Once he released it though, there was nothing left inside him to punish him for what he did, and he couldn't deal with that. He was too Catholic–he felt this was his cross to bear the rest of his life."

I eased forward to the edge of my chair as I listened to Carl ramble on about Robert, watching the words tumble out of his mouth as he desperately tried to keep his voice and lips from trembling as he spoke about his friend. I sensed that he wasn't finished so I remained quiet. He took another hefty swig and continued.

"He was my colleague yes, but also my friend, Audra. He was there for me at every marriage, every divorce and every baby born. And he was the only other partner here, like me, that was devoted to his family, that never strayed from his bounds of marriage, never chased the skirts," Carl said, his voice trailing off as he stared out the window at the teeming streets below, trying in vain to hide his face from me; which, at this point, I was sure tears were running down.

"We hated all the things that went on here and although we talked about it, never pursued an avenue to change them; but now I know we had hugely different reasons. He was under Olin's thumb, cornered, unable to stand up to him," he said, the words thick and heavy now as one hand reached up and wiped his face. "But me? What was my excuse for my silence? Sadly, I don't have one."

I took a deep breath and set my foul smelling drink on the table. I was so stunned to see this side of him that I was rendered speechless for a few moments, unsure what, if anything, I should say. Understanding male emotional breakdowns, which is what I sensed was coming, was not an arena I possessed much experience in, so I chose my words carefully, especially since the possibility was quite high that Robert's death was not some tragic accident or suicide.

"Carl, I can't imagine how hard this day must have been for you, losing your friend like this; plus assisting me in dealing with the media storm that ensued once they found out. Today, you were a staunch defender of the firm, as well as your friend, and that just shows the depth of character that you have. As for living in the past, dwelling on the "what if's" and the "what could have been's" well, although me dispensing advice on that subject is rather hypocritical, might I offer this thought, passed along by a friend, to me? Don't carry that heavy weight around with you. You cannot alter what is done, only what has yet to be."

Carl just continued to stare out the window as he quietly nodded his agreement. I decided not to touch the comment about guilt, since that was my Achilles heel, and I wasn't entirely sure that I was able to carry on a conversation about those feelings with anyone just yet. Before I could say anything else, Carl finally turned to look at me, the sadness in his eyes dancing dangerously close to bitterness as he said, "How did you do it, Audra? How did you hide for so long what happened to you? I mean, did you share your feelings with anyone? Wasn't there *someone* you felt close enough to talk to about it?"

I raised the cup to my lips again and took another sip of the pungent liquid before I answered delicately, a bit unsure of where this conversation was heading, "Carl, my reactions to my life has no bearing on how Robert, or anyone else for that matter, reacts to their own. No one can predict what one individual will do from another," I said quietly as I set the glass down, deciding that I needed to go home, the urge to leave overwhelming my mind. As I slowly stood up and reached for my purse and cell phone, I spoke quietly. "I'm sure that if Robert felt he could have shared what was in his heart with a friend, he would have. Some things are just easier left inside, Carl."

His demeanor shifted once again as his face softened and the edginess to his eyes lightened, almost like he snapped out of some odd dream as he noticed I was packing up to leave. He cleared his throat and stood up, his cheeks turning a mild shade of berry pink as the alcohol coursed through his veins. Even in his current inebriated state, I think he realized he had overstepped his boundaries with me and quickly wobbled over to my desk to retrieve the now almost empty bottle. I picked up my purse and computer bag, then gently reached over and held the bottle around it's slender neck, holding it down on the desk as I said, "Carl, I think you should let me call a taxi to take you home, or at least let...," was all I got out before the loud cackle of laughter came from the direction of my door, immediately followed by, "Well, I'll be damned, Carl. I can't recall the last time I actually remember seeing you drunk. What, maybe 15 years ago?" Nicole sneered as she walked into my office, teetering on her four inch plus heels.

God, this day must be powered by the Energizer Bunny because it just kept going and going...

Carl and I both shifted our eyes over to Nicole as she pranced her way through my office and plopped unceremoniously onto my couch, immediately kicking off her heels as she stretched her legs out. I didn't notice it when she first appeared at the door, but as she passed by us both on her way across the room, the scent of beer wafted behind her and I realized she was drunk as well.

Magnificent.

"Carl, don't you worry about driving home...you can just stay up here and drink with me tonight. We can toast to the "old" Winscott, as well as to the fall of the "new" Winscott." she slurred, her intonations heavy with her Georgia accent, which usually appeared when she had thrown one too many drinks down. Although I had seen her drunk a few times before, I had never seen her so trashed as she was now, and of course, I had never seen Carl drunk, but then again, this was not a normal day.

Not normal at all.

I took a deep breath and snatched the bottle from Carl's light grip, since he was more interested in watching Nicole adjust her muscular legs on the couch, and firmly said, "Carl, Nicole: enough. I am calling a cab right now to take you both home. The last thing we need now are two more dead partners." I knew that was harsh, as I saw both of them cringe a bit, but I knew I needed to get their attention, and quickly, before I was suddenly in the middle of a college frat party. It was quite obvious that I wasn't the only one that was struggling to deal with today's events, and we all needed to get home and try and rest, for God knows the rest of the week and weekend would probably be just as insane as today was. Nicole started to protest, but I just held my hand up, using the one piece of bait I knew she would latch onto, "Nicole, I need you fresh for tomorrow. I have a meeting at six tomorrow night with a new client, Mrs. Jeanette Lancaster, and I am going to need your valuation expertise on this one, since her husband owns several businesses that we will need valued for their divorce settlement. So you must be on your game tomorrow!" I said emphatically as I picked up the phone and buzzed security downstairs.

"I need a taxi please, we will be down in just a few moments" I said quickly to Tyson, the security guard downstairs, then hung up and turned back to my drunken colleagues. I could see Nicole processing what I said about tomorrow night with obvious difficulty due to her alcohol riddled brain, before she slurred, "You mean, Jeannette Lancaster? Wife of Tom Lancaster?" I nodded in agreement, pointing at her shoes on the floor as she was fumbling around for them, oblivious as to their location. "Oh my gawd, they are worth *millions*! This is just what we needed!"

For the next ten minutes I cajoled, begged and pleaded until I gathered all of their belongings up and corralled Carl and Nicole into the elevator, all the while listening to Nicole regale us with her tales of how she had met Jeannette Lancaster once in Palm Springs and she was the nicest lady, until we finally made it to the lobby and the awaiting taxi cab. Once the cab rounded the corner, Tyson and I exchanged knowing glances as he said, "It's late Ms. Audra. I need to walk you to your car."

After the day I'd had, I didn't protest and we walked along silently through the empty parking deck. As we rounded the corner to my level, I noticed that Gabby's car was still there, and sure enough, sporting a flat tire. Before I could turn around and ask Tyson to make sure to call a repairman when he got back to his desk, he said, "Good Lord, Ms. Tanner. What the hell happened to your car?"

ASHLEY FONTAINNE

CHAPTER 11
Olin-The Caged Snake's Musings

EARLY FRIDAY A.M.

I was so fucking sick of staring at that dingy ass cell. Nine months of being cooped up like some trapped bird was driving me bat-shit crazy. For the first few months of my incarceration, I occupied my brain by strategizing my defense plan, my head resting on the reeking joke that the guards liked to call a pillow, as I stared into the blank ceiling, going over every possible scenario we could use to get me the fuck out of here and what courtroom trickery the prosecution would use against me. Nick, Roger and I knew that the biggest hurdle to overcome would be my DNA from the crime scene and Robert's blubbering testimony. It's not like I could explain how my hairs were found on the duct tape that was at the *bottom* of the bitch's grave, securing my damnation around a plastic garbage sack's throat, and even if I could somehow conjure up some plausible scenario, Robert's tears of guilt would sway a jury full of O.J. Simpson jurors.

I lost track of how many times in the last nine months that I had relived that night, looking back on it with wiser eyes, picking up on the small things I should have done differently. Who the fuck knew in the seventies that a single piece of hair could tie you to a crime scene? And of course, getting my life entangled with such an obvious backwoods redneck was not one of the wisest choices I ever made.

Once my "brilliant" legal team (fuck, what a joke) finally stopped patting themselves on the back for pocketing huge amounts of money from me and finally formulated my defense plan, (which was SORELY lacking), I no longer found anything of interest to stimulate my brain, so I began imagining what diabolical plans Piper was cooking up in that jumbled mess of neurons in her brain, for I honestly did not have a clue. It was quite sad, really, that she was my only hope of permanently getting out of this room, since Tweedle-Dee and Tweedle-Dum were not much help.

After her early visit with me at the Summerset jail, Piper and I only talked once more, which was about three months later when she came to the Yarkema County Jail, where I was moved to about three weeks after my arrest for "safety concerns." What a fucking joke. Safety concerns: if someone had been plotting my assassination, surely my brains would already be decorating the insides of the Summerset jail, for security there truly was something out of a scene from *The Andy Griffith Show*.

I wriggled around on my lovely little strip of linen atop the rusty metal that served as my bed and finally found a semi-comfortable spot that allowed me to stare out of the cell through the bars into the dark hallway, rather than counting the spider webs that lined the decrepit walls. My Rolex was who knows where—probably around the arms of Bulging Barney at Summerset, for he eyed it hard and heavy when I was arrested—so I could only guess as to what time of day or night it was. Time took on a whole new dimension when you didn't really have anything to mark the passing of it, nor things to accomplish given a specific frame, but I was pretty adept at guessing the hour of the day based upon the noises around me. Since the only noise my straining ears heard was the occasional squeak of a rat, I surmised that it must be around one or two in the morning, which meant dinner should be arriving shortly.

Dinner. It was laughable, at best, to refer to the nasty slop that was served here as anything remotely close to edible food. Of course, I could only assume the gorillas that greased themselves down enough to squeeze into their tight uniforms were actually bringing me food, since they only brought it during the blackened, wee hours of the morning and literally kicked the tray into my cell from the hallway, thus splattering most of the swill across the already filthy floor. I would nibble on just enough to keep my growling stomach quiet, preferring to concentrate on remembering all the delicious entrees I would inhale once back out into the real world.

The world that would be minus three fucking rats.

I heard the doors unlock and the clomping of boots on the ancient concrete floor, then the clanging of my dinner tray as it came sliding into my cell, but I ignored the rank smell of my sustenance and closed my eyes and thought about Piper.

I knew the minute I looked into her glazed, over the moon, fanatical eyes that not only was she willing to kill for me, but that she would, no questions asked or even heavy prodding on my end. All it took was just one small suggestion that day so many months ago. Although I wasn't afraid of her, I knew that she was a dangerous, unstable woman that must be handled with the utmost delicacy; unlike when I previously dumped her unceremoniously and she responded by slashing her arm so deeply that my entire office required a overhaul, as her blood was plastered on not only my walls, but the rug, ceiling and couch. I remember she looked at me, her eyes so calm, so cool, almost calculated, smiled, and said, "Forever, Olin."

Crazy bitch.

I must admit though, I actually did enjoy the few months we spent fucking each other like there was no tomorrow. The woman held no qualms about dropping to the floor no matter where we were: my office, her house, the car, my yacht, a restaurant bathroom, a darkened alley at night: you name it, and she was game. She was like this little girl in a woman's body, so eager to open herself up and please her man, letting him do whatever he wanted to her without a modicum of hesitation. After our first tryst on my desk that evening years ago, I remember laughing to myself, thinking that her unimaginable amount of pent up sexual frustration had just been released all over my desk, and quite honestly, she was full of skills I thought only professionals possessed. I remember driving home that night wondering what in the hell that sexual beast was doing married to a gay man.

Poor Piper: so mistreated: so misunderstood: so consistently pointing her pussy to the WRONG men; so blinded by her unfathomable longing for a man to fill her obvious daddy issues, she seemed inexplicably attracted to ones that would never be able to fill those shoes. I still couldn't believe that she stayed with Nick for as many years as she did, because she clearly wasn't in love with him since she was absolutely gaga over Ralph, and everyone knew it. For years, she drooled over him, begging to be put on his team whenever the chance for out of town audits were available, hardly able to walk past him without creaming herself; she was always the talk of the partner meetings (at least until she became one herself).

I stared into the darkness, aware of the pungent smell of my "dinner" on the floor and the chomping of the rats as they nibbled on it. Forcing myself to ignore the rank smell and disgusting sounds, I recalled the night, 17 years ago, that changed everything and everyone at Winscott.

* * * *

It was during the celebratory dinner and drinks at the local strip club one night after tax season. Ralph, clearly drunk out of his mind and having great difficulty dealing with his surroundings, was cursing at one of the skanky dancers that was trying her best to liven him up. I remember watching him attempt to stumble outside to spew his drink after being so violated, but he couldn't really walk; so, while I held back my laughter, I got up and helped him to the bathroom, but he shoved me aside and said, "Go away you brown-nosing cocksucker," and sort of fell into the door that led into the back alleyway.

124

I decided to let the ungrateful fuck alone, so I went instead to use the john. I laughed as I thought, *Here is the mighty Ralph Winscott: Managing Partner and founder of Winscott & Associates, one of the biggest, best known names in the state; owner of not one but two private planes, several homes from one ocean to another, politicians in his pocket, card carrying member of the NRA and avid sportsman, throwing up his dinner because he can no longer handle his liquor and broads.* It was absolutely priceless to watch the pathetic joke that he had become writhe on the filthy floor like a fish out of water, and had the technology been available at the time, I would have enjoyed posting it to YouTube.

As I left the bathroom, I heard the grumblings of loud voices coming from the alleyway, one of which sounded like Ralph's loud bellow, somewhat muffled by the thumping music raging from the inside of the club. This piqued my interest as to the content of the yelling match, and the thought of possibly finding some good leverage material–as previous nights of debauchery had yielded plenty of blackmail material in the past– so I crept over to the back door, which was cracked open just enough for me to see Ralph with our legal counsel and Piper's husband, Nick Rancliff, in the small alleyway. Ralph was hanging on to the side of a dirt encrusted garbage bin for support, clearly distressed, his face so red it was almost glowing from not only the eight or nine Jack 'n Coke's that he pounded down earlier, but from sheer anger. Nick, who was quite younger, taller by at least a head and less inebriated, was wearing an odd look on his face, sort of a mixture of triumph and fear as he stood about six feet away from the raging bull that Ralph was when he became angry.

"Nick, I gave you what you wanted: Piper is now an equity partner. I gave you the cash back for her buy-in, now pony up on your end of the deal!" Ralph yelled, his words angry yet beseeching at the same time as he stared up into the face of Nick through his bloodshot eyes and his rotund head weaved from side to side.

Nick stood there and stared at him for a few seconds, the single, bare light bulb strong enough for me to see his disgust at the disheveled and reeking drunk in front of him; and even through the dismal light, I could see the internal wheels in his head spinning as he calculated his response, for I recognized that look from numerous times of performing those mental mathematics myself.

"Ralph, calm down and shut the fuck up! Do you want the entire city to hear you? For someone that is so worried about discovery, you sure aren't very skilled in the intricate art of secrecy, are you?" Nick said, his carefully chosen words his attempt at portraying authority and control over the situation; but the underlying tremor in his voice was ruining their affect, at least to my ears.

"Don't tell me to shut up, you arrogant little asshole! You don't control me!" Ralph yelled, this time louder than before. I knew the minute he uttered those words, since I had witnessed it many times before over several years, that he was going to explode and come out swinging, and sure enough, he did. I covered my mouth to control the laughter that desperately wanted to burst forth as I watched the sawed-off fuck let go of the garbage bin and lurch forward towards Nick. He threw down his drink, the glass immediately disintegrating as it met the asphalt, his Jack 'n Coke splashing all over his feet, his drink hand now a formidable fist as he attempted to take Nick's head off with one heartfelt swing. It would have been a great fight to watch if Ralph was a bit less trashed, for even at his age, he was as strong as ever and fast as a cat, which was a deadly combination and one that had inflicted much pain over the years to others; but tonight, that was not the case. Ralph immediately lost his balance as Nick deftly moved away from his swing, and the force of Ralph's momentum overtook his body as he almost did a complete 180 and fell onto the slick pavement, his head slamming hard against the blacktop with a sickening thud.

Nick quickly maneuvered his body around and was now standing over Ralph, who was just lying there, the impact of his head with the ground rendering him quiet as he blinked his eyes in rapid succession, trying to regain his composure and cognitive abilities. Before his whiskey soaked brain could comprehend that he needed to get up, Nick crouched down and said, "Awww, poor Ralph. Too much drink, too little agility. Shame, shame, Ralph. Don't you remember our night together and our mutual affinity for pain? Beating the crap out of me isn't going to change the fact that I still hold the cards here, no matter how much either one of us would enjoy it. Now, be a good boy and listen carefully; I have the tape in my car and when I leave here tonight, I will leave it in yours, and then our little "transaction" will be completed. I am a man of my word, just as you are," Nick said, the tremor in his voice no longer there, replaced with an aggressive tone that I wasn't aware Nick actually possessed.

I realized, at that moment, that my life could change if I could just see what was on that tape, so I quietly stepped back from the door and left the two of them to finish their little alleyway dirty dance alone. I made my way through the drunken crowd and out the front door to the dark parking lot, searching for Nick's Jag, and finally located it in the back of the lot, sitting alone in the darkness just waiting for someone to break into it.

Which was exactly what I was about to do.

I smiled at my good fortune of once again being at the right place at the right time. Damn, I never thought that a party down in a strip club would garner me anything except a blowjob and a hangover. I made it to the passenger door of Nick's red beauty and did a quick scan of the parking lot once more, ensuring that I was alone, and then peered in the window. Sure enough, there was a small, square package sitting quietly on the passenger floorboard, just waiting for someone to open its manila cover; which was going to be me as soon as I located something to smash the window with. I started to pull back from the window when I noticed that the door latch was up, and I did a double take.

Surely it couldn't be this fucking easy?

I reached down and tried the handle, and almost jumped for glee when it responded to my touch and opened, revealing the present inside. I quickly snatched the tape off the floor and quietly shut the door, feeling like a kid that just discovered where the Christmas presents were stored and was about to sneak off and take a peek at them, and couldn't believe my great stroke of luck!

Now that I had the much sought after tape, I needed–no, I wanted to–watch it and see just what the illustrious Nick Rancliff was holding over Ralphie's head, although I was pretty damn sure I already knew. God knows Ralph had fucked his way through just about the entire state, and I assumed it was one of these sessions with some high profile piece of ass that would burn him. Damn, I knew there was some hidden reason why Piper was now an equity partner since she sure didn't have the clientele or the high level accounting acumen to back up being a partial owner. I assumed when Ralph announced his decision to nominate her two weeks ago, as he did with all the other partners, that Piper finally sunk her claws into him and possessed something to hold over his head in exchange for her promotion; none of us dared balk at any of Ralph's decisions, lest he ruin your life, so we all signed the agreement and let it go.

I stood in the darkness for just a moment, debating upon whether I should go back inside the club and watch it on Montrae's VCR in his office—which I knew he had, since he bragged about taping the girls as they gave their client's "special" service in the back for those "rainy" days when he needed some financial leverage—or if I should just jump in my car and take my little treasure home and watch it there. Of course, if I left now, right in the middle of the party, then I stood the risk of Nick and Ralph putting the puzzle pieces together that I was the one that stole their tape, so I decided to watch it in Montrae's office and remain at the party, thereby averting any attention in my direction from a questionable absence at one of my favorite places.

I unbuttoned my shirt, stuffed the little bundle of joy under my armpit and walked back inside. I smiled when I realized no one even looked at the door as they were all engrossed in watching Shantilly, the buxom blonde that was grinding on the pole at center stage, doing her thing for the cash that was leaping out of the pockets of my colleagues and landing on stage beneath her black leather thigh-high boots. I didn't see Nick or Ralph in the crowd, but only briefly looked as I walked up to the bar where Montrae was and motioned for him. Although a rather nasty little man that would never have cut it in this world as anything other than a slimy titty-bar manager, I paid him well for the services that his club offered, as well as some "extra-curricular" activities I hosted all over the country, so he immediately began salivating like a Pavlov dog as he made his way over to the end of the bar, practically tripping over himself as he smelled the money that soon would be in his pocket.

"Montrae, I need to make a private call. Where can I go to make one around here and not be disturbed?" I said, sliding a 50 over to him. He smiled, revealing the crooked, golden teeth that gleamed under the lights and said, his Columbian accent thick and heavy, "My office, *jefe*, of course! Mi casa is su casa, amigo!" as he reached into his pocket and handed me the key. "Take all time you need! Want someone to dial the number for you, *jefe*?"

I smiled broadly at him as I took the worn down key from his greasy paw, amused at his not so demure attempt to offer up a piece of pussy to me, wrongly assuming that is what I wanted his office for, so I played along and said, "Gracias, Montrae, but no, I will supply my own entertainment," and patted my crotch with my other hand. His black, heartless eyes made a cold shiver run along my spine as they stared through me and he smiled, nodding his head as he turned and walked back to the main part of the bar, his street savvy eyes immediately recognizing that his services were no longer necessary and no more money was forthcoming from this rich *jefe*. As the crowd clapped and hollered for the next dancer, I snuck off down the hall to Montrae's office, quickly locking the door behind me. I surveyed the tiny, cramped space and immediately found the television with the VCR stashed underneath it. As I slid the tape in and pressed the on button, I felt a rush of excitement hit me as the screen lit up, hoping that things at Winscott were about to change if this tape really did hold some type of blackmail power that I could now wield instead of that bastard Nick.

I leaned against Montrae's desk and watched the images unfold in front of me, my mouth agape and heart racing as I discovered it was a sex tape alright, just not one that even I would have ever imagined. I held my breath (and vomit) as Ralph and Nick went at each other like two depraved dogs in what looked like the inside of an expensive hotel. Holy shit! I couldn't believe what I was seeing. The skirt-chasing, gun toting, beat-your-ass-to-a-pulp bull of a man, known for his roughneck upbringing and foul mouth as he courted his clients that were just as rough and crude as he was; a man who would spend thousands of dollars tonight alone on drinks and pussy for the entire male population of his firm, as well as himself; the only man that I ever felt some semblance of respect and admiration for as he took what he wanted and never looked back; was taking it up the ass from Piper's husband.

And that's when the plan formed.

As I leaned against the decrepit desk, the smell of stank, dirty hoochie and booze permeating from every inch of the filthy walls, I realized that what was on that tape held the key to my takeover of Winscott, as long as I played my cards right. I didn't have time to hatch a failsafe plan in Montrae's office because this bombshell was going to require quite a bit of finesse to accomplish.

The sounds coming from the TV were making me ill when I needed to concentrate on what I was going to do *now*, so I hit the "stop" button and ejected the tape. I held my little goldmine in my hands and forced myself to calm down and think rationally, as I began to pace back and forth in the tiny shithole, my mind racing wildly as I realized that I could own the firm within the next few days.

By getting rid of Ralph.

The sweat began to roll down my back as my excitement escalated. I glanced down at the television screen and noticed that, underneath the stand, there was additional video equipment used to make copies of tapes, and that's when the proverbial light bulb exploded in my head. I knew exactly what I was going to do to

Ralphie Boy, as I fiddled with the equipment and dug through the office, finding a blank tape and making a copy.

Ten minutes later, I slipped out of Montrae's office and stopped at the edge of the hallway, spying on the revelers from my spot, searching for Nick and Ralph. Nick was sitting at the bar doing shots with Eric but I didn't see Ralph, so I assumed he was in the bathroom, which gave me a chance for a clean getaway back outside to replace the tape.

I stopped off at my car first and unlocked the trunk and gently hid my new best friend in the darkness, then hurried over to Nick's car and slid the copy of the tape back onto the floorboard. Although it was no longer wrapped in a manila envelope, I doubted, as drunk as Nick would be if he continued to try and match Eric shot for shot, that he would be able to remember much of this night, so I smiled at my work and headed back inside once again. At the door, Shantilly was taking a smoke break, her heavy breasts spilling out over her miniscule top, her cherry red lips pulling hard on the cigarette as she eyed me like I was a walking bank. I gave her a wink and patted her ass as I walked in and told her, "Shanti, tonight I will make your month. Give me five minutes, then meet me at the bar."

And so I slipped back into the party, no one the wiser of the bomb I just planted in my car, nor the tremendous explosion it would cause later: not even me. Less than two weeks after that night, the timer on my bomb was set, just at the moment when I noticed that Ralph's demeanor changed over from stress to complicity, thinking his moral fuckup was dead and buried, and then BOOM! I lit the fuse and watched the burn.

I remembered sitting anxiously all day at my desk as, one by one, the others came in, each shocked and completely unnerved by their own personal copy of Ralph's exploits that they found wrapped in a pretty package on their desks. Of course, I feigned shock as well, touting the tape to be an obvious fake, for there was no way that our illustrious leader was capable of such atrocious acts. I nodded my head in agreement with the statements of "something needs to be done." I stayed hidden in my office all day, waiting and listening for the sounds of shame and remorse to emit from Ralph's, but by nine o'clock that night, the only thing I heard of any significance was the occasional slamming of drawers or a low grumble.

Furious that he had yet to do anything drastic in response to his starring role, I decided to grease the wheel a bit and wandered into his office, file in hand, to help perpetuate the myth (in case anyone were to walk up on us) that I was just going in to see him regarding a client. When I opened the door and saw him glued to his fine leather chair, his body almost completely sunk into the heavy cushions, I immediately noticed the opened gift on his desk. The pallor of his face was all the evidence I needed that he was well aware of the tenuous circumstances he was immersed in. The heavy smell of his favorite spirit filled the room with its sickening odor, along with the rank stench of human sweat. I had to put on my best game face as I smiled at him, my voice smooth as melted chocolate as I asked, "Ralph, you look rather ill. I hope it's not something contagious."

When he finally looked up at me from behind his sunken eyes, I knew that he was clasping for dear life to the last thin tendril of his sanity, but I also knew that he recognized a fellow bullshitter. I noticed the gun in his hand that was resting quietly in his lap, and then in one quick moment, his pupils dilated as he finally put the missing puzzle piece in place. His lips curled back into an ugly snarl as he screamed, "It was YOU!"

I smiled at him as I responded, "It was? What exactly did I do, Ralph?" I said, the chocolate pouring down my chin now as I moved, almost indecipherably, closer to him, my eyes never leaving his. "Are you accusing me of taking your little show on the road? Providing it to the masses for their entertainment? You don't really believe that I would sink that low do you? If your little...er, well, big...secret were to fall into the hands of the media, then how would that reflect upon us? You know, how the mighty Winscott likes hot weenies with a side of pain, especially the one of a colleague's husband?"

I was almost at the side of his desk. My shoes made no sound as I gently placed them, one in front of the other, on the lush carpet. I was within three feet of him and could literally feel the anger pulsate from him, rolling off every inch of his thick skin as it left his pores and adhered to his clothes. My smile was plastered across my face but never reached my eyes. Ralph's fury was past the boiling point, but he was quite inebriated. We both knew if he tried to stand, he would fall over, so he opted for only moving his arm, which shook slightly as he raised the gun in my direction. He tried to cock the hammer back with one hand, and just as he reached over with the other to lock and load, I swung into action and, grabbing his wrists, forced his hand up to his temple and helped him pull the trigger.

The sound the .45 made was deafening and my ears literally felt like blood was running out of them, almost enough to match the spurting blood from Ralph's head. I didn't care as my fake smile now was a real one and travelled to my eyes, thankful that the bastard was finally gone.

It was then time to go clean up and play the shocked employee that just walked in on his boss's suicide. My plan was perfectly executed. All the votes I needed to take over the firm after the *tragic* passing of its beloved benefactor were in place. It was neck and neck between Eric and I, and the final vote came down to the luscious little Georgia Peach that I violated a few weeks ago. I remember how my triumphant grin disappeared when she cast her vote for Eric, her eyes a pile of sweet mush while she ogled him.

Bitch.

CHAPTER 12
Sherman Fenter

I scribbled my name, *Sgt. Sherman Fenter*, on the sign in sheet in my best chicken scrawl (Mom always said I should have been a doctor with this handwriting), which officially relieved the scrawny, pimple covered boy that was desperately trying to look impressive in his uniform, from his shift. Before I could even set the pen down, ol' skin and bones was up and out of his chair in his scramble to get home, probably to eat some more pizza and chocolate to create some new additions to his face. I just stood there and stared at him, waiting for the pipsqueak to realize he forgot something before he bolted for the night. *Geez, where do they get these recruits, and what in the hell is his name?* I thought as I reached out and snagged the idiot by the arm as he rounded the desk, his eyes solely focused on the door, and, intentionally making my voice gruff, I barked, "Um, boy, aren't you forgetting something?"

Boney-Boy stared at me like I just threw scalding water on him or was speaking a foreign language, his pale face instantaneously growing even paler as his free hand, attached to his other wimpy limp noodle, reached up and did one of those "Oh, I could have had a V-8" slaps in the middle of his pasty white forehead, and he chirped, "Oops, sorry Sarge. I don't know if I will ever be able to remember that!"

I let go before I bruised the little twerp and didn't say a word as I extended my hand for him to drop the keys into, shaking my head in disgust and dismissing him as I turned and walked over to the desk to begin my long shift. I sat down and immediately began checking the logs that nim-nuts most likely jacked up from earlier. Oh well, at least it would give me something to work on tonight, because God knows the graveyard shift in this barren ward of the jail was boring as hell, except for my petty torments.

Sure enough, the logs weren't properly filled out and some weren't even signed, and I felt my irritation grow. How many times did I need to cover for his sorry ass? I made a mental note to contact our superiors before I left in the morning to request that scarecrow be moved to any shift other than the one prior to mine.

I knew fixing all these mistakes would require my full attention, so I decided to head down to the break room and snag a cup of oily coffee to rev up my brain cells. The halls were silent, save for my footfalls and the low hum of the lone television that continuously played in the break room, intermixed with a light snort from one of the numerous upstanding citizens in their new little concrete homes. I paid it no attention as I headed straight for the coffee maker, until I heard the words "…trial of Olin Kemper…" and quickly looked up, watching that pretty little reporter from Phoenix, who's name I could never remember either, as she reported on the death of Robert Folton with her sweet red lips.

Holy shit!

Since it was after midnight, I knew that this was just a repeat of the earlier news, and I missed most of her report, so I quickly poured a cup and trotted back to the control room, sloshing coffee on the dank floors behind me as I did. I sat down at the desk and quickly logged onto the Internet, intent on watching the entire news story, and as I did, I couldn't help but wonder, just as li'l Miss Cutie Pie Reporter mentioned, how Robert's death would affect the trial of the nasty bastard caged down the hall. In all my years of working in solitary, numerous sick and twisted characters had been housed in those tiny little rooms, but none of them ever rubbed me the wrong way as much as Olin Kemper did. I never could quite put my finger on the exact reason why, but there was something that leaked from him from behind those hooded, icy eyes that made me want to crack him over the head with my club, like I was bashing the devil out of him.

Of course, the fact that Gina had been my high school sweetheart didn't help his case.

Knowing that beating him to a bloody pulp was not a possibility, at least if I wanted to keep my job, I opted for my own brand of torment after he was brought here months ago, as I requested the midnight shift indefinitely, and made sure his dinner was served in the wee hours of the morning; after, of course, I made certain *alterations* to it before I slid it into his cell.

Bastard, he deserved to die for what he did and for living the high life for so long, and it was about time he was punished; but now, would that happen? I didn't know much about the legal finagling that goes on during a trial, but if the star witness was dead, I wondered if he could actually end up beating this and walk free.

I glanced back over at the computer screen and noticed a few more links to news video feeds that blared '**Recommended Stories**' and almost closed out the screen when the last link suddenly caught my attention, simply because it was about snakes. I'd had a strange love for anything scaly ever since I saw my first one up close and personal at the zoo as a young boy.

It was from a small blurb about the discovery of the body of renowned herpetologist, Dr. Dan Moore, at his tiny research and milking facility in McNeal on Wednesday. I couldn't believe it! I owned a few of his books on snakes, and just recently purchased an old copy of *Arizona's Vipers*, that he wrote over 20 years ago, at Buried Books, simply because it was chock full of fantastic pictures of some of the most venomous snakes in North America. As I sipped my coffee I listened to the report, which was rather vague and stated that poor Dr. Moore, found by a research assistant, died in a tragic accident after some of his vipers escaped from their cages and apparently bit him. I sat back in my chair and wondered how much his books would be worth now that he was dead, and then I heard the reporter say "*...inside sources tell us* *that police, although treating Dr. Moore's passing as an accident, are interested in speaking with Ms. Bridgette Summers, who had an appointment with Dr. Moore the morning of his death."*

Bridgette Summers, Bridgette Summers? Why did that name ring a bell? I closed the screen and tried to think. An old girlfriend? A high school chum? ne of Katie's friends from school? No, it wasn't any of those, and try as I might, I couldn't recall why that name triggered something in my memory. Damn, but I hated getting old.

I decided to let it go, hoping that maybe reverse psychology would work; that maybe by *not* thinking about it, I would remember. So I sat back down and began the task of finishing—Kurt, that was his name—Kurt's work from the earlier shift, and before I knew it, two hours had passed. I looked up and noticed it was almost 2:30 a.m., which meant I needed to go the cafeteria and pick up Olin's dinner.

Bastard.

CHAPTER 13
Steve-The Truth Unfolds

I finally stepped out of the shower, having exhausted all of the hot water during the 20 minutes I just stood under the stream, grateful for the refreshing water to not only rinse the filth of the desert away, but also the stench that sunk into my pores. Too bad that it wasn't possible to clean the mind the same way, for if it was, I would happily crack my head open and rinse the nasty images from the day away. It was days like that day when I started to think twice about my career choice.

I toweled off quickly and yanked on fresh jeans, shirt and socks, stumbling a bit in the darkness in my haste, then headed to the kitchen to grab a fresh cup of coffee that hopefully finished brewing while I was in the shower. God knows I needed the caffeine as I closed in fast on a 24 hour stretch with no sleep. I only got down the first swig before my cell phone rattled on the counter, and I quickly snatched it up, answering it on the second ring.

"Ronson."

"Hey Steve, it's Sandy. Got a minute?"

I really didn't, as I needed to finish getting dressed and head back to the station, but I also knew that Sandy wouldn't be calling me at 2:30 in the morning if she didn't think it was important, so I said, "Make it quick, I'm trying to get back up there. What's up?"

"I have a guard from Yarkema County Jail that insists he talk to you. He won't tell me why, but he has called twice, wanting your cell phone number, but I wouldn't give it to him. He is asking now that I patch the call through."

I set my cup down on the counter and pulled out the bar stool, cradling the phone to my ear with my shoulder as I reached for pen and paper from the edge of the counter. Yarkema County was where Olin was spending his solitary time these days, and the immediate tingle in my gut, that I had learned to listen to long ago, started bouncing around, letting me know I needed to hear what the guard had to say.

"It's okay Sandy, transfer him through. I will be there in about 30 minutes."

"Sure thing Steve," Sandy replied and then I heard the faint clicking as the call connected.

"Detective Ronson," I said, setting the phone down on the counter and pressing the speaker button, notepad and pen at the ready.

"Thank God! I didn't think I was ever going to get it through that dingy receptionist's head that I needed to talk to you." came the gruff reply from the other end, a voice full of agitation and excitement at the same time. Before I could ask his name, he continued. "My name is Sergeant Sherman Fenter. I work the solitary block at Yarkema County Jail."

I interrupted him, hoping to spur him on to the main point of his call. "I am rather swamped at the moment, Sergeant Fenter. Please, make it quick. What did you need to tell me?"

Sergeant Fenter cleared his throat, "Oh sure, sure you are, working the Folton case, I bet. Sorry. Okay, quick and dirty. I saw the news report about Robert's death earlier tonight, then saw another report of a death of a herpetologist down in McNeal, who I happen to know, well, sort of. Anyway, I watched the news report on Dr. Moore's death, and the very strange circumstances surrounding it, but what caught my attention was a name."

God, could he be any slower? I thought as I continued to scribble, raising the pen off the paper for a moment to swig another sip of coffee, wondering what part of "make it quick" he missed, so I asked, "What name?"

"Bridgette Summers," was his reply, and I decided I would get much further in this discussion if I took over and asked questions that would only require quick, short answers.

"And why is that name important to you?"

"Well, the cops in McNeal are looking for her, since she was scheduled to meet Dr. Moore the day he died, and I guess they want to ask her if she did, you know, maybe to narrow down the time of his death? Anyway, I don't know anyone named Bridgette Summers, but for some reason, my mind had memory of it. Then, it dawned on me a few minutes ago."

I had stopped writing now as I was searching for my boots and finally found them, straining to put them on and listen to Sergeant Fenter at the same time. I flopped back down on the stool after successfully getting my boots on, a bead of sweat slowly trickling down the back of my neck, my frustration with this conversation growing, but something from the pit of my stomach reached up and kept a lid on my mouth, forcing me to listen.

"I started digging through records here at the jail, and a lady named Bridgette Summers came here a few months ago." He finally spat out. "And it was to visit Olin Kemper."

I almost dropped my coffee cup.

The minute I was informed in the wee hours of the morning that Robert was missing, I knew that we would find him dead, just like I knew when I saw his horribly bloated body, rancid smelling and rank from the heat inside his tiny tent that sat for days in the brutal Arizona sun, that his death wasn't a suicide. I certainly wasn't surprised when County Coroner Rick Kensington had walked over after examining the scene and said that Robert's body exuded all the signs of a person bit by a snake, yet the horrendous wound on his neck didn't match up.

Someone had killed him, and somehow, I knew it tied to Olin, but all that knowledge was only in my head, for I had no shred of evidence other than my hunches and instincts to back up my theories.

Until now.

Fully alert now, I focused my attention back onto my conversation with Sergeant Fenton.

"Do you have access to a scanner?" I asked, glancing over my previous notes, making sure I didn't leave any of our conversation out.

"No: but I have a copier and a fax machine, and I already made a copy of the log. Give me a fax number and I will send it over right now," came the sergeant's reply, full of pride and excitement when he realized that he really *did* have a piece of important information.

I rattled off the number to him, told him to put it to my attention and not to send it until I called him back from the office, since I didn't want anyone to see this piece of information except me. He agreed, and just as I was about to hang up, he said, "One other thing, Detective. Bridgette listed herself as Olin's sister, and I checked his arrest record: Olin is an only child."

I already knew that, but was still appreciative of his attention to detail. "Thank you, Sergeant Fenton. Your detective work has been invaluable. Please remember, not a word to anyone about this. One more quick question: do you know what kind of facility it was that Dr. Moore worked at?"

"Well, his books all focus on the different types of snakes indigenous to Arizona, but in the last few years, he really focused on the Mojave Rattlers, since they are so deadly. Oh, I failed to mention, I called a friend of mine that works in the jail in Carohemia County, and he said that one of his buddies that works for the coroner heard the research assistant, the guy that found him, telling the investigator that three vials of Mojave venom was missing. Isn't that weird? Who in the hell would want to steal snake venom?"

The tingling feeling I had in the pit of my stomach earlier had just become a huge electrical surge, the voltage hitting me hard, as I could only think of one reason why someone would steal snake venom, and it sure as hell wasn't to sell it on the black market.

I thanked Sergeant Fenton and told him again to wait for my call. I sprinted through the living room, grabbing my holster, badge and keys from the bedroom, and flew out of the house. As I cranked up my Jeep, I searched quickly through my contacts until I found Rick Kensington's cell phone number, hit send, and then backed out of the driveway and headed into town. If I knew him like I thought I did, he would be at the morgue working on Robert; sure enough, he answered on the fourth ring.

"I'm not finished yet, Ronson. Geez, give me time!" he said, dispensing with the idle chit chat that he abhorred.

"Hold your pants on, Rick! That's not why I am calling," I said, slowing my Jeep down as I hit the curvy mountain roads that led into the heart of Summerset. "I need you to check something for me though."

"Ronson, I assure you that he is still just as dead as he was earlier," Rick said, the heavy sarcasm dripping from him.

I ignored his attempt to irritate me and said, "Is it possible to determine what kind of snake bit him from blood tests?"

I could hear the heavy sigh lingering in the back of his throat as he replied, "Of course. My guess is a rattlesnake, given the terrain we found him in. But there is no way that Robert was bitten by a rattler."

I almost wrecked the Jeep as I slammed the brakes on, resting the bumper inches away from the brick and mortar that made up the small morgue. "Hold that thought and let me in," I almost shouted into the phone as I climbed out and ran to the door, hanging up the phone as I pounded on the glass.

I could see Rick coming down the hallway and motioned for him to hurry up. As he opened the door to let me in, he noticed my hyped up state and said, "Alright Steve, what is going on here?"

"What the hell do you mean he wasn't bitten?" I said, my words harsher than what I intended.

"Come here, I'll show you," he said as we walked back to the area where the body was splayed out on the dissection table. He walked over to the side by Robert's swollen head and pointed to his mangled neck.

"You see this area here? At first I thought that maybe an animal did this post mortem, but after careful examination, I concluded that the tissue was still living at the time it was torn. I found no evidence of any teeth or claw marks. Under his nails, I discovered chunks of his own tissue, so he obviously did the damage to his neck himself."

I held my breath for the umpteenth time today, and even though we were in the cool confines of the morgue, the stench of the remains was beginning to make me nauseous. How Rick handled it on a daily basis was beyond me. He was bent over and examining the decayed tissue around Robert's neck again, his nose only inches from the reeking mess. I had to turn my face away and take a deep breath before I responded, "Okay, back to your original statement that he wasn't bitten by a snake?"

Rick stood up straight and smiled a bit as he walked past me to the large metal table across the room that was littered with all sorts of shiny metal devices that almost looked like medieval torture devices as he picked up a small vial of thick, coagulated blood.

"Patience is a virtue, my friend. You see, I already tested his blood to verify my initial appraisal of his demise: he had snake venom coursing through his veins, which caused his death. But," he said, pointing over to the slab once again, "he died from respiratory paralysis, and it came on almost immediately after he ripped the skin from his neck, since the bleeding stopped just a few minutes after; had he still been alive, there should have been a tremendous amount of blood volume lost, but that is not the case. A typical snake bite, while painful, doesn't cause respiratory failure in minutes, even in someone very ill or old. However, the bite from a snake that carries neurotoxic venom…well, that bite is extremely painful, yet in someone the size of old Robert here," he said, patting Robert's foot, "it still wouldn't have killed him so quick. So, I ran a few blood tests and guess what?"

Frustrated and needing to go toss my coffee up, I struggled to create a calm façade and replied, "What?"

"I found a huge amount of venom in his blood, significantly larger than what could have come from being bitten by even several snakes at one time; and of course, there are no puncture wounds on him anywhere. And, there is nothing in the contents of his stomach either other than a bit of alcohol, which means that someone injected him with a massive amount of venom, probably in the neck, and the excruciating pain from that caused him to tear apart his own neck."

Oh yeah, someone injected him, and I knew her name.

CHAPTER 14
Audra-Stress Hits Home

Home. Finally.

Purr Baby greeted my late arrival at the door with several loud meows, and I am sure that in cat language, she probably just called me several ugly names and requested her dinner, *now*. I flicked on the light as I locked the door, picking her furry mass up, cooing my apologies in her soft ear all the way to the kitchen as I prepared her long awaited meal. Poor cat.

With one last pet on her soft head, I headed to the bedroom to begin packing for my trip, but the call of the bath was too much for me to dismiss, so I gave in and waited impatiently for the hot, steaming water to fill the tub and hopefully relax some of my muscles that were way past being in knots.

I finally lowered my tired limbs into the bubbles and closed my eyes. Three o'clock in the morning and I was just now getting home, in a taxi no less, wondering who in the hell decided to completely deface my car with the huge, red spray painted letters **T R A I T O R** across the hood, every window shattered and the tires utterly shredded to pieces, like a bear had used them as a scratch pad. Poor Tyson had been so protective, he immediately pushed us into the elevator and back to the main level where he called the security desk and within minutes, the stark concrete deck was flooded with the bright lights from several police cars.

For the next two and a half hours, I answered so many questions that close to the end, my voice started to fail. The first batch of questions came from the fresh-out-of-the-academy rookie that had the audacity to ask me if I had a jealous husband or lover– I mean really, what angered ex would use the word *traitor*?– and moved on to the detective that finally arrived only after my insistence with Rookie Blue to speak with one.   The only bit of fortune that the last 24 plus hours bestowed upon me was the fact that Detective Larson actually was aware of the reputation of Winscott, plus he recognized me and knew about Robert's death, so he immediately understood that my destroyed car wasn't the handiwork of just some green-eyed ex or bored juveniles looking for some fun. This fact was hammered home with him after a quick interrogation of the on-duty parking attendant and the subsequent discovery that the camera on this level was blacked out with some type of spray adhesive.

Once finished with all the obligatory paperwork and my car doing a guest spot on *CSI:Phoenix* (I did laugh a bit at that: the black clad investigators looked like they just walked off the set, complete with 'Crime Scene Unit' emblazoned across their backs) Detective Larson arranged for Rookie Blue to take me to the airport so I could procure a rental. Of course, trying to navigate the sprawling airport and then actually find someone to help me was an episode worthy of a comedy sketch on *Saturday Night Live*, complete with an ending that had me leaving in utter frustration and being driven home in a taxi.

The bubbles were starting to dissipate and the water was tepid at best now, but I just wasn't ready to face the daunting task of packing just yet, so I drained a bit of the water out and refilled the tub with water so hot I had to pull my legs up and rest them on the cool, marble ledge until finished. I tried closing my eyes again in hopes of shutting my mind off, but of course, that didn't happen. I wanted to focus on Steve and our beautiful night together, but when I sought out those images, they were replaced by his words in my ear earlier about Robert and kept mingling with the words painted across my car, and I knew they were connected.

I opened my burning eyes and turned my head towards the bathroom door, knowing I needed to call Steve and tell him this latest little revelation, but I knew he was busy working on Robert's case and didn't want to interrupt him, or let these last few moments of hot water and fragrant bubbles go to waste. I leaned back a final time and tried to forget the gnawing guilt that was twisting in my stomach, but I lost that battle as the tears finally trickled down my cheek, quietly melding with the hot water, causing the tiny, delicate bubbles to silently burst.

CHAPTER 15
Steve-Visits the Snake

I waited for the lock to release as I stared through the metal bars, ignoring my companion; who, it appeared, had just rolled out of bed moments ago. Although he was wearing the traditional garb of a lawyer, stuffy tie and all, the wrinkles on his suit and the lines of the sheets on his face were painfully obvious; which, at four o'clock in the morning, shouldn't have surprised me, for most normal people were actually sleeping.

But not me.

The buzzer went off at the same time the lock was opened and Nick Rancliff and I waited for the steel, reinforced door to slide open. I motioned for him to go first, which he did, his limbs still asleep, as his motions were jerky and hesitant. Of course, I had yet to really inform him of the reasons behind my requesting his presence while I interrogated Olin, other than it was a matter of great urgency and couldn't wait until daylight. He had mumbled something about being glad that he was already in Summerset at a hotel so he didn't have to make the long drive, but I ignored his snide remark and just hung up, after telling him he had 15 minutes to meet me at Yarkema County Jail.

We walked silently along the corridor as the residents were still asleep, and I could tell from his hesitant footfalls that he was nervous and unsure as to why he was here. Considering that I was simply expecting the typical tyrannical attorney, preening and fussing about their client's rights being violated, I found his behavior sort of odd; Nick Rancliff genuinely seemed worried, which I found very interesting.

A burly jailor that looked like a small linebacker met us at the end of the corridor, and judging from the wide grin spread across his face, this was Sergeant Fenter. He extended his meaty hand towards me and said, "Detective Ronson. So nice to meet you. Mr. Kemper is in here."

His exuberance almost crushed the bones in my hand, which, considering the difference in our sizes was actually funny. He was like a pit bull: compact and designed to inflict pain.

"Sergeant Fenter, this is Nick Rancliff, Kemper's attorney. Please, make sure we aren't disturbed," I said as I motioned with my head towards the door, my eyes looking at the surveillance camera. Sergeant Fenter smiled wickedly and replied, "Yes sir."

I strode in first and went straight to the table that Kemper was seated at. No, he wasn't seated, he was *perched*, like a statue waiting to be admired. Even though he was sitting down and my frame towered over him, the look behind his glassy eyes managed to suggest that he was peering down at me, like I was something stuck beneath his shoe, some piece of unwanted trash that needed to be removed. For a few brief moments, we locked eyes, and I knew that mine betrayed the intense disgust that I felt for him; not only as a law enforcement officer but also as a man in love with the woman he brutally raped.

He broke the gaze first as his eyes moved over to Nick Rancliff, slowly looking him up and down in mock disgust at his disheveled appearance, dismissing him as if he were just a side show attraction before the main event, then focused his attention back to me.

"Detective Ronson. So good to see you again!" he said, his voice dripping so heavy with sarcasm that I felt the need for insulin. "To what do I owe this splendid, early morning pleasure?"

Before I could respond, Nick cleared his throat and said, "Olin, please, let me do the talking."

The look that crossed Olin's face was a mixture of primal hatred and condemnation, but the shadow of those inner thoughts faded as quickly as they appeared, replaced with his trademark icy stare as he blinked slowly and responded, "Sorry Nick, it's just an old lawyer habit to schmooze with law enforcement."

Through my peripheral vision, I could see Nick stiffen up a bit at Olin's response as he maneuvered around me and sat beside his client, his apprehension oozing out of him like liquefied syrup. He cleared his throat a few times before he finally said, "Detective Ronson, please explain to us why we were summoned here at this ungodly hour?"

"Gladly. Mind explaining this?" I said, tossing the faxed copy of the jail log on the table. This time, Olin remained silent and didn't move an inch towards it; his dead eyes never even flinched or glanced at the page as he continued to stare at me, the intensity of his gaze surprising. Nick reached across the dirty metal table and pulled the thin sheet closer, leaning his head forward a bit to read the small print.

"So, Kemper, mind telling me why 'Bridgette Summers' came to visit you, and why she signed in as your sister, when we both know you don't have one? Oh, and please explain to me how this mystery woman just so happens to be a prime suspect for Robert's murder?"

I sensed the tension emanating all around me, smelled the fear that ultimately would sneak out of the skin of someone being questioned, their body's attempt to deal with the stress forced upon them, their brains working overtime to quickly cover lies, deceits and evidence. I'd witnessed it hundreds of times over the years as I questioned people when I confronted them with something out of the blue, something they weren't expecting me to know about. Oddly, this time, the fear wasn't coming from Olin, but from Nick.

Small beads of sweat were beginning to form around his temples and all the color had drained from his fake tanned face. He had been holding the paper in his hand but quickly set it back on the conference table after realizing his hand was slightly shaking. Olin, unflinching and without turning his eyes to Nick as he continued to lock his gaze upon me, said, "Nick, I don't hear you answering Detective Ronson's question."

Nick struggled to retain his composure as he cleared his throat and refused to look at Olin, preferring to level his eyes with mine and answered, "You drug me out of bed to ask about a visitor? This is preposterous, and has absolutely nothing to do with Olin's case," he said, rising up out of his chair as he closed his briefcase with a loud snap, the tremble in his voice giving away the nervousness he was so desperately trying to hide. "So if that's the only reason we are here, this meeting is over."

"Oh, come now, Nick. He just asked a simple little question. What could be the harm in answering him?" Olin said, his face revealing a bit of amusement as Nick's obvious apprehension.

"Olin! Not another word!" Nick hissed.

Olin's eyes narrowed, but there was just enough of an opening for me to see the anger that flashed behind them for a brief second, his pride apparently irritated after being told to shut up, before his lips contorted over to a sly grin as he said, "I have only had one female visitor since my incarceration, Detective, but her name isn't Bridgette Summers. It's Piper Rancliff." He took his eyes off of mine and shot them over at Nick, eager to see his reaction to naming someone evidently connected to him. I realized that there was some unseen dynamic working between the two men and opted to remain silent and let the events unfold in front of me.

"Olin! As your legal counsel, I am instructing you to not answer any more of his questions! This line of questioning is frivolous!" Nick said, his voice rising almost as fast as the blood that now rushed to his cheeks as his anger flared as he turned to face Olin, his voice a low grumble. "You leave her out of this!"

"Why Nick, you sound almost like a jealous ex-husband," Olin sneered, his eyes bright with excitement as he was obviously enjoying his sadistic toying with Nick, and now I knew exactly why. As soon as those words left his mouth, I sensed that Nick's reaction would be a physical one and I immediately knew I wouldn't stop him, and sure enough, Nick pivoted quickly and brought his fist square into Olin's nose, the force of his anger sending Olin flying out of his chair and onto the cold concrete of the prison floor. I had to force myself not to cheer him on as the crimson liquid of the sorry bastard burst out of his crushed nose and down the front of his prison issued shirt. I embedded the mental picture so I could share it with Audra later and then shifted back from lover to cop mode as I reluctantly grabbed Nick and subdued him before he could take another crack at him.

"Sergeant Fentor! We need a first aid kit in here please!" I shouted through the bars and then turned my attention back to Nick. He eyes were wide and his pupils dilated from the surge of adrenaline, his sweat fully soaking through his thin dress shirt, his breath rough and ragged as he just stood there glowering at Olin. I gave his arm a hard yank to snap him back to reality, finally turning his attention to me as I reached around and produced handcuffs and quickly secured them around his slippery wrists and pushed him back into the chair closest to me.

"Don't move," I growled.

As much as I would have loved to just pat Nick on the back and join him in watching Olin bleed, I knew I couldn't. While I was cuffing Nick, he had scooted over to the edge of the cell and propped himself against the wall as he gingerly held his hands to his face, trying to stem the flow of blood gushing out of his arrogant nose. I heard the jangle of keys and the doors open as Sergeant Fenter arrived with the first aid kit, but knew from the amount of blood and the strength of the impact that his nose was broken and would require a trip to the prison doctor. Apparently, Sergeant Fenter recognized this fact as well, because as he knelt down to take a look, he turned to me and said, "I'll go call Dr. Patterson."

I nodded my head and waited for him to leave before I turned my attention back to Olin. I had so many questions rolling through my sleep-deprived head that I struggled to fish out just the right one to ask before he was whisked away to the infirmary. All I really knew at this point was that Bridgette Summers was actually Nick's ex-wife Piper, and that, for reasons unknown, she came to visit Olin in jail under a false name; a name that was tied to a dead doctor that just *happened* to specialize in snakes: the same kind of snakes that produced the type of venom that killed Robert. And this visit obviously rubbed Nick the wrong way, which was rather odd, since he was representing Olin and no longer married to Piper anyway. There was absolutely no way that any of this could be construed as some mere coincidence or odd accident. It was patently obvious that Olin was using Piper to rid himself of his enemies while locked behind bars in some deviate attempt to ensure that those planning on testifying against him were out of the picture.

Which meant Audra was on that list.

In the split second it took for me to link all of this together, Olin looked up at me, his eyes watering crocodile tears, and he attempted to laugh, the sound of it truly evil as it was muffled from his hands that covered his battered, leaking nose.

"Holy shit: you're fucking her! Oh, bargaining chip!"

Everything went black as my mind was suddenly under the control of a blinding rage, my fingers seeking out his neck on their own, my palms clamping down tightly. Somewhere, deep inside me, the cop was yelling at me to let go, that I had crossed the line and was too close to the situation, but I ignored my internal voice and listened to the guttural growls emanating from my lips instead. Finally, the sound of Sergeant Fenter's voice made it through the deathly darkness that my mind was roaming in as I heard him say, "Ronson! Let go!"

CHAPTER 16
Audra-Reality Check

"Rhonda, it's Audra. Have you seen Gabrielle yet?"

"No, Ms. Tanner, I haven't yet. Would you like me to connect you to her voicemail?"

"No thanks, I have already left her a message. Listen, I am going to work from home today so if anyone calls, will you please transfer them to my cell? And, as soon as you see Gabrielle, have her call me immediately," I said, irritated that it was nine o'clock in the morning and I couldn't raise Gabrielle.

"Sure thing Ms. Tanner." And the line went dead.

I made my way to the kitchen and poured my third cup of coffee. Completely packed and ready to leave for Steve's later, and my presentation fully completed for tonight's meeting with Mrs. Lancaster, I didn't really have much else to do, other than wait for the delivery of the rental car that my insurance agent just set up, so I found myself wandering around the house, stopping at the fireplace that housed Gina's urn. As soon as I saw it, I remembered that I had left the Bible that Mrs. Milligan gave me in the front seat of my car. Shit! I couldn't believe I had been so careless with something so important. I raced back to the kitchen and grabbed my phone and called my agent back.

"Melissa, it's Audra Tanner again. Listen, sorry to bother you, but would you be able to tell me exactly where my car is at the moment? I need to retrieve something out of it," I said, my words coming out faster than I intended.

"Don't worry Ms. Tanner. The adjuster just called me a few minutes ago to give me a preliminary damage and estimate report, and also to tell me he had a sack full of items that he thought you might need."

"Would one of them happen to Bible?" I asked.

"Yes, and a few other things as well, including some papers he found in the backseat that he thought you might need. Would you like for me to have them delivered to you today?"

I exhaled the deep breath I had been holding and responded, "Yes, please. I will be home all day until around 5:30."

I walked back to my bedroom and sat down on the edge of the bed, completely out of my element and normal daily routine, unused to being home at this time of the day. I was really starting to lose it, and this was not the time. *Suck it up Audra. Stop being such a wimp and pull your big panties up!*

I snatched up my coffee and made my way down the hall to my office and flicked on my computer, deciding that I should probably go over my presentation one last time, checking for any numerical errors or loss of fluidity in the wording, since my brain seemed to be misfiring quite frequently lately. Twenty minutes later, I was satisfied with its content so I quickly emailed it to Nicole for her to familiarize herself with it before our meeting tonight, then glanced over at Purr Baby. He was completely confused as well that I was home as he sat atop the file cabinet across from me, swishing his tail slowly, his two vibrant golden eyes staring back at me with an almost quizzical look on his face.

"I know, I know. Weird that I'm home, I get it. But hey, guess what? You are going on a road trip with me tonight, and you don't even know it. That will really give you something to swoosh your furry little tail at," I said, smiling as he ignored my attempts to communicate with him and just closed his eyes and for the briefest of moments, as the morning sun caressed the tips of his white fur, giving him an ethereal glow, I wanted to be him.

My cell phone rang and pulled me out of my dream-like state and I noticed it was the main office number, so I assumed that it was Gabrielle and answered a bit gruffly.

"Audra Tanner."

"Ms. Tanner, its Rhonda. Are you alright?" came Rhonda's shocked voice.

"Oh, I'm sorry Rhonda. I assumed you were someone else."

Rhonda, usually full of light banter and playfulness, was serious as she replied, "Ms. Tanner, something is wrong and I hate to bother you, but Jeff just called here looking for Gabrielle and is beside himself with worry. She never came home last night."

The last thing our office needed at the moment was more gossip, so I cringed a bit on the inside as the lie easily slid off my tongue. "I will call him Rhonda. I just heard from her. Just a lover's spat, that's all. Please, keep this to yourself, and if Jeff calls back, transfer him to me."

"Oh, gotcha. Thank goodness, I was really worried. Thanks Ms. Tanner, I sure will." Rhonda said, the relief in her voice clearly coming through the line.

I hung up and stared at the computer for a moment as a shiver of fear raced up my back and settled in the pit of my stomach. Just like when I awoke from my dreams, I couldn't shake the sense that something was desperately wrong and this time, instead of trying to chalk up my jitters to Robert's death, I decided to heed my internal alarm. I thought back to my phone conversation with Gabby yesterday. She had said she was on her way to The Castle, so the logical place to start was to give them a call. I quickly did a search for their number.

"The Castle, how may I direct your call?"

"I need to speak to your wedding coordinator please, it's very urgent," I said, hoping the perky voice on the other end of the line wouldn't ask me 20 questions before connecting me, and was relieved when she replied, "My pleasure to connect you."

As I sat on hold and nervously tapped my finger on my coffee cup, I decided to check the weather in Summerset, since it was colder at night in their higher elevation. Before I could click on the weather link, a woman's voice said, "Ms. Rosemary VanGilson."

"Good morning, Ms. VanGilson. My name is Audra Tanner," was all I could get out before the woman began bombarding me with questions about my 'upcoming nuptials.' Finally, I had to be rude and cut her off.

"Ms. VanGilson. I'm sorry to interrupt you, but I am not looking for a wedding location. I called because I am concerned about a friend of mine that came to see you yesterday about her wedding; more specifically, what time she left. Her name is Gabrielle Lincoln."

"Oh goodness," she replied, her voice quickly changing over from that of a high pitched saleswoman to a low whisper, full of jittery concern. "You are the third person to call about her today."

The knot tightened in my stomach as I responded, "Who else has called?" figuring the answer to the question was Jeff and maybe Gabby's mom.

"Her fiancé called late last night and left several voicemails, and I just spoke to him not less than a half hour ago. The other one was her wedding coordinator, Heidi. I will tell you the same thing I told them; Ms. Lincoln was not here yesterday."

I tried to control my voice from betraying my internal anxiety that was now in full swing and did my damnedest to sound nonchalant when I asked her, "Do you happen to have Heidi's number?"

"I sure do, just one moment while I find it," she said, and I could hear the shuffling of papers as she looked.

"Yes, here it is." I scribbled down the number and thanked her for her time.

"I appreciate this, Ms.VanGilson."

"I hope you find out where she is soon Ms. Tanner."

I hung up and immediately dialed Gabby's wedding planner, my hands shaking from lack of sleep, caffeine and now, my nerves. Where in the hell was Gabby?

"*The Time of Your Life*, how may I assist you today?"

"I need to speak with Heidi please. It's rather urgent."

"Whom shall I say is calling?" came the overtly perky voice on the other end, and I instinctively knew that she would ask me 20 questions before putting me through, so I cut to the chase.

"Audra Tanner. I'm calling in regards to Gabrielle Lincoln. It's an emergency."

"Um, okay, just a moment. Oh sh..." I heard her say before she hit the hold button.

"Heidi Morgan-Thomas. To whom am I speaking?"

I let the frustration out in a heavy sigh and spoke quickly. "Audra Tanner. Look, Gabrielle is my assistant and her fiancé and I are extremely concerned that she didn't make it home last night, nor did she show up for work today, which she has never done before. I have already spoken with Ms. VanGilson at The Castle and she stated that she didn't have an appointment scheduled for her yesterday. When I spoke with Gabby on the phone yesterday, she intimated that someone else was with her on her drive up there, and I was hoping that you could shed some light on whom that person might have been?"

I heard her swear under her breath, followed by a long pause before she answered, her demeanor and tone full of uneasiness.

"I'm sorry to inform you Ms. Tanner, but Gabrielle was not with anyone from my firm yesterday."

I swallowed hard as my fingers instinctively clutched the phone tighter, blood racing through my veins as the hibernating fear that had been relegated to only my stomach suddenly burst out and now filled my entire being with dread. Where in the hell was she? And who was driving yesterday when she called me? I ran through our conversation again in my head, recalling her words and her tone, thinking maybe I missed some hidden clue, but she didn't seem anything other than exuberant.

"Ms. Tanner, are you still there?" came Heidi's voice, gently pulling me back to our conversation.

"Yes, I'm sorry. I am just in a bit of shock."

Her voice took on a deeper, raspier tone as she said, "We are too. I am kicking myself for not listening to my gut yesterday."

"What do you mean?" I asked her, my head spinning with too many scenarios.

"I knew something was wrong when she called me yesterday and asked me about Diane Martin, but I was overwhelmed with too many items on my plate after our break-in early yesterday, and then this morning we found out that a former employee's daughter was murdered outside of Chandler. God, poor Angie. She had finally stopped drinking and was working on getting her GED— oh, such a tragedy! She used to work for us in the summers answering the phones," she said, her voice starting to crack under the tears that were stuck in her throat. "I'm sorry, Ms. Tanner, it's just still so fresh on everyone's mind here, so I just put my conversation with Ms. Lincoln on the back-burner. Well, that is, until this morning when Jeff called, and now you."

I sat up straighter and grabbed my pen and furiously began scribbling down what she just said as I started spouting questions out. "You spoke with Gabby yesterday? What time? What exactly did she say?"

"Well," Heidi said, clearing her throat and trying to sound more professional, "she thanked me for getting her an appointment to see Rosemary at The Castle, which I didn't do, as well as for sending Diane Martin to fetch her, and I was totally confused by that because I don't have anyone working for me by that name. Then I heard another voice in the background say something, but couldn't make out what it was; but I am sure that it was a female voice, and then, the line went dead."

I couldn't believe what she was telling me. Did this woman really think that whole conversation was normal? Why didn't she tell the police, especially after Jeff called this morning, wondering where in the hell his fiancé was? I wanted to reach through the phone and slap her for being so damned ignorant and blasé about the entire incident, but then I scolded myself for thinking so harshly of her, since she didn't have the emotional investment in Gabby like I did; plus someone she knew had suffered a terrible tragedy.

"Ms. Thomas, this is very serious. I need for you to contact the police right now and tell them what you just told me. You said you had a break-in yesterday, correct?"

"Yes," was her reply, her voice taking on the tone of a scolded child.

"Well, then you need to contact the officer in charge of the investigation, because I have a feeling that your break in and Gabby's disappearance are connected. Please, do it now!" I yelled, my own voice cracking a bit as it rose about an octave. I was shaking so badly that I could barely push the keypad on my phone to call Steve.

His phone went straight to voicemail. Damn! I disconnected and tried the station.

"Summerset P.D., Sandy."

Thank God, a familiar voice. "Sandy, this is Audra Tanner, I need to speak with Detective Ronson please. It's quite important." I said, hoping that my voice wasn't betraying the fear that now fully engulfed me.

Sandy initially treated me with an icy reception since she had such a monster crush on Steve, but somehow, the ice between us melted over the last few months and a truce was reached, which I was thankful for now because I didn't need any attitude from her today.

"Hey, Audra. Steve isn't here, but I know where he is. Hang on while I patch you through. If I lose you, call me right back."

As I waited, the infernal melodic piano notes bored into my brain made me want to scream, so I decided to use the time to finally check the weather in Summerset, as I had planned to do earlier. But before I could click on the weather link, another link caught my attention:

STORE ATTENDENT FOUND BLUDGEONED TO DEATH, POLICE BAFFLED FOR MOTIVE

The body of 25 year old Angie Heatherton, an employee of the Last Stop Exxon on Highway 367, ten miles outside of Chandler, was found late last night by another employee during shift change. Police aren't releasing much information at this time, but Cohemia County Sheriff's spokesman, Michael Clements, stated that this appears to be a botched robbery attempt, although no items appeared to be missing, according to store owner Dan..."

My blood ran cold as I stared at the screen, my thoughts literally frozen inside my mind. Not again: not another senseless murder. God, I couldn't handle another, but some inborn instinct whispered silently in the frozen tundra of my brain that the death of this poor girl was connected to Gabby. How could it not be? A break in, some fake employee taking her to Chandler, the fact that she had yet to call or come back...it all added up to a conclusion that I just couldn't bear to consider, didn't dare let the thoughts form in my head, yet I was helpless to stop.

I could hear someone calling my name and the sound finally cracked through and reached me when I realized it was Steve.

"Audra, AUDRA! Are you there?"

I shook my head to rid myself of the residual icicles and said, "Steve, Gabby's missing. I think someone kidnapped her."

CHAPTER 17
Steve-Hunting Piper

I hung up the phone from my conversation with Deputy Clements and waited impatiently for him to email me the surveillance video from the gas station. Silently, I glanced up at the clock: it was only ten o'clock in the morning, yet it felt like it was much later. My eyes were gritty and sore from being opened entirely too long, and the shower I took earlier seemed like ages ago. I thought about snagging another cup of coffee but I was jittery enough, and I needed to concentrate on the task at hand: finding Piper Rancliff.

After releasing Olin's neck from my hands...*Oh come on Steve, Fenter **made** you let go!*...I opted not to continue my interview with him, since I came within inches of actually taking his life from him, and focused my attention on Nick, for he was about to explode from stress. Getting information from him in the parking lot was a rather simple task, and one that he seemed almost relieved to release. Of course, after hearing what he had to say, I could definitely understand why.

I grabbed my notepad and flipped it open, glancing at my horrendous scribble on the pages that no one else would ever be able to decipher should I ever lose the thing, and began reading from the beginning, trying to fit all of these convoluted scraps of information together to form a cohesive flow, but my God, could this situation be any more fucked up?

Piper, once married to Nick, had an affair with Olin at work, divorced Nick because of said affair, went insane and attempted suicide after Olin rejected her, spent years at an asylum, and now her ex-husband was representing the ex-lover that jilted her...one that she had visited twice in jail; oh yeah, and under an assumed name. I felt like I just walked onto the set of a daytime soap opera and needed cue cards just to keep up. All of that information was extremely weird and twisted, yet didn't explain so many things.

Nick appeared at my office door looking dejected and slightly nauseous. As Olin's lawyer, I was still shocked that he not only cracked the bastard's nose, but at his insistence on coming back to the station to talk. He cleared his throat as he eased down into the chair in front of me, his eyes refusing to hold steady on any object for more than a few seconds and said, "Off the record, right?"

"Of course."

He took a deep, shaky breath and began to talk, his gaze finally steady as he stared at his hands in his lap, his head hung low as he spoke.

"I loved her, but not like I should have, or what she deserved. We met straight out of college at Winscott, and I was attracted to her smile and her quirkiness, which was a strange sensation for me, since I had never before been attracted to a female. But, as a gay man struggling to hide my true self from the world, I used her to hide behind, hoping that she would never find out about my *preferences*. But she did, and even though it was unbelievably difficult on her, she stayed. Oh, don't get me wrong, Piper isn't a saint or anything. She had terms that I needed to abide by to keep the charade up that we were a happily married couple, which pretty much consisted of her doing whatever she pleased and me remaining silent.

"I knew within the first year or so of our marriage that she was in love with Ralph Winscott, which deeply saddened me. Poor Piper, she gravitated towards men that would never truly be able to bestow true love upon her. She didn't know it then, and I doubt she knows it now, but Ralph was a closet gay. I found that out while working there as an intern, but I never had the heart to tell her.

Who was I to take away her fantasies?" he said, finally bringing his eyes up to meet mine.

"He was the polar opposite of what I was: gruff, short, cocky, loud and abrasive, and for some reason, she was mad about him. She would meticulously plan our entire year around her audit schedule, making sure that she went to every location he did, and would pout for days if someone else got chosen to go, rather than her.

"I think she looked at him like some sort of father figure, you know, since she grew up as an orphan, bouncing from one foster home to another." He paused, and I noticed that a few tears were floating in his eyes but had yet to spill out. "Her mother's death always haunted her, and she suffered from terrible nightmares about her for years. Her name was Bridgette Summers."

I nodded while I continued to scribble notes, understanding now his immediate reaction to the jail log.

"Ralph gave off the essence that he was stable, knew what he wanted and although wild at times with others, she mistakenly took his lack of succumbing to her advances as some sort of morality inspired strength, which made her crave him all the more.

"After she caught me with my assistant and things literally were in the open, things were tough for about a year after that, but then, we sort of worked out a sick compromise and lived together more as friends, eventually getting to the point that we could talk about *things*. She thought she was confiding in me by admitting her love for Ralph to me one night, and I didn't have the heart to tell her that not only did I already know that, pretty much everyone else that knew her did as well. I mean, she was so obvious!"

God, could things get any weirder? I thought to myself as I continued to write.

"When she failed to make equity partner the third time she was up for it, she was devastated, and even though our relationship probably seems quite odd to you, I still loved her and felt like her big brother; like it was my job to keep her from harm, so I decided to intervene. I scheduled a lunch date with Ralph and, after a few drinks, took him back to a hotel and videotaped our tryst."

167

I shouldn't have asked, I thought as my hand briefly paused, not sure I wanted to write down what I knew was coming next.

"A few days later, I contacted Ralph and told him that if Piper didn't make equity partner, I would make sure our tape became public. Of course, he freaked, and sure enough, Piper was promoted. A week later, I attended the end of tax season party at a strip club that Ralph threw, you know, to celebrate his hetero lifestyle, and gave him the tape back. Unfortunately, Olin found out about the tape, we just didn't know it at the time."

Things were clicking now.

"To this day, I am still not really sure how he found out or how he accomplished the feat of getting a copy, but he did. The day before Ralph killed himself, all of the partners at Winscott received a mysterious package; a courtesy copy provided to me too, that contained a copy of the tape. Ralph flipped his lid, as you can imagine. He called and accused me of doing it, for not holding my end of the bargain up. He was absolutely beside himself, rambling incoherently about his life being ruined and vowing to kill me. I tried to calm him down, explain that I had nothing to do with it, but I was in just as much shock as he was, for I *never* intended to make that tape public, I just used it as leverage" he said, the tears finally spilling out of his guilt-ridden eyes and sliding down his cheeks. He looked me straight in the eye, his beseeching mine to believe him as he said, "But I swear, Detective, I did not do it."

I believed him.

"Less than 24 hours later, he killed himself. Or, at least, that's what everyone believed, myself included, until I received the jailhouse phone call from Olin, requesting me as his counsel."

He paused again, his body lightly shaking, his face as pale as a ghost. I remained quiet, waiting for him to continue. "He told me I had to, or he would make sure that the extra copies of the tape would be released to the media and that he would testify that he saw me go into Ralph's office that night and fake his suicide." Openly sobbing now, he clasped his hands around his head and muttered, "I knew then that Ralph's death wasn't a suicide at all, and that I was trapped: the blackmailer was being blackmailed. Fucking ironic, isn't it?"

I could count on one hand the times in my 44 years have I been stunned into silence, but this one surged to the top spot, surpassing all others with ease. I stared at Nick with a mixture heavy in disgust, light in sympathy, letting his words sink in, mulling over each bit of unbelievable information. God, Audra wasn't kidding when she referred to Winscott as a pit full of vipers.

And she was right smack dab in the middle of the pit.

"At what point did Olin and Piper hook up?" I asked, prodding Nick to finish the story.

"Piper went into a deep depression after Ralph's death. It took years for her to come to terms with it, because she never knew about the tape. She thought he killed himself over her, you know, the whole *Romeo & Juliet* type saga of unrequited love. It sort of became an inside joke at Winscott with all the other partners. I can only assume no one ever let on about the tape to her because she was so unstable at that point; I don't know, maybe they feared telling her the truth would break her, and she would taint the founder of the firm's image even more. That's what I always assumed, since every single one of those bastards only care about money," he said, anger beginning to take control over his emotions, drying his tears and replacing them with vibrant anger.

"About seven years ago, Piper followed her same pathetic pattern and fell for a man that would do nothing but bring her harm: Olin. Oh, and that greedy bastard played right along, knowing damn well she had fallen in love with him. He didn't care, he just used her as an extra vote to take over Winscott and oust Eric. And it worked: she cast the deciding vote. That's when she came to me and said she wanted a divorce to be with him. I will never forget the look on her face when she told me. I didn't even recognize the woman behind those eyes. That's when I realized she was slipping deep into insanity. I felt partially guilty for that trip, since I started the entire ball rolling with the tape, so I let her go. But then Olin's true colors emerged, and when she realized she had been duped and that he didn't really love her, something inside her snapped, and that's when she tried to kill herself. That bastard drove her to insanity's edge, kicked her over and then laughed when she hit the bottom!" Nick seethed, his anger fully engulfed now, and unable to remain seated any longer, he stood up and began pacing in front of me, his fists clenching and unclenching at his sides.

"Somehow, he is still slithering around inside her poor fragile brain, controlling her like some twisted puppeteer. I can't believe—no, I *won't* believe—that she could be responsible for hurting anyone like you seem to think she has. The only person she ever hurt was herself. But," he continued, his face glistening with sweat and so red, he looked like at any moment he was going to have a stroke, "if she is somehow tied to Robert's death, then it is only because he is controlling her."

I took a heavy breath to control my own raging emotions, for I was being bombarded with all sorts of thoughts now after hearing this incredibly sordid story. The two strongest were an unbelievably intense hatred towards the monster that sat in the Yarkema County Jail's infirmary, and the other, sheer panic for Audra's safety.

"Nick, sit down. You need to clear your head and think. We need to find her, and I mean right now. I need every bit of information on her you have, such as addresses, phone numbers, make and model of her car..." I said, and he nodded his in agreement as I shoved a piece of paper in his direction, pointing at him to get started.

As he wrote down the answers to all my questions, a heavy knot of dread had formed in my gut and a cloud of worry slowly swirled around my head, making me feel slightly dizzy. The enormity of the depths of Piper's insanity pounded through my mind.

CHAPTER 18
Audra-Terror Rises

Oh my God, would the rental car ever get here? It was 3:30 already and I was starting to panic since I had to meet Mrs. Lancaster and Nicole in two and a half hours. I was sure that I had made a lifelong enemy after my last conversation with the harried representative, who assured me that my rental would be arriving any moment. That last call was 20 minutes ago and still, no vehicle.

Tired of pacing in front of the window waiting for the car, I decided to recheck all my packed bags for the trip to Summerset tonight, since I had nothing else to occupy my time with. After my conversation with Steve a few hours ago, I was a jumble of nerves and eager to get out of this stuffy house. When he told me he wanted to send an armed officer down to retrieve me and bring me to Summerset, I told him he was overreacting and that I would be fine on my own, and promised to text him every hour until I left. I did my damnedest to placate his fears by reminding him that I was surrounded by a security gate that no one knew my pass code to (not even him!) and I wasn't going alone to my meeting tonight. I could hear the stress seep through his voice, and I knew he was genuinely concerned about my safety, but I wasn't.

I was concerned about Gabby's.

Steve promised me after our conversation that he would make the appropriate phone calls to get her disappearance listed as a kidnapping, rather than just some routine missing person, and sure enough, less than ten minutes ago, there was a breaking news alert by none other than Jan Patakee. For the first time in years, I was actually glad to see a news report tied to Winscott, since I was going bat-shit crazy with worry. If something happened to her because of me…

I shook that thought of my head and continued packing, unable to finish that thought for fear of where my mind would wander, so I focused my attention to my overstuffed suitcase and almost jumped out of my skin when my cell phone rang.

"Hey, Carl," I said, grateful for the distraction.

"Are you okay? I just saw the news report about Gabrielle," he said, his voice low and full of concern.

So much for not thinking about it.

"I'm fine, Carl. Really; just finishing a few things up here, then off to a meeting with Nicole and Mrs. Lancaster and then heading to Summerset. Will you please make sure to keep the troops in line while I'm out of town?" I said, hoping that he would take the hint that I didn't wish to discuss Gabby's situation. There was a long pause on his end before he replied, "Of course I will, Audra. Just know, we are all praying for her safe return."

I felt the tears well up in my throat, but I choked them back down, refusing to give them freedom to overtake me. Fortunately, before I could come up with some excuse to hang up, my phone beeped with another call, and noticing that it was Steve, I quickly said, "Carl, I appreciate it, but I have to go. I will call you later." I clicked over to Steve's call without giving Carl the opportunity to respond.

All I got out was "Hey" before Steve cut me off. I could barely hear him and could immediately tell he was driving, for cell phone service in Summerset was spotty at best.

"Audra, listen closely….surveillance…Piper…lock your…on my…" and then the line went dead.

I tried calling him back twice but it went straight to his voicemail, which meant he had no service at all. I called once more and left him a message, telling him to call me back, because I didn't hear everything.

I felt shaky and a bit dizzy, so I sat on the edge of the bed and thought about what little I did hear. He said earlier that he was following a lead on Robert's killer and that it might very well tie into Gabby's disappearance, and that he was waiting on a something from the detective in Cohema County that was working the murder of the grocery store clerk. Was that something surveillance footage of the grocery store? And then, the realization hit me that he said *Piper* and finally, the garbled phone call made sense; Piper was on the surveillance tape at the grocery store.

The same store that was only a few miles from The Castle where Gabby had been heading yesterday with the fake Time of Your Life employee, Diane Martin; the same woman that had been so disturbingly in love with Olin that she had slit her wrists in his office.

My heart began to pound wildly in my chest as the puzzle pieces began to form a solid image in my head. This revelation about Piper was the last missing link, and as the image solidified in my mind, I realized Piper was the weapon Olin was wielding to strike us all down.

Oh dear God.

My hands were shaking so badly that I couldn't dial my phone. *No, it isn't going to end like this!* I screamed inside my head as I stood up and grabbed the suitcase off my bed. *That sonofabitch won't win!*

I drug the heavy bag down the hall to the front room and ran back to the bedroom for my purse and shoes, quickly sliding them on as I scooped up Purr Baby off the bed and shoved him into his carrier, despite his loud protests, then raced back to the living room. I checked the security system to make sure it was fully armed, even though I knew it already was. Satisfied that we were safe and the rush of activity steadying my hands, I sat down on the couch and dialed the car rental company again.

"I'm sorry, Ms. Tanner, but we are extremely shorthanded today and won't be able to deliver your car until tomorrow."

I hung up before I went ballistic on the woman.

I was trapped; a sitting duck waiting for the hunter to come along and tag me.

Fuck no, not today! So I quickly disconnected the call and typed "taxi service" into the home screen, but before I could even locate one, my phone rang. *Damn, I do not have time for her right now!* I inwardly groaned when I saw that it was Nicole's cell.

Unable to hide my irritation, I answered abruptly, "Yes Nicole, what it is?"

Nonplussed, she said, "Well now, don't you sound frustrated? Getting cold feet before tonight's meeting?" she said. I could just picture her face. I knew she was relishing the stress in my voice when she almost purred, "So, what may I do to help? Hold the meeting without you?"

Her laughter in my ear almost made me launch my phone into the wall. Instead, I said, "Nicole, I am in a bit of a bind here and need to call you back, as I was just about to call for a taxi so I can make it to the meeting tonight, on time. Seems my rental car will not be available in time. Will you be in your car…?" I said, before she cut me off.

"You don't have a car? Damn, I thought you were the gal that could get things done. This meeting with Mrs. Lancaster is too important to us to put into the hands of some slimy cab driver. I am coming to pick you up. Be there in a few."

Before I could offer up any argument, she was gone. I stood there in the middle of my living room and fiddled with the phone, debating whether I should call her back. I almost called for a cab anyway, since the thought of relying upon Nicole was never a position I wanted to be in. The nervous chill then dancing up my spine made me change my mind, so I quickly gathered my gear and stood by the couch, watching the window for her car, and smiling as I looked at Purr Baby and realized that Nicole had no idea that she would be included in her chauffer service.

CHAPTER 19
Piper-Phase III

Ah, finally, it was time: straight up twelve o'clock. I adjusted the laces on my boots once more, making sure they were securely knotted so they wouldn't come loose and trip me, for I had one busy day ahead of me, and needed to make sure that even the slightest detail was taken care of.

As I left the confines of my temporary home, or what I liked to call Bates Motel II, I mentally kicked myself for not retaining my composure better yesterday as I reached my car and the smell exploded into my nostrils. God, but that bitch's corpse started stinking fast!

"Sorry *Gabby*, I didn't mean to bash your skull in. You are going to miss the party." I said as I backed out onto the desolate highway, rolling down the windows and turning the air conditioner on full blast before my eyes became so full of tears from the smell that driving would become impossible. "But don't worry, even in the rancid condition you are in, I am sure you will be a hit."

I drove in silence for the next 20 minutes as I went over every detail for today's activities. I was almost giddy (or maybe just high from the fumes from my passenger, Lil Miss Rotting Corpse?) with anticipation, because tonight, the one I wanted most was going to be mine.

And I couldn't wait to kill her.

"Steady girl," I said out loud, "You must not make any mistakes. Look, you have already screwed up part of the plan: you don't get to enjoy watching the Harvard Harlot cry and beg for Gabrielle's life. You must be more careful!

"Shut up! This idea is much better! Stinky bitch back there wouldn't have had the impact on her as much as *this* one will, so it all worked out for the best. Besides, you enjoyed demolishing that face of hers just as much as I did."

I smiled at that one, because yes, I did enjoy watching her face explode in front of me, the sound of the metal crushing into her skull and then her faint grunt and loud thud as her body crumpled to the floor.

I passed my mental checkpoint sign and knew I was close, so I began my charade of the "stranded motorist" as I intermittently changed from neutral and gunned it to tromping on the brakes while in drive, finally jerking my way to a stop at the shoulder by the mailbox; nothing like renting a piece of crap clunker to make the whole scenario seem realistic. But just in case my intended target was suspicious by nature, as I stepped out onto the pavement I lit the smoke bomb that I brought with me and dropped it by my foot, then gently scooted it under the front of the car; the effects were fantastic.

I made my way up the twisting driveway and climbed the front steps, the weathered boards groaning in protest, and knocked on the door. I scrunched up my face and carefully displayed the hapless female in need of help, even managing to extract a few tears to run down my dusty cheeks, just as the door opened.

"I'm sorry to bother you ma'am, but can you help me? My car," I said, pointing to the end of the driveway to my vehicle that sat motionless, the smoke rising from under its hood, "started making an awful racket and then all that smoke, and I don't know what to do. I don't have a phone, so would you mind calling someone for me? I can just wait out here."

"Oh, I'm so sorry. Goodness, that is a lot of smoke. Don't be silly, honey. You come in and sit down and have a nice glass of iced tea while I call Denton's Towing. They will come right away." she said as she opened the door and moved aside to let the snarling wolf inside the unsuspecting sheep's pen.

I smiled at her as I said, "Oh thank you. So kind of you. My name's Clarisse. It's a pleasure to meet such a kind soul," I said as I walked in, extending my hand towards hers.

"Think nothing of it, Clarisse. Have a seat and I will go make some tea, and that phone call," she said as her wrinkled nub reached out. "Nice to meet you as well. I'm Rosemary. Rosemary Milligan."

"Yes, I know," I said as I shut the door.

ASHLEY FONTAINNE

CHAPTER 20
Audra-Apologies

"Your mom was about as happy to have that hairball in the house as I was to have it in my car," Nicole said, her eyes still a bit red from the few stragglers of cat hair that floated around inside her car, all seeming to aim straight for her irritated nostrils. She sneezed violently. "I hate fucking cats!"

"You really don't know how much I appreciate this Nicole. I was beginning to feel like I was in prison, trapped in my own house. You never realize how much you depend upon your vehicle until suddenly, you don't have it anymore," I said, trying to sound nonchalant, but failing miserably. What I didn't tell her was how much I needed to escape the confines of my walled prison, as the walls in my house had started closing in around me. Had I not had Purr Baby there, I would have probably just called a cab and wandered around the city aimlessly for hours until tonight's meeting, but after Steve's call, I realized that would just be an added burden, so I decided to leave her with my parents.

It was 5:30 and we were stuck in the heart of downtown traffic as we headed towards Zargento's. Funny, a few days ago I was actually looking forward to this meeting, but now, I wanted nothing more than to get it over with and get to Summerset, and Steve. Earlier, after I found out that I would be carless, I was almost in a state of panic at the thought of having to stay with my parents until tomorrow when my rental would be ready, but thankfully, Steve had finally reached a spot that had cell coverage and called me. He was on his way down here, along with Nick Rancliff, to execute a search warrant for Piper's house, so he was just going to pick me up when they finished.

I still couldn't believe that I was sitting in the passenger seat of the car of a woman that most likely hated my guts. I was still astonished that she agreed to pick me up, much less take Purr Baby and me to my mother's house, but she did so with surprisingly little complaints. Initially, I assumed she was just making sure that this big fish we were meeting at dinner didn't slip through our hands, since we needed the revenue so desperately, but then, after being in the car with her for a bit, I came to the conclusion that she really was just trying to be nice to me without having to say nice things, probably because of Gabrielle's disappearance. My thoughts were confirmed on this point when earlier, she turned and looked at me while sitting at a red light and blurted out, "Gabby will be okay, Audra. If anyone can take care of herself, that girl can."

The afternoon heat was rolling its heavy haze through the valley from the asphalt and the stalled cars, so Nicole reached over and cranked up the air conditioner a bit more; thank God, because I was not only hot from the heat outside, but from the intensity of my frayed nerves. I wanted this day over and to be in the relative safety of Steve's arms, and for Gabrielle to call me and spin some long, drawn out tale of where she had been for the last 24 plus hours.

"So, I heard about what happened to your car. Is it repairable or are you going to have to buy another?" Nicole said, leaning her face over to the nearest vent and lifting the hair off the back of her thin, damp neck.

"Well, the insurance adjuster seems to think that it's worth salvaging," I said, grateful for the conversation, rather than swimming in my own dark thoughts. "He said it will take about a week or two, but should be as good as new once finished."

"Hmph," she said, her manicured hand fluttering in the air like she just swatted a fly. "I would have insisted upon it being totaled and held out for a new one. I mean, really, from what I heard, the damage was quite extensive."

As we continued our idle chit-chat about mindless drivel, my thoughts went back to my conversation with Mrs. Milligan earlier in the week, and her tenacious encouragement for me to rid myself of heavy "guilt" garbage that I was carrying around with me, so I decided that now was as good of a time as any to make my first foray, since I had a captive audience.

"Nicole, I need to tell you something," I said as I turned in my seat and faced her.

She was still holding her face to the vent as she replied, "Shoot."

I took a deep breath and said, "I'm sorry."

I saw an almost imperceptible twitch splash across her face, her muscles in her throat and neck tightening up as she slowly pulled her head back and turned her attention to me. "Excuse me?" she replied, her voice barely above a whisper.

Before I could stop myself, the words just leapt out of my mouth. "I'm sorry for what I did to you, Nicole. I should never have gone after anyone else except Olin. He is the one that deserved all my anger, not you or anyone else. Granted, I was furious at the time that none of you helped me–and honestly, I still think it was morally reprehensible to turn a blind eye–but that anger didn't give me the right, or the justification, to seek out and destroy so many other lives in the process of trying to recapture my own. I just…well, I just became so single minded, so focused on revenge, that nothing else mattered to me," I said, my voice quiet yet steady. "I was in so much emotional pain that I wanted everyone to suffer, and that was wrong of me."

Her eyes wide with shock, Nicole just stared at me for what seemed like an eternity, and I fought the instinct to just bolt out of the car and take my chances on the highway rather than face the wrath I knew was going to explode out of her mouth, but I opened this can of worms, so I just sat still and waited.

I couldn't believe my ears when, after a full minute of just staring at each other, her eyes huge as a vast array of emotions

181

jumbled together behind them, and mine probably reflecting the same, she finally leaned back in her seat and said, "You have got to be the strangest woman I have ever met, Audra. You engineer possibly one of the most outrageous corporate takeovers ever accomplished, the likes of which someday I am sure will make it into a novel, expose a killer and bring him to justice, and then apologize to a *female* that knew you were raped but didn't come to help you? What kind of drugs are you on girl, because I want some!" she said, as her nervous laughter filled the small interior of her car, but the tears that twinkled in her eyes gave her true emotions away. I was completely taken aback and rendered dumbstruck, so shocked myself that literally, I could have been knocked over with a feather had she touched me with one. "You did me a favor anyway. I was tired of Eric's cheating old ass; I just didn't know how to tell him that. Besides," she said, turning her head to look out the window, but not before I caught a quick glimpse of a fully formed tear precariously sitting on the corner of her eye, "Olin needed to finally pay the Piper. Oh, Freudian slip." as a forced laugh emerged, filling the car with its cackle.

The thick glacier of hate that separated us finally began to melt, and I couldn't stop myself from laughing with her as well. As the traffic eased slowly forward, so did the course of our conversation, as we tentatively started to walk on this new road forged between us. I decided to steer the conversation back to Piper, since I wanted to know as much as I could about her to pass along to Steve, hoping Nicole would offer up something that we could use to help find her.

"I am so glad that I was out on an audit when Piper slashed her wrists. All that blood would have made me ill," I said, surprised at the sound of my nonchalance that I was definitely faking.

"It was just like walking into a horror movie," Nicole said, keeping her attention on the road as we finally were making some headway as the traffic began to thin out. "But it paled in comparison to the mess in Ralph's office." She paused as a small shutter passed through her. "*That* is a day that I will never forget, nor Piper, I'm sure."

Piper?

"Oh, I wasn't aware that you both saw his, um, *remains*. I was under the impression that Piper was out of town on an audit."

"She was, but that's not what I meant," Nicole said, her eyes cutting over at me sharply, like I was some sort of muttering dolt for not understanding her hidden meaning, which I was beginning to feel like myself because I had no clue what she was intimating.

"So, what did you mean?" I said, willing to sacrifice some of the ground I just made with her if it would procure me some leverage on Piper.

Nicole huffed loudly as she replied, "Jesus, Audra! After all your stealthy 'research' on all of us, you never discovered anything about Piper's obsession with Ralph, or the video tape that was sent to all of us, including the waste of manhood hunk, Nick?"

Stunned yet completely absorbed by this newest twist, I said, "Nicole, I have no idea what you are talking about. Piper was obsessed with Ralph? And what tape?"

Nicole threw her hands up in the air dramatically, her mood quickly shifting from agitation at her previous misconception of my idiocy to excitement at realizing she had the opportunity to share something that I was oblivious to and said, "Wow, *The Warrior of Winscott* doesn't know the history of *Winscott*? Now that is classic!"

For the next 15 minutes, Nicole talked non-stop about the twisted triangle between Ralph, Piper and Piper's ex-husband, Nick. As her words sunk in, they became the concrete that fully set my newly formed pieces of the pie together, providing a rock solid understanding into Piper's psyche, and the disgusting tentacles that tied all the deviate monsters together, forming one cohesive mass of pulsating evil, each feeding off of the others' pain.

And it made me hate Olin even more, which I never thought would have been possible. My mind was truly overwhelmed by all of this newly acquired information, my stomach in one gigantic knot from this startling revelation. I sat in stunned silence and just listened, absolutely petrified for poor Gabrielle if she truly was in the midst of these monsters' plans.

At 6:10, we finally pulled into the parking lot at Zargento's and hurried inside, Nicole rambling on about whether or not we missed Mrs. Lancaster. I had tried calling her cell phone twice but it just went straight to her voicemail, so we were both a bit concerned that she had become angry and left. As we walked inside and requested our table, the host informed us that she called only moments before, saying she was experiencing car trouble, and would arrive shortly.

"Well, thank God for small favors." Nicole said as we headed to our table. "After all that girly bonding shit, I need a drink. Whiskey, on the rocks please!" she said, as she flopped down on the supple leather seat, scooting around to the middle of the u-shaped booth. "Chop chop!"

For the next hour and a half, we went over our presentation once and then, in between drinks and ordering some incredible dish that I couldn't begin to pronounce, we found ourselves discussing Ralph again as the drinks loosened both of our tongues. I looked at my watch and realized it was almost eight o'clock, that we were both trashed, and that Mrs. Lancaster had stood us up.

"Well, I hope her husband takes ALL their fucking money." Nicole said, her words slurred and her southern accent melding them together, which apparently, it did not only when she was angry, but drunk as well. The waiter came over with the check and offered to call us a cab, to which Nicole replied, "Honey, I am more than capable of driving anything with a stick right now, including you AND my car." and the poor waiter turned three shades red and turned to leave the table with the two crazy drunk women.

"No, no, wait, please do," I said, catching him before he scurried away in his embarrassment.

I was tipsy and just past the point of being able to drive, but Nicole was absolutely sloshed and could barely walk. No wonder: her miniscule frame was full of about six shots of whiskey and at least two glasses of wine. She was loudly berating the rudeness of the "bitch" that stood us up as I tried to give directions to the cabby to my house, and I had to shush her twice.

As the driver made his way towards my house, I internally scolded myself for drinking too much; but then again, I wasn't going to be driving to Summerset, Steve was, so I tried to cut myself some slack. After all, the last two days had been full of such an emotional roller coaster ride, it was actually surprising that I wasn't a raving lunatic at this point. And even though Nicole was a bit over the top for my tastes, I was beginning to discover that she possessed a wicked sense of humor, and God knows, I needed a good laugh.

The cabbie finally pulled us into the driveway and up to the gate, and as I punched in my pass code, the gate slowly rolled back. As we wound our way up the steep driveway to the front door, Nicole blurted out, "Oh boy, cat hair!" and then burst out laughing.

The cabbie helped me get her out of the car and up to the front door while I fumbled for my key fob in my purse, and in my furious searching, I guess I pulled too hard on the strap and it ripped, spilling the contents of my purse all over the entryway and into my pea gravel flower beds. I bent down to search for the stupid thing and finally found it at the edge of the concrete and pressed the button, not realizing that the cabbie had propped Nicole up on the front door while he was helping me search for the key, and Nicole immediately fell forward, arms and legs flying as she landed just inside the doorstep flat on her face. In my inebriated state, I couldn't stop the laughter that escaped my lips at not only her ungraceful entrance into my house, but the look on the cabbie's face as he quickly retreated and said, "no charge" as he slammed his car door and flew down the driveway, probably thinking it was high time to leave before somehow, he ended up being blamed for the two drunks really hurting themselves.

I turned around and stepped over Nicole's thrashing body as she tried to stand, but she was so out of it that it came out more like a baby's crawl, so I set my purse on the chair by the front door and reached down to grab her elbow. She was laughing so hard that she had the hiccups now, and I smiled and said, "Well, good thing I cleared the air earlier and apologized, or we would still be enemies, and I wouldn't be here helping you stand up."

She finally stood up, threw her arms around me, and put her face within inches of my own, as drunks tend to do, and said, "One apology does not a friend make, Audra. Oh, wait, who am I kidding? You are so funny and I could use a good laugh now and again. And, I am sorry too, Audra, really, I should have stopped him. But girl, you got him good!" and then dissolved into a sputtering pile of giggles once again.

Eventually, I maneuvered her over to the chair by the front entrance, her body almost as pliable as melted rubber and told her, "Stay put. I have to go get my stuff off of the porch."

Her head was rolled back and resting on the wall and her eyes were now closed, her hand covering them as she moaned, "Oh, not to worry. I have the spins." And then she passed out.

As I walked back out the front door and began retrieving the spilled contents that exploded out of my purse, I started smiling at the look of shock that would be on Steve's face when he finally arrived to pick me up. Not only had he never seen me drunk before, but the fact that Nicole was here would probably be just as unreal to him as it was to me.

I grabbed the last little straggler and stood up, eager to get inside and lock the door. But just as I turned to close the door, I felt the hair stand up on the back of my neck as I realized, a split second too late, that I wasn't alone. The rustle from the bushes announced his presence, and then suddenly, he was on the doorstep facing me. In that split second, I realized I recognized him, and my first urge was to say hello, but then I also realized that he shouldn't be there, and my mind sort of stuttered; and in its confusion, I said, "Kevin? What are you...?"

But that's all I was able to get out before his fist exploded into my jaw, knocking me backwards into the foyer. My head slammed down hard on the marble floor, and my vision swam in a mixture of darkness and bright and colorful flashes of light as I heard him say, his voice gravely and distant, "That one was for what you did to me. Wait until you see what's in store for what you did to my family."

And then I heard no more.

CHAPTER 21
Steve-Into the Lair

"It looks and *smells* like she hasn't been here in months."

I looked over at Detective Vargas, who was holding one of his meat hooks–that functioned as a hand when not pummeling something to death with it–up to his nose, his eyes immediately blinking as the smell hit him with full force. It was the pungent mixture of rotted food and garbage, which was rather disgusting, but for a Phoenix detective to have such a low threshold for smells was pathetic. Geez, where did they find these guys?

I stepped past him into the kitchen, my flashlight illuminating the various array of bugs that quickly scuttled away from the intruding beam, as Nick followed behind me. He had remained quiet up until this point, but once the smell reached his nostrils, he grumbled under his breath, "Oh dear God" as we finally made it completely inside. We stopped and listened for a moment and heard nothing, no sound except for the scurrying feet of insects. Nick reached over to the wall and turned the kitchen light on and gasped, "Holy shit!"

The mess was unbelievable: it was like stepping into an episode of *Hoarders*, just with more room to walk. Piles of rotted food littered the countertops and overflowed onto the floor, which crunched under our feet from months of neglect. The refrigerator door was open and all the contents inside were a ruined mass of stinking liquid. We quickly picked our way through the kitchen and into the formal dining area, Nick mumbling the entire time, "Oh my God" as each step brought us in contact with more filth.

The dining and living room were just as cluttered, except it was piles of newspapers, books and magazines, some stacks as high as two feet. I heard the sadness in Nick's voice each time he commented on something, the shock of the deplorable conditions of his former home and the depths of madness that his former wife was obviously in hitting him hard. Had he not been such a manipulative prick, I might have felt some sympathy for him; but as it was, I didn't.

All I felt was jittery and apprehensive, eager to find something to lead us to Piper.

Detective Vargas remained in the doorway into the living room and radioed for backup as Nick and I continued to sweep the house, Nick's continual comments on the state of it beginning to wear on my nerves. Finding nothing other than clutter, we headed up the stairs to the main bedroom, which, considering the disgusting display downstairs, was actually clean. Obviously, Piper spent most of her time in this room, which meant that if any clues as to her whereabouts were to be unearthed, the most likely spot was here.

I scanned the room quickly, trying to pick up on anything that I thought looked out of place or odd. Seeing nothing out of the ordinary, I holstered my gun and walked over towards the dressing table to retrieve the wastebasket that was sitting next to it, hoping some sliver of paper might have been carelessly thrown aside, but it was empty. Nick was struggling with maintaining a control on his emotions and sat down on the edge of the large, king sized bed, his arms reaching up and cradling his guilt ridden head in his hands as he slowly shook his head back and forth, mumbling quietly to himself as the notion of just how fucked up his life was hit him square in the face.

I set the empty garbage basket down in its original spot and pulled out my rubber gloves before rifling through her drawers, their loud *snap* reverberating through the quiet room, which made Nick almost jump out of his skin. The black shadows that settled under his eyes reflected just how much stress he was experiencing, and his overly exaggerated reaction to a small, sudden noise told me how frazzled his nerves were.

Serves the idiot right. I mean really, who are these people? All of them were demented, playing with each other's lives like they were controlling life-size dolls for their sickening amusement.

I gently opened the drawers that contained more makeup than I had ever seen in one place in my entire life, except maybe for a department store. Growing up with a single mom, I knew what most of it was, or had a vague idea of which part of the face it was supposed to go on, but the amount in front of me was staggering; but it was just makeup, which didn't tell me much other than the fact that this Piper chick had some serious issues with her looks.

Suddenly, Nick jerked his head up and focused his eyes on the closet to my right, and immediately stood up and walked over to it as he said, "I just remembered the closet!"

Baffled, I queried, "What about it?"

"It has a hidden room." he said as he jerked the door open to reveal a closet that was as big as my bedroom. "She thought she had it secretly installed while I was out of town on a case," he said, his hands fumbling around the walls, knocking clothes off their hangers as he went, "but I ran into the builder not long after and he asked me how she liked it." he said, almost out of breath now as he was frantically searching for something.

I was a bit amused at his sudden burst of energy and it was rather humorous to watch him run around in circles in the closet, but this was wasting precious time, so I stepped inside and grabbed his shoulder, forcing him to turn around and face me.

"Nick: stop. Look at the mess you are making. Whatever you are looking for will be all that much harder to find if you proceed with pulling all of her clothes off the hangers. What are you looking for?"

"The button to open it."

"You don't know where it is?" I said, dumbfounded that he wouldn't know everything about his home, especially something as important as a button to a secret room for Heaven's sake.

"No. I never asked Bill," he said, his eyes scanning the walls while he answered, "I didn't want to arouse any suspicion by asking him questions that I should obviously know the answer to. I didn't want him telling Piper."

What? I thought as I shook my head in disbelief.

Apparently, Nick read my face and said, "I tried to give her as much space as possible, remember? Oh, it doesn't matter now. Just help me find a way to make the door open."

"Nick, we can't go about this like crazed drug addicts looking for a fix. Now, stop for a minute and let's think," I said, trying to keep my voice from betraying the irritated edge this man was driving me to. "Think about the design of this room and the layout of the rest of the house. The room has to be located on the other side of that wall," I said, pointing behind him. "There is no other place that it could be, which means the button or lever must be over here somewhere."

I moved past him and slowly ran my hand around the door jam, feeling nothing. I looked around quickly and noticed there was no stepping stool of any kind, so I asked Nick, "How tall is Piper?"

He looked at me like I just spoke in another language before answering, "Uh, around 5'4" I think."

I turned back around and lowered my gaze to what I surmised would be her maximum extended reach, reaching behind the clothes as I went, and just as I made it all the way around to the left side and was about to just take my gun out and start shooting holes in the wall, I felt it. Silently, I pushed in on the indentation and with whisper quiet stealth, the back of the closet opened up, revealing a room just as big as the closet.

As the door finished sliding open, the room lit up automatically, revealing what to me looked like the backstage of a theater. There were hats, shoes, dresses, purses and even costumes, all arranged by color and style, along with a rectangular table down the middle that served as not only a staging area for numerous pairs of glasses and wigs, but held numerous drawers underneath it as well. I heard Nick sigh heavily under his breath as he followed in behind me, realizing that this room was used for much more sinister purposes than what he always had envisioned.

As Nick stared at the clothes and rummaged through some of the more worn purses, I focused my attention on the drawers. I pulled open the long middle one only to be greeted with dust from the emptiness inside, but something told me to reach in and feel around all the way to the back, and that's when I felt the small knot in the pit of my stomach immediately tighten when my fingers touched something; I pulled it out.

It was a tattered section of an article that looked like it had been ripped it out of a magazine and then crumpled up and shoved inside this small drawer. Gently, I set it on top of the dresser and began to smooth out the wrinkles as easily as I could without tearing the worn section. Most of the writing was illegible, but one part stood out as a glaring beacon of guilt: the name of Dr. Moore circled in red ink. As I continued to peer at the crushed paper, Nick finally noticed I wasn't moving or saying anything and his curious legal mind finally took over as he strode over to where I was, his voice shaky as he asked quietly, "What is it?"

"The nail in Piper's coffin." I replied.

CHAPTER 22
Audra-Dreams Are Now Reality

Oh man, my head is throbbing! How much did I have to drink last night? Why am I so sore? I don't remember doing anything strenuous? Oh yeah, I did have to lift Nicole off the floor, but wait, that wasn't too hard....oh, Jesus, what is that smell? Why can't I move my arms? My feet? What is that stench?

Then suddenly, my blurred vision burst through the vaporous mists of alcohol and pain and I immediately had full clarity. I remembered Kevin standing in my doorway and the image of his fist coming towards my face, his eyes black with anger, and then nothing, until now. Some primal fear deep inside me told me not to open my eyes or move a muscle, which was near impossible as my panic started to rise from within my chest, its cold, icicle-like fingers paralyzing my body as they ran rampant through my veins and gripped my heart like a frozen vice. *Oh Jesus, think Audra, think.*

Okay, I needed to assess the situation. I needed to rely on all my other senses at the moment, since I was petrified to let on to whoever might be watching me now that I was conscious. I felt a chair under me and realized that I was sitting and that my arms were tied behind my back, and something was wrapped around my ankles. Obviously, Kevin hit me quite hard, enough to knock me to the ground and render me unconscious for...oh God, how long had I been out? What time did Nicole and I make it to my house? Eight? Nine? And why in the hell did Kevin hit me? What was he doing at my house? What was that horrific smell? Where the hell was I?

I felt my blood pressure rise exponentially, right along with my heart rate as it thumped loudly as fear overtook me, so I forced all of my energy to my ears, making myself listen to my surroundings rather than to the rush of blood pumping in my ears, promising myself that if I could determine I was alone, I would open my eyes. It was quiet save for a light, rustling sound coming from my right, sort of like feet shuffling with slippers on a slick floor. I heard the lonely, distant cry of a coyote from my left and realized it must still be night, but that cry didn't help me in terms of my location, for God knows those things were all over the state, which meant that I could be anywhere.

I heard a light groan from behind me and recognized it as that of a woman, one still asleep but in obvious pain. Was that Nicole? It was almost impossible to tell since all I heard was a brief moan followed by the faint sounds of struggling respirations. I held my own ragged breath for as long as I could, straining to hear any other noise that would indicate someone was near me or provide some fleeting clue as to where I was, and finally, hearing nothing, I slowly opened my eyes to view my prison. For a split second I completely panicked because I was in utter darkness, but some small voice of reason whispered in the back of my mind to give my eyes a moment to adjust to the darkness.

After about a minute they did, just enough for me to determine that I was in a small room of some sort, my feet and arms tied with what felt like a piece of cloth to a thin, wooden chair and sitting near the middle of the room, wearing the same clothes I had on before, surrounded by what looked to be a couch on one side and a bed or another couch on the other. I winced in pain as I tried to turn my head to look behind me to see if indeed it was Nicole that I heard moments ago, for even though I wasn't able to use my trussed hand to feel the egg sized knot on the back of my head, it surely was there, the pain so intense that it made bright bursts of light splash into my vision, momentarily blinding me. *Work through the pain Audra. Now is not the time to cry over a bump.*

I inhaled deeply and quietly and forced myself to twist my neck further than even my toughest yoga workout ever required me to do, and I caught a glimpse of Nicole's shoe and lower leg, crudely tied to a chair just like mine and about six feet behind me. I turned my head back to the front and stared at the door in front of me, a small sliver of dim light barely visible through the crack at the bottom. A million thoughts raced through my head, each of them clawing for the forefront of my attention. I felt the perspiration seep out of my skin as my heart pounded, even though I was silently begging it to slow down. I was having difficulty forming a cohesive thought with the loud *whooshing* sound in my ears.

I blinked back the burning tears of fright and focused on what I did know, which wasn't much other than, obviously, Nicole and I had been kidnapped. By Kevin? Why? It was Piper that killed Robert and probably snatched Gabrielle, so just what in the hell was Kevin's involvement? *No, not the time to figure the puzzle out Audra. Get loose and get the hell out of here, wherever that may be!*

I clamped my jaw down and gritted my teeth, focusing my rambling attention on freeing myself from this infernal chair. After a bit of slow movements, I determined that the cloth binding my hands behind me wasn't as tight as I first thought, though it was now thoroughly soaked with my reeking sweat, making the material's grip on my skin a bit stronger than when I first woke up. I struggled quietly in the darkness as I tried in vain to maneuver my wrists out of their cloth shackles, but to no avail, and I knew that the more I struggled, the tighter I was twisting the cloth. If I could just get my arms *in front of me*, then I could use my teeth, but accomplishing that was going to be near impossible, especially without alerting wary ears that I was awake and trying to escape.

Think girl, think!

There was only one way I could come up with to free my arms from the back of the chair, and the thought of that much pain made my stomach lurch in protest. *You have no choice, just do it!*

197

For the first time in my life, I closed my eyes and said a silent prayer to a God that I really hoped existed, hoping it would extend past the dark ceiling above me, asking for the ability to withstand the inevitable pain. I slowly released my breath and forced my muscles to heed my instructions as I slowly leaned sideways in the chair, aiming for the couch/bed next to me, hoping beyond hope that I judged the distance correctly so that I would land on it rather than the hardwood floor. Suddenly, my weight shifted too quickly and before I could even really register that fact to react to it, I landed silently on the couch. I fought hard to keep the joyful yelp that wanted to burst out in check.

I held still and listened for any telltale sounds of discovery that my movements might have incurred, and upon hearing nothing but the beating of my heart, I held my breath and forced all my energy and weight on my shoulder, waiting to feel the sickening crunch and lightning bolt of pain shoot through me when I dislocated it. But then I realized my left foot was dangling free and touching the cool floor below it.

Oh, thank God for thin ankles!

I planted my left foot on the floor and slowly pushed myself until I was completely on the bed flat on my back. Once fully there, I stretched my left leg around the chair leg over to the right one, loping my toes around the cloth as I began to wiggle and tug at the cloth. A few minutes later, fully engulfed in sweat now, my right leg was free, so I quickly stood up, my sweaty feet making no sound as they touched the floor. I squatted a bit and weaved both legs around each leg of the chair and then pushed and stood up, and thankfully, the chair remained in place as my arms slid over the back of the thin wooden spindles. Oh God, I was free!

I stood still for a moment and listened, my ears greeted only by silence and Nicole's breathing, then I immediately sat on the floor and rolled onto my back, twisting and stretching my arms until I could get my butt through their ready-made opening and around the back of my legs. Thankfully, the sweat that was now pouring off me made this process a bit easier and suddenly, my hands were finally in front of me, and I brought them up to my mouth, yanking and pulling until they too, were free.

I stood up from the floor and padded silently towards the still knocked out Nicole, and just as I made it to her chair, I heard a male voice that I recognized as Kevin's, coming from the other side of the door.

"Oh my God but does she stink! Must this be part of your plan? I mean, can't we just tell her you killed Gabrielle? Must she see this, this *mess?*"

My heart shattered into a million pieces. *Gabby was dead? That was what I smelled, her rotted corpse? Oh, dear God, please, let me be dreaming! Please, please let me wake up and this all be some horrific nightmare!*

I felt a heavy lump in my throat the size of a baseball as the tears spilled out of the corners of my tightly closed eyes. Gabby, my friend, my comrade in arms, the girl whose energy and love for life made me smile every day, even when my moods were overshadowed with sadness or stress. Dead. Gone. Poor Jeff. He would be devastated. He was absolutely wild about her. My hand involuntarily flew to my mouth to cover my sobs and contain the vomit that was dangerously close to coming out.

"Yes, you idiot, she needs to see this *mess*," came the voice of a woman, barely audible and highly agitated, "you want every bargaining chip available to ensure her signature, don't you? This ol' bitty here might not be enough."

My heart sank as I recognized Piper's voice. I felt lightheaded, sweat dripping down over my brow and my body involuntarily began to tremble, and tears sprang hotly forth and raced down my face. Gabby was dead because Piper killed her, just like she killed Robert, which meant Nicole and I were next. Oh God, why didn't I see this before? Why wasn't I more vigilant? Why was I so damned stubborn, unwilling to let Steve send an officer over to watch over me? Why did I always feel the need to handle things myself?

Ol' bitty?' What the hell did she mean...?

Suddenly, through the stench that was still swirling in my nose, I caught a faint wisp of another smell, a scent that made my blood almost leap out of my skin, and a small whimper left my lips: the warm, sweet smell of lemon infused tea and brown sugar cookies.

Mrs. Milligan's house.

The tears dried up as the resolution took control over my body, almost like what some would call a religious experience. This was my destiny; Mrs. Milligan said it herself: I was her Avenging Angel and my love for her would be my guiding light. My purpose in life had never been clearer than it was right at this moment: this was my penance for the mistakes of the past, because I knew that none of us would be here, no one would be dead, if it weren't for me. My selfish actions, brought on originally by another's, started a ripple in the pond that was now nearing the size of an enormous tidal wave, swallowing up people in its voracious path, almost like it was hungry for their blood. And only one person could end it.

Me.

Unsure of how much time I had before Kevin or Piper came in and found me free, I reached up and clamped one hand over Nicole's mouth as the other grabbed her shoulder and shook her, hoping to God that however long we had been unconscious had allowed plenty of time to elapse for her to sober up, at least enough to comprehend the situation we were in. Suddenly, her eyes flew open, their sheer panic almost shooting out of them and her body instantly struggling from my grasp.

I gripped her shoulder harder and leaned over to her ear, my lips pressed up against it as I whispered, "Nicole, it's me, Audra. Hold still and listen to me. We are in trouble, and I need you to focus, okay? I am going to let go now, but you can't make a sound. Promise?"

I felt her slowly nod her head in agreement while her chest heaved as she struggled to control her panicked breath. I released her shoulder first and then my hand from around her mouth. I took another deep breath and whispered again, my words short and to the point.

"Are you still drunk?"

She nodded her head no, fear snatching her tongue from answering.

"Are you hurt?"

Again, she nodded no.

"Okay, listen, I am going to untie you and help you out the window. We have been kidnapped and you will need to go get us help. Gabby is dead and we are next if you don't make it. We are in Summerset at Rosemary Milligan's house, which is about five miles from town. When you get to the road, turn right and follow it."

Nicole nodded in agreement again, and I could feel her body shaking as the odor of her fear mixed with the flowery scent of her hair in my face, which was a welcome relief from the rancid odor coming from the other room.

"Stay on the road, don't veer from it. And Nicole, run faster than you ever have, for the devil truly will be chasing you now," I said as I pulled away from her ear and bent over to untie her arms. We worked in tandem silence and I was grateful that she was intelligent enough to grasp the gravity of our situation and not ask any questions. Once her arms were free, I paused again and listened, my ears only greeted by the quick breaths of Nicole as she fought to unknot her restraints. I slowly walked over to the window and eased the heavy dark curtains back, praying that my recollections of her windows were correct, and thankfully, they were: the old swing out windows that were as long as they were wide, which meant Nicole would have no trouble making it out to the short drop below.

I looked back over at Nicole and she just freed her other leg and slid off her heels and stood up, and as she did, I could tell from the horrified look on her face that she finally caught a full whiff of the smell. She froze for a brief second, processing the information, and I knew that since she grew up on a farm, she would recognize the sickeningly sweet smell of death.

And she did.

With grace and stealth that someone her age shouldn't possess, she was quietly by my side and we traded glances for the briefest of moments as I slowly turned the ancient handle and held my breath, hoping that it wasn't sealed shut from years of neglect. To my surprise, it moved with ease and opened soundlessly, and I felt Nicole's hot breath release with almost as much force as my own. She grabbed my shoulder for support and like a cat, she leapt up on the open sill and then turned and faced me, her mouth silent but her eyes screaming for me to follow.

I shook my head and waved her away, almost pushing her out of the window. With one quick glance back, she jumped and landed in the hardened earth below, her feet barely touching it as she burst into a full sprint, and then I lost her in the darkness; the only confirmation that she was out there was the fading sounds of her feet attacking the road.

God, please let her make it!

I refused to let my mind wander anywhere except where I explicitly allowed it to, forcing myself to concentrate on one task at a time. I crept across the room and knelt down by the door, my cheek lightly grazing the floor as I cocked my head and listened, but all I could hear was the faint mumblings that sounded like they were coming from the other side of the house. I sat back on my haunches and mentally toured Mrs. Milligan's home, realizing that I was in the spare bedroom towards the back, which meant that the hallway that led to the kitchen was on the other side of this door and that Kevin and Piper were probably in the front room, since their voices were so muffled.

Which meant that a brief window of opportunity to find a weapon just presented itself.

I stood back up and surveyed the room the best I could in the darkness. Mrs. Milligan had been alone for a long time, and I recalled her telling me that she rarely came in here anymore and it had become more of a guest room. As I squinted my eyes and scanned the room, I noticed that only one small, twin sized bed was in here and one loveseat. Of course, the chairs that Nicole and

I were attached to moments ago were here, but that was it. No phone to call for help with: no closet where an old gun might be hidden up on a shelf; no dresser drawers that might miraculously contain a pair of well-worn scissors, or even a hunting knife. Hoping against hope that either my purse or Nicole's was in the room, my heart sank when I realized there was nothing in here to aide in my rescue. *Damn, why couldn't this moment be like in a movie?*

I realized the only way I would have an instrument in my hands that would give me some sort of stabilizer against Kevin and Piper was to silently creep into the kitchen and check the drawers, where surely my protection awaited, and the kitchen housed a phone to call for help; or at the very least, to dial 911 and let my silence urge the operator to dispatch a patrol unit. Even if I did manage to accomplish that, Mrs. Milligan's house was miles from town, which meant that the police aide wouldn't be arriving anytime soon. Frustrated that arming myself seemed my only viable option, I tiptoed across the room yet again and listened at the door. Faintly, almost as if they were standing on the front porch, I heard the echoing of voices, yet was unable to match a face with the voice since it was so garbled. I held my breath again, praying once more to the God that seemed to have heard my inner screaming a few moments ago, and slowly turned the door handle, closing my eyes almost completely shut as I cringed, waiting for the sound of the ancient metal to give my plans away with one high pitched squeak.

As I twisted, the metal did make a small grinding noise, but it was barely audible to even my ears. I finally pulled the door open just a crack so I could peer out, and scanned the hallway. There was just enough light streaming from the dimly lit kitchen down the length of the corridor to allow me to determine that the other bedroom doors were closed, giving me a straight shot into the kitchen, which was roughly ten to 15 feet away.

I cracked the door open just enough for me to contort my body through and pulled it shut quietly behind me, a faint *click* of the locking mechanism the only sound heard in the empty hallway. I crouched low with my back against the wall, and unsure as to how much time I had to accomplish securing a knife and dialing 911 before Piper and Kevin found me, I scurried quickly into the kitchen when suddenly, almost as though I hit an invisible brick wall composed of sights and smells, I came to a forced stop, my brain unwilling to compute the images my eyes were sending to it.

I knew from my own nose what the smell was, plus from the conversation I overheard moments ago between Piper and Kevin, I knew that Gabrielle was dead, but seeing her lifeless, limp body secured crudely to a chair under the bright glow of the kitchen light was more than I could bear. Her once beautiful face and body were now a swollen mass of unrecognizable, decaying flesh; her glorious mane matted from dried blood and solidified, unmoving, to the sides of her ruined head. The light from above reflected off of the large section of exposed skull, illuminating it, almost as if the light was coming from the inside of her brain, like some deadly beacon forcing my eyes to look in its direction. She was dressed in sweats that looked like they once had been lightly colored, but now appeared dark and grimy from the stains of her leaking body fluids.

Both of my hands flew up and clasped around my mouth to stifle the scream that was forever stuck in my throat. My knees waivered and my body instinctively leaned back against the kitchen wall for support. Clenching my eyes shut, I tried in vain to wipe out the ghastly image as tears spilled down my face and onto the cold linoleum floor. *Oh God, Gabby!* I tried to control my breathing, but it was coming in great heaves now as I began to hyperventilate, and as much as I didn't want to uncover my mouth, I had no choice but to let go as the roiling vomit burst out of me all over the floor.

This isn't happening. This is another nightmare! Oh God, please, let it be another nightmare! Let me wake up! Please! I can't live with this, I can't! It's my fault she's dead! No, no, NO!

The release of my stomach's contents was loud and I knew that any moment, Piper or Kevin would find me, so as tears blurred my vision, I stepped over the vomit and crossed the kitchen floor over to the countertop and reached for the huge knife that was sitting in Mrs. Milligan's cutlery set. The sound the sharpened steel made as I yanked it out screeched across the neurons in my head, and I knew then that I wouldn't stop until I killed them both. *Screw 911. This is your mess to clean. Turn around and walk past her, Audra, don't look at her. Just go avenge her now and find Mrs. Milligan, if it isn't too late. Focus!*

It's funny how the trajectory of your life path can shift so quickly, the dizzying motion of such huge leaps almost stifling, forcing you to take on a journey that you are woefully ill equipped to navigate; unprepared; unsure of your footing and direction, stumbling through each day just to be able to say you forged some new ground on the trail. Other times, like right now, the journey slams you face down in the muck-covered path and forces you to stay where you are, the weight of discovering your purpose in life finally coming into focus; crushing you to the ground, unyielding to your desperate pleas; your direction already preordained; no amount of fear, anger, sadness, love or any other emotional state able to change your circumstances. This is where I suddenly found myself as only two thoughts remained clear and strong in my mind: I knew that there was a real possibility that I wouldn't leave this house alive, but I didn't care: I needed to save Mrs. Milligan.

My internal monologue was controlling my tension filled body now, the voice of my inner animal fully in control as my destiny settled roughly on top of my heavy heart and shoulders. I gripped the handle of the knife with my sweaty palms, ready to find my prey and eviscerate them both, when I heard the floor creak behind me. I swung quickly around with knife at the ready as my face contorted into an angry sneer, and I locked eyes with a pair of dark brown one's that matched the madness of my own.

"Well, lookie here. Someone thinks they are going to play the hero!" Piper growled out the last word as I heard a *click* of the hammer on the gun that was aimed directly at my chest by hands I assumed belonged to Kevin. "Not today, bitch; your *Warrior* days are over. Drop it," she sneered, just as Kevin appeared right next to her, the gun shaking slightly in his effeminate hands. "Or I'm afraid I will have to make poor ol Mizz Milligan suffer greatly."

Her words slid easily off of her tongue as she held up a syringe full of thick, creamy colored liquid that almost glistened underneath the bare bulb dangling from the ceiling, as she gently swayed it back and forth across her chest. "And trust me, Robert didn't enjoy his death at all. I'm sure you don't want that poor bag of bones in there to suffer such a painful fate, so sit!" she barked. As much as I wanted to launch myself across the kitchen and bury the blade up to the hilt into her blackened, twisted heart, I calculated my advantages at this point, which were basically nil, and slowly leaned over and placed my chance at freedom on the table, then stepped back and leaned against the cool counter.

"Now, there's a good little escapee. Kevin, go get our other guest. We don't want her to miss out on tonight's festivities, do we?" Piper directed her words to Kevin, but her darkened eyes never left my own. For the first time I had a clear glimpse of them, and it was obvious to even me that she was gone. There wasn't much lurking behind her eyes except utter madness, and although I knew I should be scared, a strange sensation spread through me as I realized I could be just as cold and calculating as she was, but for completely different reasons.

"Where is Mrs. Milligan?" I said slowly, never taking my eyes off of my newfound nemesis.

"She is *resting* in the other room. You ask about that ol bitch first, but have yet to comment on your other friend here. Don't you think she looks…well, better? It's a nice change from before," Piper said, her arm that held the syringe flamboyantly swaying in front of Gabrielle's corpse, almost as if she was a morbid version of Vanna White. "That lying mouth will never utter another lie again. I made sure of that when I bashed her face in," Piper sneered, looking down at the matted corpse almost like she was a proud parent displaying her child's artwork to her friends.

Before I could respond, the sound of Kevin's voice came barreling down the hall, followed quickly by his footsteps as he burst into the kitchen. His sudden outburst startled Piper, who dropped her focus on me and turned it to him as he yelled, "She's gone!"

"What?" screamed Piper.

"She's not in there!" he said, turning his attention, and the gun, on me. "Where the fuck is she?"

Nicole had been gone for less than ten minutes and I knew that she probably hadn't made it very far towards Summerset, but still, she did have a lead on him, but I needed to buy her some more time, even if it only consisted of seconds, so I replied, "Oh, she just went out for a night stroll, you know, to get some fresh air after waking up with a hangover."

Before I could finish the last word, Kevin was suddenly upon me and the back of his hand caught almost the same exact spot on my face that it had earlier that evening, but this time, I was not only ready for it, but almost craved the pain to give me strength of my own. The loud smack of his skin against mine reverberated through the kitchen only to be outdone by Piper's shrill shriek, "Don't waste your time with her! Go find Nicole!"

Kevin was breathing heavy, his hair mussed and falling into his reddened face as he nodded at Piper and quickly spun around, slamming the front door behind him as he headed to search for Nicole. Piper's eyes immediately converged upon mine again, a hint of laughter twitching at her lips as she moved slowly towards me, her limpid pool of sanity not disturbed by petty blinking.

"Clever girl, but it won't matter…now, let's have a seat in the living room by your other friend. I have some papers that require your signature. It's up to you whether we use ink or blood."

CHAPTER 23
Steve-Desperation

"Yes, that's the correct VIN number, I'm sure of it. I am looking at the purchase documents right now," Nick said, his voice cracking slightly as he tried to focus on the buyer's order in his lap. He was pale and shaky, gripping the phone tightly in one hand, the other buried in the door handle of my car as I sped through the streets of Phoenix towards Audra's house.

"I'm sorry sir, as I said earlier, the GPS on that VIN number is not locating anything."

"Fuck!" Nick yelled, slamming his phone shut, his frustration overwhelming his normally calm, attorney-like demeanor. "That was a complete bust. I can't believe we couldn't find any records of her phone number! How in the hell are we going to find her? She could be anywhere."

"The crime scene unit will hopefully uncover something, soon. I was really hoping that we could get a trace on her car. Think Nick: you know her best," I said, the knot in my stomach now the size of a basketball. Twice since leaving Piper's house a few minutes ago I tried calling Audra, but her phone was going straight to voicemail, which it never did. For the first time in my career as a cop, I overrode my instincts and told myself that she was fine.

But I knew better.

Nick let out his breath in a huge burst of frustrated air as he replied, "I only thought I knew her. I knew she was unstable and a danger to herself, but I never would have imagined that she was a danger to others."

As I exited the freeway towards Audra's, I snatched my cell phone from my lap to call her again, ignoring the panic that was rising in me. A crazed, psycho killer bitch, armed with rattlesnake venom, that had killed one person already and kidnapped another, was God-knows-where in this sprawling state, and she was after the woman that I loved. *Jesus Steve, you just admitted it: you love her.*

And I did. I loved every single thing about that feisty sprite of a woman, from her bravery and strength down to her hidden fears and flawed character. The first time I saw her truly smile I felt it pierce through my own armor, and I knew then that she was something special. Our night together seemed eons ago after all the craziness of the past few days, but I could still remember watching her sleep, her face calm and relaxed as her body curled around my own, her breathing deep and heavy. I knew then that I wanted to experience that every single night for the rest of my life.

My heart was beating fast as I dialed her number again, and it then went into overdrive as the call went straight to her voicemail again. *Where was she?* Then I remembered the dinner date.

"Nick, what is the name of that overpriced Italian joint downtown? I think it starts with a Z?"

"Zargento's?" Nick responded, looking at me like I just lost my mind by asking.

"Yes! That's it!" I said, slowing down a bit as I rounded the corner into Audra's neighborhood.

I dialed information and within seconds, was connected. It was past ten o'clock and I hoped they were still answering the phone. On the fifth ring, I was just about to hang up when someone picked up.

"Zargento's."

Thank God. "My name is Detective Ronson and I need to speak with the manager, now please. It's urgent."

"He has already left for the evening sir, as we closed at ten. I am the host, Renaldo, may I help you with something?"

Damn it! "There were reservations this evening for around six for Audra Tanner. I need to know if she made it?"

There was a pause on the other end as I heard paper being flipped as Renaldo was searching. "You say you're a detective? Is there something wrong?"

"Yes, there is something wrong, or else I wouldn't be calling to ask! Time is precious here, so please just answer my question: did she show up?"

I heard him clear his throat, his voice betraying his hurt at my chastisement, "Yes, Audra Tanner, party of three, only two checked in at 6:30, and they left at eight in a cab."

"Only two? Was the other woman older with a head full of curly blonde hair?"

"Yes, as a matter of fact she was. Very funny lady, especially when I helped them both to the cab. The one you just asked about was pretty drunk and, um, rather flirtatious."

So, Audra and Nicole left together, drunk, around eight, yet their meeting with the rich bitch never happened. Either the rich bitch stood them up, or this was a set up. I chewed on that for a second when my thoughts were interrupted by the host who said, "Funny, I just noticed a note here that the third party *did* call at six and left a message saying she was delayed with car trouble, but on her way."

Bingo.

"Did she by chance leave a call back number?" I asked as I turned onto Audra's street.

"No, but I could check our Caller ID. Hold on."

I put the phone on speaker and set it down in my lap as I turned into Audra's driveway and stopped quickly, digging through my console for a pen and paper in case luck was with me, and just as I found a pen, Renaldo clicked back on the line.

"There was one call at exactly six o'clock from a cell phone, the number is..." and I quickly scribbled it down, my heart beating from excitement now. I thanked Renaldo and hung up and said to Nick, "Hey, I think we have our first lead..." but I stopped short of finishing my sentence when I noticed the look on Nick's face, so I followed his gaze and looked out the windshield.

My stomach dropped like I was riding the biggest roller coaster of my life as I stared at the open gate. A cold fear swept up my back as I shut the car off and reached under my seat for my revolver. I didn't even look at Nick as I opened the car door and said, "Do not follow me. Call 911 and stay put."

Nick just nodded his head and began to dial as I quietly shut the car door and headed up the drive to the front door. I didn't notice anything amiss until I hit the peak of the driveway and looked at the front door, which was wide open, the glaring light shining alone in the darkness. I made my way through the front door and inside, crouching by the door and listening for sounds of life. I glanced down and saw two purses next to a chair, the contents of both strewn all over, and as I followed their scattered path, my eyes stopped on a smear of blood on the floor and the remnants of two shattered cell phones.

Oh God, I was too late.

On autopilot now, I quickly cleared the house and determined that no one was there. Once back to the front door, I bent down and opened the other bag, assuming that it must be Nicole's, and upon finding her driver's license, realized I couldn't escape the instincts I had been born with and that had been honed to razor sharp accuracy as a cop: Piper had Audra, and it seems, Nicole as well.

I walked back out the front door and was greeted by Nick's hulking figure walking up the driveway, and thought how ironic that two completely different men were in this life and death struggle for two completely different women for polar opposite reasons. I heard sirens in the distance heading in our direction, but it brought no comfort to my pounding heart as I looked at Nick, who was now standing directly in front of me, his eyes a rampant mess of emotions, and said, "We're too late."

"Oh God" Nick said, his voice choking back the tears that were in his throat.

"Where is my cell?" I barked.

He produced it silently from his pocket, the tears flowing freely down his face now. Quickly, I ran back to the car as I dialed the station, praying that Sandy would answer because God knows the rest of the staff didn't have the brains or expertise to help me.

"Summerset Police Department, Sandy."

"Sandy, I need you to run the following number. Get someone to ping it so we can locate where it was last used. Get Judge Hall patched through to my cell. We need a warrant to trace this number," I said, snatching the paper off my console. "And I mean NOW!" I yelled, cringing a bit on the inside for my outburst at Sandy, but unable to hold back my nervousness anymore.

"Sure thing, Steve. Hold on," Sandy responded, thankfully realizing that this was truly an emergency.

The first of five Phoenix police cruisers came screaming down Audra's street as I finished giving the phone number to Sandy, and before my voice was lost over their wails, I said, "Hurry Sandy, please."

CHAPTER 24
Audra-Showdown

I sat in the very same spot that I did days ago, and so did Mrs. Milligan; only this time, she was unconscious and bound tightly to a chair less than three feet away from me. When Piper led me to the living room moments ago, I thought my heart would burst from agony as I gazed upon her aging frame, unmoving and pale as death's shadow, until I saw her chest rise and fall faintly. Knowing she was still alive, even if her heartbeat was faint and her breathing shallow, caused my nerves to settle somewhat. My mind focused on setting her free from this nightmare that I inadvertently drug her into.

Piper was perched in the chair between us as her eyes burned into mine, watching every reaction and movement from me as I looked at Mrs. Milligan, just waiting for me to mentally cave and become some blubbering idiot; putty in her hands.

Bitch picked the wrong woman for that.

Barely perceivable, I drew my breath in slowly through my nose and leveled my eyes and stared straight into her pools of madness. Her right hand still held the syringe that was uncapped now, a few drops of the liquid dripping slowly off of the sharp end. The edge of the needle was dangerously close to Mrs. Milligan's limp arm, while Piper's other one reached out to the papers on the table and pushed them towards me slowly.

"Sign," she purred.

My window of opportunity was a cracked sliver at best. Kevin could walk in at any moment, and Piper could break from reality at any second and stab Mrs. Milligan with whatever poison she held in her hand. The thought crossed my mind briefly that I could just leap across the table and knock her down, thinking that we were about well-matched in height and weight, but I tossed that plan out as quickly as it entered my head. Her insanity obviously made her a very strong woman if she took down a man, even though I wasn't quite sure of exactly the way she had accomplished that. I didn't want to deal with what if scenarios or thoughts and decided to use the one weapon against her that was stronger than any gun or knife: Olin.

Forcing my facial features to contort into a snide grin, I glanced down at the papers and responded, "Exactly what am I signing here, Piper?"

Her wicked grin matched my own as she replied, "Oh, just a few little loose ends. You know, an affidavit stating you are resigning as Managing Partner and that you are nominating Nicole as the new one. Of course, if she is unable or unwilling to carry out those duties, the firm will then be under the control of Kevin." The pools were writhing in glistening madness now, almost making me dizzy, but I never looked away, deciding to dive right into their darkened waters.

"Really? So that's what this is all about? Kevin wants Winscott? Jesus, Piper, he could have just asked. Running that hellhole isn't what it's cracked up to be. So, what's this?" I said, my head nodding slightly towards the other piece of paper.

"Your suicide note."

My heart quickened but I kept on swimming.

"Oh, suicide! What a brilliant plan! So let me guess; the note rambles on about my guilt and sadness, and I decided to drive all the way to Summerset and stop here, at this house of all places, to kill myself, after dragging the rotting corpse of my assistant with me? And Mrs. Milligan? Come on Piper, you can do better than that!" I said, taking another stroke in the blackened water.

Her eyes narrowed a bit at my affront to her planning capabilities. "No, actually, you admit to killing Robert, Gabrielle, Mrs. Milligan *and* yourself because you couldn't stand your life anymore, and they needed to pay for their lying, sinful deeds. You realized that you couldn't live with the fact that the filth you spouted about Olin caused a chain reaction for others, forcing an innocent man to be arrested. Your thoughts on this were solidified after Robert confided to you that he, in fact, killed that trollop so long ago. Oh, and you also felt so guilty about ruining Nicole's life that you wanted to leave her the company...you know, as some sort of final peace offering. Female to female bonding shit. Of course," Piper's smile was so inherently evil that the chill from it shot straight through me, almost as if the Grim Reaper himself reached inside my chest and squeezed, "Nikki was supposed to die in a terribly tragic car accident shortly after becoming top dog, but look at you! You brought her to us and saved me from having to dirty up my hands! I will admit, her presence threw a small rock into my well-oiled plan, but Kevin and I decided we could use this to our advantage. Now that we have her... well, had her," she said, glancing quickly out the picture window into the stillness of the night, "she will mysteriously disappear, leaving the authorities to assume that you had something to do with her death, since she was last seen with you. It's perfection!" she said, her breath coming heavier now and her voice almost sultry as she cooed the words, "Oh, and the best part? I get to kill you and that obnoxious Southern Belle myself once Kevin finds her!"

My God, she was certifiable. Not that I had any doubts about it before, but watching her almost salivate over the thought of ending the existence of more human lives was beyond frightening. There's nothing like having the eyes of a demented, psychotic killer staring you down like you were a wounded bird that they toyed with before ripping it to shreds.

Except I wasn't wounded.

"Wow, I'm impressed Piper. You have it all figured out, right down to whatever drug or poison is dripping out of that needle, just waiting to enter my veins" I said, hoping she would take the bait and give away what toxic substance I was up against.

"Kevin told me about your fascination with snakes and the last thing you said to Olin, so I thought it would be a really nice touch to end all of your pathetic little lives with rattlesnake venom!" she said, her lips curved into a wicked grin that never reached her eyes, which were almost pulsating with a strange mixture of excitement and anger.

At least now I knew what I was up against, although that knowledge made my skin crawl and my stomach drop to the floor. I forced myself to keep my gaze steady and not look over at Mrs. Milligan, who was still unconscious, but whose arm was dangerously close to the venom.

"Of course, I have an extra vial now since I accidentally bashed that lying whore's face in. I worried that it would go to waste, but now that Nikki is in the picture, it won't!"

Dear God, please give me strength.

"So, if you are planning to kill me anyway, what is my incentive to sign?" I said, struggling to keep my voice steady and strong as fear thumped through me.

"You are such an accountant Audra! You must know every little detail, even when it comes to your own death," she said as she reached inside her purse, which until now, I hadn't noticed hanging on her chair, and extracted another syringe. "Well, you get to make the epic decision as to which way this old prune dies; the painful death from this venom, or a nice peaceful slumber from this little vial of painkillers," she said, holding up the newest syringe in front of me, its silver tip inches from my nose. "So, which is it, Audra? You want to watch the old bag writhe and convulse on the floor, which believe me, after watching Robert, wasn't a very pretty sight, or will you take on that pain for her and let her drift off into nothingness? You have exactly ten seconds to make your choice, bitch. I am tired of talking to you."

Without blinking an eye, I reached out and pulled the papers to me, along with the pen that rested on top of them. I grabbed the suicide note first and scrawled my name across the bottom. I could sense the electricity level in the room soar as Piper's excitement level was oozing out of her. I knew her thoughts were running at full speed, so, as I pushed the suicide note in front of her, holding the pen over the agreement and said, "All of this for the man that never loved you, dumped you once, but that also killed your one true love, Ralph."

I knew it was coming and I steadied myself for the sting. In one swift motion, her left hand immediately dropped the syringe that contained the drugs in it and her palm slammed across my cheek as she screamed, "Don't you DARE speak his name you fucking bitch! Ralph loved me!"

She's on the ropes now. Steady.

"Loved you? Are you kidding? He never touched you because he was too busy wearing a dog collar while Nick screwed him."

Her face instantly became pale as the blood rushed from it, the shock of my words having exactly the calculated effect on her I'd hoped, and for a brief second, she took her eyes off of mine as she stared off into some demented internal mental room, trying to process what I said. Her body, which before had almost been reverberating with adrenaline-infused jitters, slouched a bit in her chair as her head slung violently back and forth, her mouth silently forming the word No over and over.

That's when I lunged.

The guttural scream that erupted out of my throat was so loud that Piper actually jumped. I flew across the table and lowered my head, aiming directly for her chest as I plunged the pen deep into her back. The velocity of my attack knocked her out of the chair and we both tumbled to the floor with a loud crash.

And then, like an erupting volcano, every wretched emotion ranging from intense rage to utter sorrow spewed out of me, and all over Piper. My vision truly did go black as my body took control and closed my mind down, using my senses instead to fight. I straddled her and my fingers wound tightly around her hair. I slammed her head over and over into the hardwood floor, my ears relishing the dull thud each time it hit along with her grunts of pain. Sweat was running down my back and my arms were aching from the force of my muscles but I didn't care. I just kept trying to crush her head in so her disturbed brain matter would spill out.

My own ravenous thoughts were abruptly cut short as I felt her weight shift under me, and for a split second, I lost my balance; as I started to lean to the side, Piper used it against me and threw all her weight in the same direction. We rolled over, her legs now pinning me to the floor. The black haze that overtook me only seconds before was now replaced with bright, white raw fear as I realized she had the upper hand.

Her empty hands.

I quickly turned my head and caught a glimpse of the shimmering syringe to my right just as Piper raised her arms over her head to pummel my face. Muscles screaming in protest, I reached over and grabbed the syringe, praying to God that it was the right one. The grunt that escaped my mouth as I buried the needle into her thigh was abruptly silenced as Piper's fist made contact with my face, my nose exploding blood in every direction.

Her screams of pain as she clawed at her thigh echoed through my head and I almost smiled. She crumpled over and rolled off me, her body convulsing and contorting like Satan himself had possessed her.

I knew then that I grabbed the right one.

As quickly as they started, her screams stopped, almost as if unseen hands were around her throat and cut her air supply off. I scrambled to my feet and clamped one hand over my gushing nose and tried to move away, but the sick fascination of watching her suffer overcame me, and even though I willed myself to, my eyes just wouldn't close, nor my feet move.

It took less than a minute for the last, labored breath to escape Piper's lungs and her eyes to remain locked in eternal pain that stared into Mrs. Milligan's dark, empty ceiling. The house was eerily quiet now, save for my ragged breathing through my mouth. Watching her last moment here on Earth end finally snapped me back to the present, but I still felt like I was viewing myself from a distance. For some odd reason, my head was suddenly filled with the voice of one of my college professors, his lecture on stress and adrenaline chasing the last of my disconnecting cobwebs out of my head.

It was time to get the fuck out of there.

I spun around so fast that I almost tripped over my own unsteady feet. I bobbled a bit and then raced to the kitchen and grabbed a dishtowel, holding it to my nose as I picked up the phone to dial the police. My hands shook as I held it to my ear, the pain from my wounds suddenly coming to the forefront of my attention.

My heart sank when I realized that no noise, not even a tone, emitted from the ancient phone. I looked down and saw the cord had been severed, which didn't shock me as much as it angered me. I knew Mrs. Milligan had no other connections in the house and my phone was probably shredded into tiny pieces and strewn across three counties by now. Damnit!

Think! Breathe and think! Don't look at Gabrielle. You can't do anything for her now, but you can for Mrs. Milligan!

Piper.

To pull all of this off with Kevin, communication was vital, so surely she had a cell phone on her, or maybe even in her car. I ran back into the living room and found her purse on the floor; its contents still oddly intact. I yanked open the zipper and flipped it upside down, dumping the few items onto the floor, only to become furious at the lack of a phone. My vision starting swimming in black again, overwhelming fury pounding through my head, and I took it out on Piper's body. I stood up and strode over and swung my foot directly to that worthless bitch's stomach with every bit of strength I had…and that's when I felt it.

I bent down and reached into her pants pocket and sure enough, there was a tiny cell phone tucked away inside. Dear God, I had never been so glad to see a piece of plastic in my life.

I flipped it open and prayed that I didn't just destroy the miniscule thing and that it had power. I almost jumped up and down with excitement as I heard the line connect.

"9-1-1. What is your emergency?"

Thank you, God!

221

"Sandy, it's Audra. Listen, I am at Rosemary Milligan's. Need an ambulance and police. There are people dead here," I said, my voice muffled and crackling as I held my nose shut, the blood flowing down the back of my throat. I wasn't sure she heard or understood me until she began barking directions and dispatching units.

"Audra, are you alright?" came Sandy's reply as she focused her attention back to me.

"Pretty sure my nose is broken. Bleeding, but I am okay. Mrs. Milligan has been given some sort of drug that knocked her out, at least that's my understanding. Otherwise, she seems to be fine. Listen, she is still tied up and I need my hands free to help her. How long will it be?"

"Honey, the entire force is on its way, as well as every citizen that has a CB radio around here! About ten minutes, max," Sandy said, trying her best to be cheery.

"Where is Steve?" hoping that he wasn't still in Phoenix trying to find me.

"On his way, don't you worry, hun. You just take care of Rosemary. The cavalry is coming!"

For the first time since I awoke to this nightmare, I closed my eyes and let a few tears trickle down my face. "Thank you, Sandy." Before I could tell her about Gabrielle, Robert and Nicole, the line went dead as the last of the battery power faded. Shit!

I launched the useless thing at the wall, smiling a bit at the sounds of it shattering into tiny pieces, and went over to Mrs. Milligan's side. She was still sleeping hard, thank God. The things that happened here tonight in her once peaceful home were not the types of things she should ever witness. I knelt down and worked quickly, gently untying her from the chair, and slid my arms under her limp body, groaning as I hefted her to the couch. Her dead weight made the few steps seem like miles. My nose turned into a faucet of hot, squirting blood that left a cavalcade of crimson on my shirt and the floor. Choking on it, I finally lowered her to the couch and eased her back into the soft pillows, the rusty taste trickling down my throat. I reached for the afghan that was draped

222

across the back of the couch and quickly covered her still frame. The blood was hitting my empty stomach now and I felt the urge to throw up again. I rose to my feet with the intent of heading to the bathroom, my hand instinctively rising to cover my mouth. It froze in mid-air when I saw headlights coming up the driveway.

It was Kevin's car.

I dropped back down to the floor, praying he hadn't seen me, all concern about vomiting gone as my fight or flight response took control. My heart was pounding so hard that I feared it would send me into cardiac arrest at any moment.

I crawled across the floor over to the other syringe, snatching it up in one quick motion, my eyes scanning the room for another weapon. I needed something to stun the bastard before I could get close enough to put him into la-la land. I heard the car door slam and footfalls coming towards the porch, which didn't give me time to scramble to the kitchen and retrieve a knife. Panic pulsated through me now and I realized that my dreams of being trapped in a crushing room were about to come true. Hysteria almost won out, but then I saw the candlesticks on the mantle.

Not caring whether he heard me or not, I shot up off the floor and ran to the fireplace, snatching the heavy silver candlestick. I knew I only stood one clean shot, so I flicked the cap off of the syringe, gripped the end in my mouth and ran back to the front door. He was right on the other side. My grip tightened as I raised my iron tool above my head, my body poised just like a baseball player waiting for the final pitch in the World Series. The knob turned and the door swung open, just as Kevin yelled, "Piper! I found her!"

Nicole's disheveled body came crashing through the door, landing with a loud thud on the hardwood. She cursed and yelled, "No need to be pushy, you bastard!"

My heart almost stopped beating when I saw her. She was covered in dust and dirt, bleeding lightly from her knees and hands. More blood, more mayhem.

More rage.

Through my open mouth, I sucked in a lungful of air, steadied my weight on my back foot, and brought down the candlestick. It made a swooshing sound as it broke the air, followed by a loud, gut jolting thud as it made full contact with the back of Kevin's head. Silently, he stumbled forward one step before his knees buckled, falling face first onto the floor, his head bouncing off the hardwood once before coming to rest by Nicole's left foot. His body only inches away from me, I suddenly found myself standing over him, the candlestick held high over my head, ready to bash his brains in and end his pathetic life; payback for all the damage and destruction he and Piper were responsible for. I wanted all of this to end, to finally close this God-awful chapter in my life. So many lives ruined; too much heartache. Lives intertwined that never should have even touched. Innocent ones that paid the ultimate price for a roller coaster ride they never should have been on. I wanted this to end, but I realized that I was the one that started it all. If I had just gone to the police, none of this would be happening. My dear friend wouldn't be rotting in the kitchen and her fiancé wouldn't have his life ripped to shreds when he found out his betrothed was gone. Robert wouldn't have been hunted down like prey. Nicole wouldn't be sprawled out on the floor like a ragdoll, bleeding, a victim of a kidnapping, if it weren't for me.

So, I ended it, but this time, the right way.

I dropped the candlestick to the floor, barely noticing the noise it made as it rolled across the shiny wood. I grabbed the syringe from my mouth and reached down, burying it into Kevin's rump. Carefully, I injected a small amount of the medication into his system, just enough to keep him unconscious. I already killed one person today in the heat of battle and I couldn't bring myself to do it again.

"Well now, you don't have the balls I thought you did girl," Nicole said, her voice hoarse.

I pulled my eyes away from Kevin's limp figure and stepped away from him. Nicole was still on the floor, so I made my way over to her and held out my hand. As she stood, her gaunt face covered in dirt, she smiled at me with dry, cracked lips. I tried to bring a smile to my face but it would not come. It just did not feel right to smile at this point. I looked over with hardened eyes at the violently contorted corpse of Piper and replied, "He wasn't an immediate threat, Nicole. I am certain that candlestick cracked his skull. Now he can just sleep until the cops get here. I am out of the revenge business; for good."

I walked slowly over to the couch to check on Mrs. Milligan. Thankfully, she was still asleep, completely oblivious to everything. I could hear Nicole moving around behind me, surveying the after effects of what she missed while she ran for help. I knelt down beside the couch and stroked the delicate skin on Mrs. Milligan's arm, thankful that I felt the warmth of her blood flowing just below the surface. Although I had a lot of blood on my hands now, at least I did not have hers. Exhausted, I closed my eyes for just a second and forced my breathing to slow down, ears aching to hear the sound of sirens so this nightmare would cease.

I heard Nicole let out a low whistle as she stopped moving around. "Looks like your battle with Piper was epic! Hey, what is this?"

I forced my burning eyes open, turning my head to see what she was referring to. She held a piece of paper in her hand and was studying it in the dim light, her brow furrowing as she tried to read the print.

"Well, that is either my suicide note or the agreement installing you as the new managing partner, I am not sure which," I responded, my voice barely above a whisper. The constant draining of blood down my throat made it raw, and talking only made it worse.

Nicole extended her long arm out as far as it could go and replied, "Oh, yes, I see now. It is your suicide note. What the hell? Why did you sign that?" she said, her voice grating on my nerves.

"I did not have much choice, Nicole. It was either sign it or watch Mrs. Milligan die."

Nicole dropped the note like it was on fire and quickly bent over and picked up the other. I quietly watched her scan it, wondering what she must think about being a pawn in all this.

Bitterness and confusion flashed across her face, so I cleared my throat and explained.

"Piper said that was their plan all along: to make it look like I killed everyone over guilt, and left the company to you as some sort of apologetic token for ruining your life. They planned on killing you in a car accident shortly afterwards, which would then give Kevin the reigns of the firm," I said, the image of Piper's distorted face flashing through my mind. "Of course, their plans changed a bit when Kevin found you at my house."

Nicole's eyes grew huge with shock, her body slightly trembling, causing the dirt to loosen from her clothes and float to the floor around her. Oddly, the image of *Pigpen* crossed my mind. She took a few halting steps backwards and rested her exhausted form against the wall for support. Her voice was quieter now as she replied, "So, they were going to kill me tonight so Kevin could run the firm? Oh my, what a plan."

I silently nodded my head, my heart too heavy to speak.

"So, basically, you just saved my life. God Audra, I do not know what to say," she said, the utter absurdity of the entire plan finally sinking in.

Tears welled up in my eyes so I turned my face back to the window, relishing the silence between the two of us now. Both of us were lost in our thoughts, digesting the events of the past 24 hours. Even though it was hot as hell in the cramped living room I still felt chilled. I knew it was a reaction from the rapid descent of my previous adrenaline surge and my blood loss, but that did not make me feel any better. My entire body ached. Muscles that I wasn't aware I had or what their function was throbbed in pain. I shuddered slightly and rubbed my arms.

I stared into oblivion, my eyes focusing on the bright moon above, trying to find the words to thank whatever entity resided up there for allowing me to survive. Unfortunately, prayers of thanksgiving were overshadowed by other thoughts. All I could think of was, why did I stay? Why did I subject myself to the torture of working at Winscott for so long, dragging everyone down in the end? What was wrong with me? Why did I opt to take this path, rather than a more moral one?

Stop it Audra!

Walking down this path was not going to help, at least not at this moment. What was done was done, and although I desperately wanted to, turning the clock back was not a possibility. Now was not the time to fall into the trap of rancid thoughts again. I resolved right then to make the trip back to the therapist and work on my broken soul. Gritting my teeth, I focused my thoughts elsewhere. God, when would the police arrive? How long had it been since I called? The Snow Queen didn't need to see me cry; especially now since the possibility of forging new ground in our relationship seemed probable. A small glimmer of hope for the future, since working as a team would be much easier than as forced colleagues. I blinked back the tears and focused on the highway, hoping that the lights that just appeared was not an optical illusion.

It wasn't, for as soon as I saw the blue shimmering in the distance, the faint whine of the sirens met my ears. Oh God, it was finally over! Suddenly, I was filled with adrenaline again as the excitement took over, a smile breaking free. I turned to Nicole and said, "Thank God, they are coming!"

Nicole wasn't leaning against the wall anymore, and it took me a second to realize that Kevin was not lying in the doorway either. He was propped up against the far wall about 20 feet from me, his body sagging against it, his head lolling at an unnatural angle, almost touching his right shoulder. A smeared trail of bright blood marked where he had been to where he was now. I tried to make sense of what I was looking at, then I realized that Nicole was sitting on the floor next to him, her clothes completely drenched in red from dragging him. It looked like she was holding his hand, which of course, was impossible. Before I could form a word, she spoke.

"I figured out what to say," she growled, her voice oddly low, her jaw clenched together so tightly that the veins in her thin neck were bulging. "The difference between the two of us is quite simple: you wanted revenge. I want blood. And for the balance to be zero."

Movement caught my eye. She was not holding hands with Kevin; she was holding his wrist and using both of her arms to raise his, the gun in his hand pointed straight at me. "Get over there and sign that piece of paper, now."

Instinctively, my hands moved to protect my elderly charge from harm as I moved my body to shield hers. Even from across the room, I could see the anger raging behind Nicole's light eyes. *What in the hell is she doing?*

Dumbstruck, I could not form any words. Seconds passed as we stared at each other, the unreal scene making me dizzy. Realty came crashing back when I heard the hammer click on the gun. "I said MOVE!"

Suddenly, I found my voice again. "Why, Nicole?"

Her words reverberated through the room as she yelled. "WHY? You have to ask why? Are you fucking kidding me? You destroyed everything! Poor little Audra could not stand the heat, so she burned us all. You truly are naïve if you deluded yourself into believing that your little dramatic plan to make us all pay would not come back to bite you in the ass! This is real life, Audra, not some schoolyard grudge. What made you think you had the right to ruin us? Because Olin fucked you?" she hissed, her words like daggers slicing through me.

"Welcome to the real world, baby doll. You are just now reaping what you've sown. Now, enough chitchat; move your ass and sign that form! I did not spend the last nine months waiting for this day to end it empty handed!"

My body betrayed me as it shook in fright. The sirens were getting closer, but they still were far enough away that I knew I was on my own. I slowly stood up and made my way across the floor to where the papers rested. What choice did I have at this point? The only hope for salvation seemed to be fading, for I doubted I could stall for time. Nicole was too smart for that.

I bent down and picked up the agreement. Nicole's eyes never left me. The paper lightly fluttered in my shaking hands. "I need something to write with," I said, my voice throaty and low.

Nicole cut her eyes over to Piper's body. "Use that."

I followed her gaze, my stomach lurching when I saw the pen sticking out of Piper's back; then it settled a bit when I noticed another one on the floor to my left. It must have been inside Piper's bag that I riffled through earlier. My movements controlled, I took a few steps and squatted down to retrieve it, my eyes never leaving Nicole's. I made my way slowly to the table and sat down, pen at the ready, trying to determine how far the sirens were now. They sounded much closer, but not close enough.

"It was you, wasn't it? My car?" I said as I signed my name, hoping that I could tap into her vanity.

"Gee Audra, if I could clap right now, I would give you a round of applause. Bravo! Of course it was. How else would I have insured that you would need a ride? Do you have any idea how many hours I spent making fake reservations for rental cars all over town? I can assure you, it was a lot!" she said, her eyes twinkling at the memory. "Destroying your car was just an added bonus."

I never looked at the page as I signed my name. I had her talking now.

"You knew all along what Piper and Kevin had planned, didn't you?"

She rolled her eyes at me like I just asked the dumbest question in history. "Ding, ding, ding! Give the twat a prize! From the moment Eric walked out of my life, I began planning my own revenge; one that ended with your death. As fate would have it, I wound up in the same downtown dive bar late one night that Kevin was at. I overheard his phone conversation, although at the time, I did not know he was talking to Piper. But I picked up enough to realize he was talking about you and the firm. Because of you, he lost his wife, and he wanted you dead; he was just too much of a whipped pussy to do it himself.

"So, I hope you don't mind," she said, those words spat out with emphasis, "I used a play from the 'Audra Tanner School of Revenge' and began my own surveillance. Once I deciphered what he was up to, and with whom, I just watched and waited."

The sirens were closer now. *God, please let them hurry!*

"I am impressed, Nicole. It is a perfect plan. You get the firm, I am out of the way and your hands are free of all the blood that Piper shed. Brilliant! But, what are you going to do when Kevin wakes up and starts talking?" I said, standing up slowly. She eyed me with caution but let me move.

"The dead do not speak," she said, the words cold and calculating as they left her lips.

I swallowed hard and shifted my eyes over to Kevin. From this distance, it was impossible to tell if he was still breathing, but judging by the pallor of his skin, I took her words to heart.

"Oh, yes indeed, dear. I do believe the correct term the police will use when they write this report up will be 'blunt force trauma' as the cause of poor Kevin's death. Guess your pathetically small body belies the strength within honey, because you bashed his skull in! Thank you for not making *me* kill him. Not that I wouldn't have, but this is much easier on me, since your fingerprints are on the weapon and not mine."

I was about two feet from Mrs. Milligan when I heard the shift in her voice, her southern drawl dripping with sarcasm. "Ah, the cops are here. Guess I learned a lesson here today as well: revenge really is sweet."

My peripheral vision caught the lowering of the gun, but this time, it was not aimed at me. Dear God, she was going to shoot Mrs. Milligan first. The room suddenly filled with the strobe light blue from the police cars that were careening up the drive, the sound of their tires crunching on the gritty dirt driveway. It didn't matter though, because they were too late.

I closed my eyes and launched my body in the air at the exact same time the sound of the gunshot hit my ears. The intensity of it inside the miniscule living room was deafening. The pungent aroma of the gunpowder hung in the air and filled my lungs as I inhaled a huge gulp of air. I felt my trajectory shift violently as magma hot pain shot through me, the bullet tearing through my flesh. I landed on my side by the couch, the pain rendering me motionless, my mind shutting down as the room spun, my vision blurred. I heard multitudes of footsteps on the porch and voices outside the window, but I could not speak. *Please God, save her,* I prayed, hoping He would answer one final plea and spare my friend.

The last thing I heard was Nicole screaming "Oh my God! He shot her!" as the door was kicked in by men in uniforms. My final thought before darkness overtook me was *I'm sorry.*

CHAPTER 25
Steve-Broken

Nick and I did not speak as I turned the car into the driveway, fishtailing slightly as I jerked the wheel hard. The yard and house were coated in a sea of blue and red lights from too many units for me to count. News vans lined the highway about 60 yards away, held at bay only by dutiful officers.

I shoved the car into park and jumped out, Nick following quickly behind me. The thumping of helicopter blades above almost drowned out the crackling of the radios. As a cop, I was used to being in the midst of this type of ruckus, but experiencing it from the other side was gut wrenching, since it involved *my* loved one.

My throat closed shut as two assistant coroners wheeled out a gurney with a body bag that from the looks of it, held a small corpse.

Oh God, please, don't let that be Audra!

When Sandy called me back earlier and told me that the last ping of Piper's cell phone came from Summerset, my world changed. Like the proverbial bat out of hell, I pushed my patrol unit to its limits, at times exceeding over 120 miles per hour as Nick and I raced to Summerset. Thank God I knew the roads like the back of my hand. But when Sandy called and said that Audra called from Rosemary Milligan's house, I thought my heart was going to burst from my chest.

Now, seeing all this chaos, my mind whirred with questions. The first one that needed answered was, where was my Audra?

I spotted Rick Kensington coming out of the house, and I almost knocked down two deputies in my zeal to climb the stairs.

"Where is she?" I stammered, my eyes affixed on the body bag being loaded into the van.

"Steve, that's not her. She has already been transported to Mercy General," he said, almost yelling.

"Is she..." I could not finish my question.

Rick shut the door behind him as he stepped fully onto the porch, his other arm reaching out to touch my shoulder. "She was shot in the shoulder, Steve. She lost a lot of blood. When they loaded her in the ambulance, she was unconscious."

My shoulders stiffened at his words, my questions short and to the point.

"Piper?"

Rick cut his eyes quickly behind me to the coroner van, and as he did, I heard Nick wail behind me. "Oh God, Piper!"

I ignored him. Even though I knew I should, I felt no pity for his loss. I was glad she was dead so at least I didn't have to kill her.

Before I could ask anything else, the front door opened and Nicole appeared on a stretcher, only her face visible above the pile of blankets on top of her. I moved towards her, but Rick put his hand on my chest.

"Steve, don't. She has been through a lot as well. We have this under control here. Go. Leave the investigation in the hands of the state boys and the Feebs. You know you are too close anyway. Get your ass out of here and get to Mercy General. Audra needs you now. There is nothing here for you to do."

I knew he was right, and had I been in his shoes, I would have said the exact same thing. But that knowledge still did not stop the anger surging through me. I nodded in silence and spun around, determined to leave before I exploded. I took the steps two at a time and noticed Nick was leaning against the van, talking to a face that looked vaguely familiar. I did not feel right just leaving him here, knowing he was dealing with his own tragedy. I shifted direction and stopped beside him, recognizing the face of his companion as Trevor Milligan, Rosemary's nephew.

"Nick, I need to get to Mercy General. Can you catch a ride to your car with someone?"

Nick nodded, his tear-stained face betraying his pain. He looked like he just aged ten years.

Trevor said, "Don't you worry, Detective. I will take care of Nick."

The tone in his voice belied his emotionless expression, so I asked, "Trevor, is Rosemary…"

His stony face never changed as he replied, "She is at Mercy too. Shaken up, but fine, I'spose."

Thank you God.

I gave a quick nod and ran to my car, nearly jerking the door off. The engine roared to life, I backed up and started down the driveway, thinking what an odd conversation must be taking place between the two of them.

And how guilty I felt for not being there to protect her.

A beautiful Arizona sunrise began to peak as I sped into town, hoping it was a sign of another new day for my Audra, my guilt-laden foot pushing hard on the accelerator.

CHAPTER 26
Olin-Freedom

The throbbing in my nose woke me up from the first night of sleep in what could actually pass as a bed. The prison infirmary was certainly not the Ritz, but it was much better than the dank hole I was used to.

The brightness of the room made my eyes water. Of course, my bashed nose was not helping either. I tried to reach up and touch it, but my hands were strapped to the bed. Fuck. I closed my stinging eyes and vowed to myself that once I was on the outside again, I would anonymously post Nick's video to YouTube. I still could not believe that the little fag punched me.

Opening my eyes again, I searched around the sparse room for a clock. It was impossible to come to a conclusion, since the only light was the glaring fluorescent ones above me. Thankfully, the room was fairly quiet, which was a good thing, since my head was throbbing in agony.

A small television set was crammed into the corner of the ceiling so I tried to sit up, hoping I could find the controls. Moving around was nearly hopeless, since I was trussed to the bed like a common criminal. Ridiculous. I mean, seriously, I was in prison for God's sake. Where was I going to go? Another cell?

Squirming in the bed like a child that cannot sleep, I felt something push against my side. I stretched my fingers out as far as I was able and touched it. It was one of those call button controllers. Latching on to it, I raised it enough where I could see it, and noticed that there was a button that controlled the television right next to the "call" button. Well, I did not need any company right now, although some pain medication would be a welcome relief, but that would mean some grunt lowlife would come in here, and I wanted to be alone in my misery.

I pushed the 'on' button and the television came on. My God, how many months had it been since I watched television? I decided to pass my time with some mind numbing entertainment.

The only channels available were the three local stations. Of course; why should I have expected this hellhole to indulge in anything else?

My irritation quickly fled as I settled on Channel Six. My jaw dropped, literally, as I watched that hot little dish report on the most recent news story.

In shocked silence, I stared as images of a house flashed on the screen, followed by a picture of Piper from her days as a partner, immediately followed by pictures of Gabrielle and Audra. So many thoughts raced through my head that following the mumblings of the reporter was damn near impossible, so I focused my attention on the scrolling ticker at the bottom.

Holy shit! Piper was dead. Kevin was dead. Gabrielle was dead. Audra was in the hospital, her condition unknown. The crazy bitch did it! She just wrote my ticket out of here! The best part was, now I did not have to kill her once I was free! Could this day get any better?

I think not.

CHAPTER 27
Nick-Bitten

Roger Clanton stood out like a sore thumb in his sleek, Italian suit. His outfit probably cost more than what any of the local cops made in a year. And he knew it too, evidenced by his carriage and demeanor as he waited impatiently for the jailers to bring out his client.

It was late Sunday evening and we sat quietly next to each other in the visitor waiting area. The dummy car carrying the decoy had left about an hour ago. Roger considered it his idea that one should go out, since Olin was truly a targeted man now. Once the news in this small town spread that the kidnapping and near death of one of its most beloved citizens was tied directly to Olin, the risk of some crazed person coming after him was at an all-time high.

Even with the air conditioner blaring, the heat in the small room was almost unbearable. I noticed that small beads of sweat were beginning to form on Roger's brow, and my armpits were saturated. Finally, the door clanged open and Olin appeared, wearing a bulletproof vest over his lovely prison orange. His face was swollen and both of his eyes were a dark shade of blue and purple. I could barely contain the smile that wanted to burst forth. Yeah, I did that.

Roger and I rose quietly and followed the jailors out to the Sally port as they loaded Olin into the back seat of the unmarked cruiser. Olin let out a small grunt as he was forced to sit down, the jailor on his right shoving his head down a little too forcefully as he flopped into the backseat.

"Was that really necessary?" Roger said to the young jailor.

"Sorry, sir, just trying to keep him from hitting his head," was the sarcastic response.

Roger sat in the back next to Olin and I climbed into the front, next to the burly deputy that was our driver, and buckled my seatbelt. The windows were tinted so black that it looked like they had been painted, which probably held dual purposes: to keep the heat out and others from looking in.

The metal door rose slowly and we made our way out into the night. The drive to Summerset from here encompassed about 50 miles through nothing but sparse desert and sporadic areas of forest. I was lost in thought about the trial tomorrow, and it seemed that Roger was as well, for none of us said a word. Finally, after about two miles, Olin broke the silence.

"So, Roger, what's the plan? I mean, is that not why you are here, to talk about strategy?"

Roger took a deep breath and said, "Sorry Olin. I was just rehearsing tomorrow in my head. Yes, that is why we are here. There has been an incredible amount of things happen in the last 48 hours that we plan on addressing in court tomorrow. At this point, the prosecution is hobbled. Two of their three witnesses are dead and the remaining one is unconscious in the hospital. That means they will have no choice but to request a continuance. We will not object; in fact, we will welcome it, since your time is almost over. It has been nine months already, and by the time they sort out all this mess and construct some sort of new strategy, the speedy trial rule will be close to expiring; maybe already expired, depending upon how quickly the witness wakes up."

God, he was so matter of fact, so nonchalant about the whole debacle. I guess it is always like that, but when you have a personal stake in the outcome of things, you notice more. I forced myself not to let my true emotions splay across my face as I stared into the darkness out the window.

"That is your plan Roger? Jesus, I am paying you a small fortune and that is the best you have to offer me? To hope that the prosecution fucks up? Wow, I am impressed with your legal expertise," Olin snapped, clearly irritated. "What do you have to offer?" he said, directing his attention to me.

I turned my body towards the back and addressed them both.

"Based on the events of yesterday, I say we attempt to introduce Audra's suicide note that contains her admission that she lied about the rape, and that Robert confessed to her that he killed Gina, and thereby request that the judge throw out the DNA evidence. That leaves them with nothing."

Olin looked over at Roger and said, "Now there is a stroke of legal genius! You should learn from your *younger* partner."

Roger seethed in his seat, unaccustomed to someone talking to him like he was a first year law student. I smiled and turned back to the front.

We had traveled about 15 miles and were now on the darkest stretch of the highway. The radio had quietly buzzed with typical radio traffic earlier, but now was more just static as we truly were out in the middle of nowhere. The moon was full and shining brightly through the front windshield and the only sound now was the hum of the engine and our breathing.

We had not passed a single vehicle the entire time. The desolate area felt like we were driving on some unchartered planet, devoid of any life forms. Suddenly, the interior of the unit lit up with bright light, the sound of a roaring engine railing behind us.

"What the fuc...?" was all the deputy could get out before the entire car shook from the impact with the vehicle behind us. The light was blinding as the headlights blared into the car. Although he tried valiantly, the deputy could not control the car and we veered sharply to the right, the car careening violently down the slope and heading straight for a cluster of small juniper trees.

"Hang on!" the deputy yelled.

Before we hit the trees head on, he jerked the wheel with all his strength and the car spun out in the dirt, the back end coming about so fast I felt sick, and finally slamming into the trees on the driver's side. Roger and the deputy were on that side, and they absorbed the majority of the impact. Roger's head smashed into the passenger window with such force the glass shattered, and the deputy's did the same. Although I was sore from the bouncing around, the seatbelt kept me in place and free from any major damage. I looked back quickly and noticed that Olin was snow white, the fear in his eyes emitting his shock.

The vehicle stopped moving and the motor made a sick noise, sputtered once and then went silent. I looked over at the deputy, whose head was bleeding, glass covering his head, face and shoulders. He was groaning slightly, but his injuries did not appear to be life threatening. I unlatched my seatbelt and reached back to check on Roger, but it was obvious he was dead. His head was sticking through the gaping hole that once contained the window, now covered in his blood and brain matter.

Olin finally found his voice and said, "Get on that fucking radio and call for backup or something! Someone is trying to kill us!"

I glanced away from his ashen face and out the rear window. The headlights from earlier were now headed our way, slowly, down the embankment. My heart skipped several beats as I fumbled blindly with the radio.

"I can't get it to work Olin!"

"Fuck!" he screamed. He turned his head as far back as it would go and saw the lights coming, his face covered in sweat now. "Hurry up and find the keys! I have got to get out of here!"

I dropped the mike and reached over and patted down the deputy, finding the keys to Olin's shackles on his belt. I opened my passenger door and climbed out, opening his door and reaching down to unlock his chains in the dark. He was trembling as he yelled, "Hurry the fuck up! They are almost here!"

"Hold still, Olin! I can't see!" I said through clenched teeth, sweat already pouring off of me.

Suddenly, the lights that had been coming towards us were extinguished, along with the sound of the growling engine. I finally unlatched the last of his shackles, and Olin knocked me over in his quest to exit the vehicle. I stood up and brushed myself off, my heart pounding wildly.

"It's no use, Olin. Time's up," I said, turning towards him.

The sound of pump action shotguns locking and loading followed my words, and Olin froze.

He did not turn around; he just stood there, back erect and trembling, as footsteps behind us came closer. I nodded at the two men, completely encased head to toe in black, both wearing ski masks, and the one closest to me caring a long lead pipe. I reached into my pocket and pulled out the pair of surgical gloves that I hid earlier and snapped them on.

"You can turn around now, Olin," I said as I secured the second glove.

Slowly, he turned his body and faced me. The look on his face was absolutely priceless.

"Controlling an unstable individual with empty promises? Expensive. Laughing at her death once she accomplishes your dirty deeds? A luxury. Paying for your sins? Absolutely fucking priceless," I said, smiling as masked man number one handed me the lead pipe.

"Now, walk, you bastard," I said, enjoying the stinking fear that was exuding from him.

"Nick, can't we just..." Olin started to plead before I cut him off.

"Shut up, Olin. Walk, right now, or he will shoot your kneecap off right here," I said, jerking my head toward masked man number two. I could see the wheels spinning as he tried to calculate his odds of running, but in the end, like the coward I knew he was, he put his arms down and began to walk deeper into the woods.

No one said a word as we walked. After about ten minutes, we reached an open area where the trees parted and the moon shone, revealing two freshly dug graves. As soon as Olin saw them, he pulled up and swung around, facing me. I smiled. *Now, for the fun part.*

"Nick, come on, are you kidding? Buried alive? For things I did not do? That does not seem like a fair punishment! For God sakes, you are a lawyer!"

"Shut up Olin! I am not ready to hear you talk just yet," I said, raising the lead pipe in the air like a bat, motioning for him to continue closer to the graves. "You will get your chance to speak in just a second," I sneered as he moved closer to the hole. "Now, stop before you fall in." Lowering the pipe, I rested it against my leg as I reached into my jacket pocket. "So, would you like the chance to make this right? To, for once in your miserable existence, be honorable?" I asked, removing the hidden recorder.

His eyes wild with fear, he looked down at the recorder and then back between the two masked, gun toting goons and the graves. He nodded his head 'yes.'

"Whoever said you were not reasonable just didn't know you like I do, huh? Okay, here is the plan. If you would like to have your life spared, Olin, you need to start talking. Clearly, concisely: enumerating, without omitting any details, every single tidbit of your derelict transgressions. Start with Gina and end with Piper," I said, holding the recorder out to him.

He stared at it for a full minute before responding. "The truth, that's it? Then I am free to go?"

"The truth Olin, and not *your* twisted version of the truth, the actual truth. We will be the judge of your words, so chose them carefully," I said, waving my other hand at the goon brigade. "If they don't like what they hear, I am not responsible for their actions." For emphasis, goon one lowered the barrel of his shotgun to aim at Olin's chest.

Olin nodded once and took the recorder from me, his fingers cold and clammy. For the next 30 minutes, I listened to him recount everything, and as he progressed, I swore I heard an undertone of pride seep through his words. When he finished, his voice was hoarse and barely audible. Holding out my hand, I took the recorder from him, and I quickly stuck it into the hand of goon one, where it disappeared into the depths of his pocket.

Reaching down, I grabbed the pipe that had been leaning against my leg. I raised it high and smiled at Olin, burning the fear in his face forever into my memory. One predator to another, he was fully aware of what I was about to do, but the slimy worm tried in vain one more time to weasel his way out.

"Nick, I did what you asked! You gave me your word! You are a lawyer; you can't just kill me in cold blood! I know you; this isn't who you are! Please!" Olin said, his hands instinctively rising to protect his face as I leaned back, the lead pipe dancing around in small circles behind my head.

"Lawyers always lie to get the outcome they want, Olin. I wanted a confession, which now I have. Yes, the old me would never kill someone in cold blood. But the new me, the one you created, has absolutely no qualms about doing so," I said as I swung the pipe and landed it squarely between his legs, the force so intense that his breath was completely stripped, unable to even cry out in pain. He dropped to the ground and rolled onto his side, his face contorted in pain. I moved to the other side and raised the pipe again, bringing it down this time on the side of his kneecap, smiling as I heard the bone crack. The pain from that blow allowed Olin to find his voice and he screamed out in pain. I moved slightly back and brought the pipe down again, smashing his ankle bone into pieces, laughing like a maniacal fool as he continued to squeal like a little girl. He finally removed his hands from his crotch and grabbed his ankle, snot and tears mingling down his face as he begged for his pathetic life. I answered his pleas by crushing his hands under the weight of the pipe.

As he writhed in the dirt, I stepped back and nodded at my companions, setting the pipe against my leg once more. Silently, they moved past me, handing me their guns. They each took position at his feet and head. In tandem silence, they hefted him into the grave. The sound of his body making contact with the bottom made me laugh out loud again, and something in the back of my mind told me I was enjoying this a bit too much.

I didn't care. I might have to pay for this lack of moral compass sometime in the future, but at this moment, relishing every single whimper of that bastard was worth it.

Piper deserved no less.

I walked over to the edge of the grave and peered down. Broken and unable to move, he finally stopped screaming, for the realization that his life was almost over hit him. Our eyes locked and I literally felt the raging anger shoot out of them. I shot my own back as I said, "This is for Piper," and kicked the first pile of dirt straight down into his lying face.

Shovels appeared in the hands of Trevor and Frankie, Rosemary Milligan's nephews—or as I like to call them, the goon squad—and they began to fill the grave. With each shovelful, Olin screamed obscenities like only he could. Silently, I watched until I could no longer see his body or hear his muffled voice. Satisfied that he was gone, I turned and began to make my way back to the wrecked car. Stumbling a bit through the darkness, I eventually found it, and set the guns down by the back tire as I peered inside. The deputy was still unconscious and Roger was still dead, so I sat down in the dirt and waited, hoping beyond hope that Piper was enjoying this.

I sure was.

An hour later, I heard the footsteps of Trevor and Frankie coming through the brush. I stood up, patted myself off and opened the passenger door, draping my arm across it for support until they appeared. They were silent, covered in dirt, and no longer were wearing their ski masks. Really, what would be the point now? I sure as hell wasn't going to give them up.

Trevor was the older one, and much stronger. We had already agreed that since he had been in plenty of bar fights over the years, he would be the one. I reached inside my coat pocket and pulled out my cell phone and handed it to Frankie, who promptly threw it on the ground and crushed it under his black boot. Trevor stood in front of me now, he eyes full of emotions that I could not begin to decipher. This was the one part of my plan that he had an issue with, which I found rather ironic; no problem burying a guy alive but issues with beating one up.

Steadying myself against the doorframe, I took a few deep breaths. Trevor finally spoke and said, "Ready?"

I sucked in one more huge breath and said, "Ready" just as the first blow landed. Funny, instead of seeing stars, I saw Piper's face.

CHAPTER 28
Steve-Grief

The sound of the door opening jolted me out of my restless sleep, my hand instinctively reaching for my gun on my hip. For a split second, panic overtook me when my hand found nothing but an empty holster. Then I remembered where I was.

The young nurse smiled apologetically at me while she moved over to the left side of Audra's bed. Embarrassed, I rose and stepped outside, letting her finish her job while I stretched my legs. Wiping my sleep-encrusted eyes, I tried to focus on my watch, shocked when I realized 24 hours had passed.

Twenty-four hours spent beside my silent Audra, listening to the humming machines keeping her alive.

The nurse was changing her bandage now and I knew I could not handle seeing any more of her blood, so I turned around and headed down the hall, my nose following the smell of coffee. The black bag that belonged to Audra's mother was still setting in the chair by the door, which meant she was still here somewhere. She and Dr. Tanner were probably in the cafeteria, which meant that was not where I would go to find coffee. Jesus. Those two were the epitome of phoniness. No wonder Audra stayed away from them! If I had to hear one more round of "Where in the hell were you?" from that woman, I was afraid of what I might do. My own immense guilt was enough to make ten grown men weary.

The yellow plastic chair was uncomfortable as hell but I ignored it and sipped the steaming concoction that sure didn't taste like coffee. I wanted this to be a dream, and was wishing I would just wake up from this God-awful nightmare in my own bed, my arms protectively around my love. Dreams dissipate quickly upon awakening and the images do not remain embedded in your mind.

In a daze, I replayed the events of the last two weeks over and over in my mind, reliving every word, every emotion, every place I went wrong. So many varying emotions were vying for my attention right now. I felt nauseated watching them spin around in my head at supersonic speed. The one that was hardest to control was unadulterated, raw anger.

Just a few short days ago when my hands were clasped tightly around that bastard's neck, I came closer than I cared to admit to killing him. Part of me wished that I had finished what I started and snapped his neck in half, leaving his body in a crumpled heap on the jail floor. The other part of me was sort of glad he was still breathing so I could make a fresh trip to the jail and beat him to a bloody pulp, since I couldn't very well beat up the corpse of Piper.

Rubbing the back of my neck, I closed my eyes in an attempt to chase those thoughts out of my head. They went against every fiber of my being; the polar opposite of not only what I was brought up to believe, but trained to do as a cop.

But God, I wanted that sonofabitch dead; more than anything, other than for Audra to wake up; a horrible, painful death. One full of screams of pain, interspersed with pleas for mercy. *Oh God, I am way too emotionally involved.*

Before I started seriously planning ways to circumvent the cameras at the jail, my devious thoughts were interrupted by footsteps moving fast down the hall. I looked up to see Deputy Sullivan running towards me.

"Detective! Finally! We have been trying to call you for hours now," he sputtered, his breathing heavy and his face flushed a light red.

Sensing his emotions, I stood up and braced myself. "Sullivan, what are you doing here?"

He took a deep breath and said, "What's wrong with your phone?" I quickly shook my head in irritation and motioned with my hands 'continue."

"Olin is dead. They just found his body about four hours ago." He paused, letting me digest that bit of information before he continued. Good thing he did, because it took a full 30 seconds for me to really comprehend his words. He waited for the color to come back to my face before he continued.

"They never showed up at the Yarkema jail. A search party found the transport car about 50 miles from the prison down in a gully. One of the attorneys is dead, the other unconscious, and so was poor Randy." I looked quizzically at him, not recognizing the name. "The deputy who was driving. Anyway, Olin was nowhere to be found, so they called the dogs in. They found him about a mile from the car. Buried."

I stepped back and sank down into the chair. Dead: no, not just dead...*buried;* which meant someone else was involved. But who in the world...?

"You said an attorney was dead. Do you have a name?" I said, the puzzle pieces coming into view.

Deputy Sullivan consulted his notes, flipping the pages of his small pad. "Clanton. Roger Clanton. Nicolas Rancliff is the other one. He is here in room 537. Poor guy took one helluva beating."

Thankfully, Deputy Sullivan's radio sparked to life and he stepped out into the hall. Immediately, my brain began to analyze all the individuals that wanted Olin dead, their reasons and their availability to accomplish an obvious hit. The list was long in terms of the willing, but short in terms of the able, and one name blinked like a neon sign in my head.

The pretend coffee was immediately tossed in the trash when I stood up. Motioning to the deputy that I would call him, I excused myself quietly, moving down the hall at a quick pace. I reached the elevator banks and punched 'up' and waited impatiently to ride to the fifth floor. Once the doors opened, I made my way to room 537 and walked in.

Nick was an absolute mess. Bandages adorned his head, nose and neck. His left arm was in a cast, and his eyes were almost completely swollen shut. Purple and black replaced the majority of his fair skin, making him look like some alien from a B movie.

I walked to the edge of the bed, unable to determine if he was awake or not from the door. He turned his head slightly towards the noise of my footfalls and damned if he didn't try to smile when he recognized me.

Pulling a chair up next to yet another hospital bed, I crouched on the edge, studying his facial expressions intently. Even though they were hooded and engorged with purple flesh, his eyes spoke volumes.

"Looks like that accident really messed you up" I said, my voice devoid of emotion.

He nodded slightly. "Yes, it did. Not as much as the beating though. Good thing I played dead convincingly, or I would have been buried right next to Olin in the other grave by those masked vigilantes."

I didn't trust my voice with anything except for a quiet "Hmm."

It was impossible to determine if the gleam in his eye stemmed from the pain medication in his I.V. or from the fact that he knew he just handed me a steaming pile of lies that I chose not to question.

Or that he was staring into the eyes of a sympathizer, one that could keep a secret.

"How is Audra?" he queried, the look of genuine concern passing across his face.

"Serious, but stable," I replied, unwilling to speak the word *unconscious* out loud.

He tried to sigh but it came out more like a grunt. "Maybe she won't remember any of this either. Sometimes, it's just best to let the sleeping snakes lie."

Looking down at him, a vague hint of a smile niggled at the corner of my mouth. I replied, "Nick, I believe you just hit the nail on the head with that bit of introspect."

He silently nodded and I turned and walked back to the elevator and left him with his own internal pain. I didn't know how he did it, nor did I want to. It was enough to know it was done, and once Audra woke up, she could finally have some peace in her life.

I was on Audra's floor again and made my way down the hall, my thoughts spinning wildly. When I rounded the corner, I came face to face with Nicole.

"Nicole! Should you be out of bed?" I questioned, noticing her appearance. She looked like a dried out prune, no makeup and her hair was plastered to her head like a dirty helmet. She was wearing standard hospital issue scrubs and several bandages on her arms.

"Why, there you are! I have been looking all over for you! Did you hear about Olin?" she said, her voice full of excitement.

"I did. Terrible tragedy," I replied, still walking towards Audra's room. I stole a quick glance inside the intensive care window and saw the nurse was still working on her, so I slowed my pace a bit.

She snorted. "Terrible tragedy my ass! No one is happier than I am that the bastard is dead. Except maybe poor Audra," she cooed, turning her face towards her room. "How is the dear? Is she awake yet?"

"No, not yet. The doctors said she lost a lot of blood, but any minute now, she will wake up."

I wasn't sure if, in my sleep deprived state, I dreamt it or not, but I swore I saw a flash of anger behind her eyes right before the tears came.

"She was so brave. She tried to save me! If only she would have listened and come with me out the window, but, oh, that wouldn't have made a difference anyway!" she cried. "Oh God, if only I was stronger! I tried so hard to stop Kevin from shooting her!"

Before I could respond, the door flung open and the nurse came out, searching the corridor frantically until her eyes landed on mine.

"She's calling for you!" she said, her voice the most beautiful thing I ever heard.

Racing past Nicole, I headed to my love's side. Her eyes were still closed but her body was moving slightly, her right hand gripping the sheet. The monitors were beeping frantically, her heart rate soaring. I felt a knot the size of a baseball form in my throat, making speech damn near impossible. I leaned down and whispered, "I'm here baby. Just rest, sweetie. Shhh. It's all over now. You're safe: no one can hurt you, I promise." My voice caught in a choking spasm.

Her hand squeezed mine with urgency as her lips moved silently, but her eyes were still closed. I put my ear next her lips, trying to make out her feeble words over the infernal beeping of the machines surrounding her.

"Oh my God, is she awake?" Nicole asked, now standing in the doorway.

I waved my other hand up in the air to silence her, cooing quietly into the ear of my love as I gently stroked her knotted hair with my other hand.

"What baby, what did you say?"

It took almost a full minute for the word to fully form on her parched lips.

"Nicole."

Before I could fully process what she said, the heart monitor's alarm blared, and the nurse screamed out the door, "She's coding! Crash cart!"

Instinctively, I grabbed Nicole by her arm and moved her out of the way from the stampede of help that came barreling through the door. A loud, high-pitched scream drew my attention to the door. Mrs. Tanner rounded the corner, Dr. Tanner right behind her, barking orders to no one in particular. The sheer look of terror on both of their faces made them, for once, look almost like caring human beings. I shoved Nicole out the door and into the hallway, quickly shutting it behind me and stood in front of it.

"Let me see my baby!" Mrs. Tanner screamed, tears rolling down her cheeks.

"Get out of my way you imbecile!" Dr. Tanner grunted, his eyes wild with fright.

The doctor working inside yelled "Clear!" and we all heard the sound of the shock. Thankfully, my back was to the door, but Mrs. Tanner saw it all, and her face immediately went ash white, her eyes rolling back in her head. While I maneuvered to catch her, Dr. Tanner ignored her and slid past me, barging into Audra's room.

Lowering Mrs. Tanner's limp body onto the cool linoleum floor, I yelled, "Nicole, I need a blanket and some water!" When I heard no response, I looked up, thinking maybe she'd snuck back inside the room as well.

She was just standing there, her body trembling and her hands clenched into tight fists at her side. It took me a moment to realize that the look on her face wasn't just fear.

It was anger.

ABOUT THE AUTHOR:

This is the second novel in the *Eviscerating the Snake* series by Ashley Fontainne. The third and final novel, Adjusting Journal Entries, is in process.

An avid fan of classic literature and stories that deal with revenge, Ashley spends as much free time as possible reading, gaining insight into the delicate world of the human psyche.

CPSIA information can be obtained at www.ICGtesting.com
Printed in the USA
LVOW081427120312

272702LV00001B/42/P